Written in Stone

Quarry Press

Written in Stone
A Kingston Reader

Edited by Mary Alice Downie and M.-A. Thompson

The publisher gratefully acknowledges the financial assistance of
the Ontario Heritage Foundation, The Canada Council, and
the Ontario Arts Council.

Canadian Cataloguing in Publication Data

Main entry under title:

Written in stone: a Kingston reader

ISBN 1–55082–063–X

1. Kingston (Ont.)–Literary collections. 2. Canadian literature (English).
I. Downie, Mary Alice, 1934– . II. Thompson, M.-A., 1951– .

PS8257.K46W74 1993 C810.9'3271372 C93-090070–7
PR9194.52.K46W74 1993

Cover art by Gwyneth Travers, reproduced by permission of Peter Travers.
Graphic Design by Peter Dorn RCA, FGDC.
Typeset by Quarry Press, Inc.
Printed and bound in Canada by Webcom Limited, Toronto, Ontario.

Published by Quarry Press, Inc.,
P.O. Box 1061, Kingston, Ontario K7L 4Y5.

Contents

2. SYMPHONY IN STONE

3. NEIGHBOURS

Acknowledgements

OUR thanks to the staff of Special Collections, Douglas Library, Queen's University; to Dorothy Farr, of the Agnes Etherington Art Centre; and to the staff of Queen's Archives. Special help was provided by Paul Banfield, Jane Errington, Barbara Robertson, Donald Swainson and Douglas Stewart.

We are grateful to the Ontario Heritage Foundation for generous financial assistance; to our editor, Betty Corson for her cheerful guidance and to Bob Hilderley, our publisher, for his extraordinary patience and helpfulness.

Introduction

IT'S always difficult to explain to visitors the perennial fascination of life in this small city, once a colonial outpost for two empires, quiet key to the heart of the continent. After all, any place that announces its population as 60,900 when you approach from one direction, 160,000 from another is not your typical metropolis – especially when you consider that almost 15,000 of that flexible population arrive in September and leave in May, while yet another couple of thousand are incarcerated and can't leave at all.

Kingston was founded with considerable pomp and cunning in 1673 by a French count, captured and burned in 1758 by a British colonel, refounded in 1783; then for two heady years in 1840-1842 it was the capital of Canada. After these early brushes with history, the town snoozed through much of the nineteenth and early twentieth centuries, serene in its beauty and a legacy of stone and brick. Then came changes, welcome and unwelcome, and citizens from all over the world who have added spice and colour to the stately – some would say stuffy – pleasures of the "Old Stones."

From the beginning, Kingston has received (chiefly) favourable reviews: "the meadows are clear and fit for the scythe" wrote one observer in 1783. We knew when we started *Written in Stone* that writers and artists, both transient and permanent, had recorded the life of this city, but we were startled to discover just how many had portrayed the handsome streetscapes, the beguiling natural setting of water, woods, and sky, the pastimes and escapades of its inhabitants – a bracing mixture of upright and raffish.

Kingston provides the invigorating experience of being in a living museum, where things happen still. It is fun to be part of the pageant. As Tom Marshall has written: "It is like living in a monument, a large outdoor sculpture, or like being on a ship that travels through time and never arrives anywhere."

As we dug deeper into the treasure mine of the Douglas Library at Queen's finding constant interconnections, characters appearing and reappearing, we came to see the city as one of those many-volumed historical sagas, filled with high adventure, low comedy, romance, intrigue both political and academic, bursting at the seams with eccentric characters – mad La Salle, dreaming of China, Tonti of the Iron Hand, our patron Puck, Sir John A. himself, that ambiguous cleric Bishop Strachan, Dollar Bill...

Written in Stone is a handbook, a reader, a guide to this swirling panorama. It is not an anthology for the *illuminati*, the denizens of Sydenham Ward or those who live within spitting distance of Queen's – addicts already converted to their own euphoric view of the city – although we hope they will enjoy it too. It is meant for all those who live in the Swamp Ward, in Bayridge, Elginburg, and Amherst Island, and for the families and friends of inhabitants, who may never visit the city. It is also addressed to a greater invisible Kingston, to those thousands who have passed through for varying lengths of time, people in the army or at the universities – Kingston's foster children who are scattered around the world.

Reviewers – anthologers *manqué* – always find that a particular favourite piece has been overlooked. From the large selection of impressions of Kingston – poems, diaries, novels, sketches, watercolours, photographs – we could select only a sampling. We also had to decide what qualified as Kingston life: people from the centre of town go out to visit friends, to pick apples, to canoe, to enjoy a Chinese meal in a township mall. Others come in to the heart of the city, to work, to market, to school. We have not restricted ourselves to official boundaries.

The order of the selections presented a dilemma: should it be chronological, alphabetical, topical? At one desperate point we contemplated asking our publisher to issue the book in a looseleaf binder so that readers could create their own anthology. Or, we thought one compiler could stand at the top of the stairs and fling the manuscript down for the other to pick up – fortune would determine the arrangement.

In the end, we have settled on three sections, each devoted to a central theme, but inevitably, like life in Kingston itself, they overlap. For some of the writers we have selected, Kingston was not much more than a passing phrase. For others it has been a lifetime commitment – occasionally an obsession.

Thomas Moore, Charles Dickens, Walt Whitman and Rupert Brooke have left comments. Alas, there seems to be no characteristic quip from Oscar Wilde.

The Salterton novels of Robertson Davies are still read by inhabitants "with shocked delight and glee" and a fresh crop of young writers – Steven Heighton, Diane Schoemperlen, Kate Sterns and Judith Thompson – continue the tradition of chronicling their city, favourably and otherwise.

We have a confession: neither compiler can muster a single grandparent in Cataraqui Cemetery, much less the requisite four. We are converts (always the keenest), not cradle Kingstonians. One of us lives outside the city in what was once a stagecoach inn, the other in a high Victorian house in the centre of the city built, according to an unreliable legend, "by the president of the Pickle Works." We positively look forward to haunting them, joining the throng of friendly ghosts who roam the streets engaging in "invisible psychic encounters." Meanwhile we remember Bronwen Wallace's comment that in Kingston "you never end up where you think you're going to."

First Impressions

Preface

KINGSTON is where the St. Lawrence River and Lake Ontario meet, a natural rendezvous, and as Robertson Davies has observed, things happen where watercourses join. A romantic might expect, in this city defined by water and stone, to see a flotilla of one sort or another – Frontenac's expedition rounding the bay, Iroquois canoes splintering the mist, batteaux heavy-laden with ragged Loyalists – and to hear the chant of the *voyageurs*, the echo of shots fired from wooden men-of-war, the roaring of sea shanties from the decks of a grain ship steaming into the harbour.

Early explorers sailing up the river through the maze of islands must have been astonished at the huge inland sea that opened up before them, and felt both wonder and terror at the deep silent forests sheltering the native people who dwelt along the shore.

Not surprisingly, there is a pronounced military presence in Kingston. The town began as a fortress and is still ringed by Fort Henry and various martello towers, Vimy Barracks and Fort Frontenac, the National Defence College and the Royal Military College.

Following the explorers and the armies came the victims of war, the United Empire Loyalists, fleeing from the American Revolution into British territory. They were given land along the north shores of river and lake. Despite the rigours of life in scattered little settlements and the misery of the so-called "Hungry Year" in 1788 when all crops failed, the memoirs of settlers describe feasts of wild rice, berries, and salmon, and report the arrival of co-operative pigeons that settled in the trees by the thousands, seemingly eager to be eaten.

In the midst of neighbourly barn raisings, sleigh rides, and weddings, there were inevitable tragedies. The water and the forests could take away too. And if today, you drive through the back roads of the area, the little lost graveyards attest to the hardships and sickness that swept away the young, the frail, and the elderly.

Merchants brought supplies for the new settlements upriver and sent the great lumber rafts back to Montreal and Quebec. More settlers came, refugees from the famines of Ireland and the enclosures of Scotland. And then the tourists came, to watch the sailboat races, to tour the Thousand Islands, drawn by the prospect of a land rimmed by water.

"Kingston and the Islands" – the grandeur of the riding name causes a *frisson* on every election night. The romantic spell cast by the Thousand Islands seldom failed to influence visitors as they approached the city in the past. Nowadays, less fortunate travellers must whiz along the boring stretches of Highway 401 (The Macdonald-Cartier Freeway), unless they sensibly take the old road that winds beside the river.

Because of both geography and scenery, Kingston was an essential part of every colonial grand tour that provoked tourists' comments, lively or dyspeptic, on the magnificent site of Quebec, the spirited social life of Montreal, the mud of York, the stupendous falls of Niagara, and even the most noted seldom failed to scribble a line or two about Kingston. Although the usual responses recorded tended towards the ecstatic, other visitors, embittered by bloodthirsty mosquitoes or a night spent in one of the unspeakable Upper Canadian taverns, saw it as a place set in a hard and dangerous land, a tediously provincial city, a howling wilderness.

As one reads the journals and travel books of army officers, government officials, and their wives, there are amusing recurrences and contradictions. One complains that there is "nothing to do but sail." Another, in a city now well-endowed, remarks on the shortage of schools and surgeons. In a remark that will sound eerily familiar, he adds "they, who assume this appellation, contrive to get well paid for their trouble." Sir George Head warns emigrants to beware of unscrupulous land speculators.

Now, visitors come in spring and summer, for conferences, for the sailing, enjoying the oldest marketplace in Ontario, filling the streets with colour like exotic birds. In the fall, another flock descends on the city – students enrolling at Queen's University, St. Lawrence College, and the Royal Military College. If anything unites modern Kingstonians, it is the passion with which they debate the pros and cons of this rambunctious and temporary population. Whatever the length of their stay, many have found Kingston a memorable part of their lives. Indeed, some surprised visitors may find themselves returning, transformed into inhabitants.

The journey through the dreaming luxuriant scenery of the Thousand Islands – "The Venice of America" or *Manatoana*, the Garden of the Spirits, as the native peoples called it – has sparked countless professional literary imaginations. Octave Crémazie, "the father of French-Canadian poetry," wrote ecstatically of "The Thousand Isles! magnificent necklace of diamond and sapphire that those of the ancient world would have preferred to the brightest gold of Ophir!" A nineteenth-century writer claims that the legend of Hiawatha originated in the area. Whitman extolled it, Anthony Trollope unkindly thought that the islands would not be noted "by any traveller who was not expressly bidden to admire them." Rupert Brooke, because of all the castles built on them by rich Americans, thought them "not much more beautiful than Golders Green!"

In this section, Samuel de Champlain, one of our most distinguished (and earliest) travelwriters, records an adventure worthy of *A Midsummer Night's Dream* as he wanders, astrolabe-less, through the forest in pursuit of a fabulous bird – which inspires the meditation of the twentieth-century poet Douglas LePan. Thomas Moore, struck by the haunting music of the voyageurs, pens a song which in turn moves the modern Joan Finnigan to "invoke the ghosts." This artistic conversation through the years is a strong force.

As to the city itself, Charles Dickens deplored it. Oscar Wilde, nattily attired in a travelling outfit of "tweed trousers, brown velvet coat and green velvet tie" with a "huge theatrical cloak" looking "like a thatched roof over a delicate strawberry" advised that Kingston should have night classes in which drawing should be taught.

The difficulties and tragedies of early settlement graphically described by the modern poets Frances Itani and Eric Folsom contrast strangely with Mrs. Simcoe's account of settled activities – walks, teas, and forgotten umbrellas – or the ennui suffered by the French aristocrat La Rochefoucauld-Liancourt. There is pain of another sort in the moving account of the death of a young rebel by Linus Miller and the horrors of malignant cholera described by the redoubtable Surgeon Henry.

The waterfront works its magic upon poets Gail Fox, Allan Brown, and Jean-Jacques Hamm, while in yet another conversation with the past, Tom Marshall considers Robert Frost's visit to the city and wonders, "Did he see/domes and towers and spires?"

JOAN FINNIGAN

The North-West Passage Is Here

JOAN FINNIGAN (1925–) was born and raised in Ottawa but has spent much of her life in Kingston, first as a university student and then as a parent raising a family. Since 1966 when she began to write full time, she has published many books of poetry and oral history, including *Some of the Stories I Told You Were True*; *Legacies, Legends & Lies*; *Tell Me Another Story*; *Old Scores, New Goals: The Story of the Ottawa Senators*; *Finnigan's Guide to the Ottawa Valley*; *The Watershed Collection*; and *Wintering Over*. For her poetry she has been nominated for the League of Canadian Poets Pat Lowther Award as well as the Ontario Ministry of Culture and Communications Trillium Award. Kingston, she says, has been the creative milieu for much of her work: "It continues to be inspirational for me."

Skating on Navy Bay

I

Invoke the ghosts!

Send runners to tell them
the North-West Passage is here,
here amongst the Thousand Islands.

By looking up they missed it.

In maple leaves and fronds of ferns,
in cat-tail stems
are tangled
the cities
of voyageur's dreams.

Spires and minarets of India,
the diamonds of Maharajahs,

and silver-paved are the streets
going down-hill to the locker
where the boots
of the drowned sailors
lie.

II

Silver is the colour of this sepulchre,
swords of New Brunswick Fencibles,
slumberous timbers of the Frigate
and the St. Lawrence,
bones of Ophelias
from Rockwood.

by framed snowflakes
of two storms ago,
the finished summer of a hyacinth,
hair in shut locket.

the water-lily world descends
to Prevost's cannons
lying with rockets of ice
in their mouths

and further to fossils
of kingdoms in caves;
Thomas Moore sang here
at this Meeting of the Waters
to snow-blind
Irishmen

the lake is a crystal of frozen voices
and tears

but the frog breathes below
in channels of mud

and vigilant the stalled fins
of the fish.

III

We move to our own music;

the wind is at our backs
   and the pair of blades
   is a hypnotic spell
      of sun
and the drive is to go on,
         and on,
absorbed by the flow
      of ice.

We walk on water;

and the sirens call from the islands
   like bell-birds
   in the wilderness
   of Yucatan

Which shall it be?
   Howe,
   Garden,
   Amherst?

We choose Amherst;

it is so far that night
   will have to gather us in.

and coming back there shall be
fallen stars
underfoot.

Excerpted from *The Watershed Collection*

DOUGLAS LE PAN

Anything Might Happen, Anything

DOUGLAS LE PAN (1914–) left a distinguished career in the Canadian diplomatic service to become Professor of English at Queen's University in 1959. From 1964-70 he was Principal of University College at the University Of Toronto. He has twice won the Governor-General's Award, for his novel *The Deserter* and for his book of poetry *The Net and the Sword.*

Astrolabe

Now it seems almost as easy as breathing
this commerce of bodies and souls, unlicensed.
There was a moment, though, when it cost almost
everything – the explorer, tense, frightened, resolute,
with his cargo of musket, memories, diaries,
astrolabe, committing himself to the tender
skin of a birch-bark canoe, and a new continent,
and a new world, where anything might happen,
anything, not knowing that the thin skin of birch
might hold the weight of a lyric future
as well as the weight of suffering Europe on its ribs.
They grew to each other, though, slim lyric sweetness
and grim tension of the malcontent, till they
worked out new terms of trade, the musket
melting beside the pile of beaver pelts
till it rose again as a rod of almost god-like strength
and sweetness, and the pile of musky pelts flowered into
an ineffably golden fleece. At last the moment came when
he searched no longer for the stars, throwing away
his astrolabe to rust beneath a pine-tree,
and moved at last at ease in a world he never dreamed,
this new world, ours, where savagery and sweetness melt as one.

Excerpted from *Something Still To Find*

SAMUEL DE CHAMPLAIN

Lost in the Forest

SAMUEL DE CHAMPLAIN (c.1570–1635), geographer, explorer, colonizer, and creator of the jovial Order of Good Cheer, is a man all Canadians can be proud to claim as the founder of their country. His journals and logs have been collected in *The Works of Samuel de Champlain*.

...IN the beginning, when we set out for the hunt, I went off too far into the woods pursuing a certain bird, which seemed strange to me. It had a beak like that of a parrot, and was as big as a hen and yellow all over, except for its head, which was red, and its wings, which were blue. It made short flights, like a partridge. My desire to kill it led me to follow it from tree to tree a very long time, until it flew away. Then, losing all hope, I wished to return upon my steps, where I found none of our hunters, who had been constantly gaining on me until they reached their enclosure. In trying to catch up with them, going, as it seemed to me, straight to where the enclosure was, I lost my way in the forest – going now one way, now another – without being able to see where I was. As night was coming on, I passed it at the foot of a large tree. The next day I set out and walked until three o'clock in the afternoon, when I found a little stagnant pond, and seeing some game there I killed three or four birds. Tired and worn out, I prepared to rest and to cook these birds, from which I made a good meal. My repast over, I thought to myself what I ought to do, praying God to aid me in my misfortune in this wilderness; for, during three days, there was nothing but rain mingled with snow.

Committing all to His mercy, I took courage more than before, going hither and thither all day without catching a glimpse of any footprint or trail, except those of wild beasts, of which I generally saw a good number; and so I passed the night without any consolation. At dawn of the next day, after having a scant meal, I resolved to find some brook and follow it, judging that it must empty into the river on whose banks our hunters were. This resolution once made, I put it through with such success that at noon I found myself on the shore of a small lake about a league and a half long, where I killed some game, which helped me very much; and I still had eight or ten charges of powder. Walking along the bank of this lake to see where it discharged, I found a rather large brook, which I followed until five o'clock in the afternoon, when I heard a great noise. Listening, I could not discern what it was until I heard the noise more distinctly, and then I concluded that it was a waterfall in the river that I was looking for. Going nearer I saw an opening and when I had reached it, I found myself in a very large, spacious meadow, where there [were] a great many wild animals. And, looking, on my right, I saw the river, wide and big. Wishing to examine this place, and walking in the meadow, I found myself in a little path where the savages carry their canoes. When I examined this place well, I recognized that it was the same river, and that I had been that way. Well pleased at this, I supped on the little that I had and lay down for the night. When morning came, and I had studied the place where I was, I inferred, from certain mountains that are on the border of that river that I was not mistaken and that our hunters must be higher up than I by four or five good leagues, which I covered at my leisure, going along the bank of this river, until I caught sight of the smoke of our hunters. I reached their place, greatly to their happiness as well as to my own. They were looking for me, and had lost hope of seeing me again; and they begged me not separate from them any more, and to take my compass with me, which I had forgotten, which could have put me back on my way. They said to me: "If you had not come, and we could not have found you, we should not have gone to the French any more, for fear of their accusing us of having taken your life." After this, Darontal was very careful of me when I went hunting, always giving me a savage to accompany me....

Excerpted from *The Works of Samuel de Champlain*

JEAN LE CHASSEUR

Delighted at Finding a Place

JEAN LE CHASSEUR (c.1633–1713) came to Canada with Count Frontenac in September 1672 and served faithfully as his secretary for ten years before becoming secretary to the Intendant of New France. It is thought that he wrote the unsigned account of the journey to found Fort Frontenac. He later became lieutenant-general of Trois Rivières and seigneur of Rivière-du-Loup.

Louis de Buade, Comte de Frontenac at de Palluou (1622–1698) served as governor of New France from 1672 to 1682 and then again from 1689 until his death in Quebec. He was a controversial and energetic figure whose qualities are debated still, but no one questions his significance in expanding the French fur-trading empire in North America – the fort at "Katarakoui" was an early link in the chain.

12th [July]: Broke camp early in the morning and after having travelled until ten o'clock, halted for three hours to eat and rest. As they approached the first opening into the lake, the Count wanted to proceed with more uniformity than had yet been done, and in full battle order. Therefore, he arranged all the squadrons in the following manner:

Four squadrons, making up the vanguard, went in front in line abreast.

The two flat-boats followed next.

Count Frontenac travelled with his retinue at the head of all the canoes of his guards, those of his staff, and the volunteers who were near his person, having on his right the Three Rivers squadron and on his left that of the Hurons and Algonquins.

Two other squadrons travelled in a third line, making the rear-guard.

They had scarcely gone half a league in this formation when they saw an Iroquois canoe appear with the abbé d'Urfé, who, having encountered the Indians above the Cataraqui River, and having advised them of the Count's arrival, was coming to meet him with the chiefs of the Five Nations.

They came alongside the command vessel and paid their

respects with many signs of happiness and trust, swearing to him the obligation they owed him for having spared them the trouble of going farther and for really wishing to receive their submissions at the Cataraqui River, which is a very suitable place to lodge, as they were going to show him.

After Count Frontenac had replied to their civilities they placed themselves in front to serve him as guides, and led him through the mouth of the Cataraqui River into a bay about a cannon shot from the entrance, which forms one of the finest and most pleasant harbours in the world, since it could hold one hundred of the largest ships, having there sufficient water at the mouth and in the basin whose bottom is only mud, and which is so secure from every wind that cables would scarcely be needed for mooring them.

Delighted at finding a place so appropriate for his plan, the Count immediately landed and after having inspected the woods and terrain for two or three hours, he re-embarked in a canoe to examine both sides of the river entrance and some points that jut out into the lake so that he only returned about 8 o'clock in the evening.

The Iroquois impatiently waited for him in order to pay their first respects at his tent, but as it was late, they were requested to postpone them until the next day when there would be time to visit each other and to converse more comfortably, to which they willingly agreed.

13th [July]: They beat a salute at dawn and about seven o'clock everyone was under arms according to the orders that had been issued the previous evening. All the troops were ranged in two rows which circled Count Frontenac's tent and extended to the Indian lodges. Some large sails were laid in front of the tent for them to sit on; and they had to pass along the two rows. They were surprised to see such pomp which seemed new to them, in the same way as all his guards with their tunics which were something that they had not yet encountered. There were more than sixty of the oldest and most eminent, and after taking their seats and following their custom having smoked for some time, one of them, named Garagontié, who has always been a strong friend of the French, and who ordinarily is their spokesman, paid his respects on behalf of all the Nations: swearing to the happiness that they had felt when they learned, from Sieur de la Salle,

Onontio's plan to come and visit them; that even though some ill-disposed spirits had tried to cast suspicion among them at his approach, they had not hesitated to obey his orders and to come and meet him with the assurance they had that he really wanted always to maintain peace with them, and to protect them against their enemies, while treating them as a father ought to treat his children; that they came, therefore, like true children to guarantee to him their allegiance and to swear to the complete submission with which they would always carry out his commands; that he was speaking in the name of the Five Nations because they were all of the same mind and thought; and in order better to bear witness to it the chiefs of each nation were going to confirm what he had just told him in the name of all.

Thus, each chieftain came individually to pay his own respects and to tell him the same thing in substance, but in varying and very eloquent terms.... Count Frontenac, having had a fire lit nearby where they were seated, replied to them in the following words which he adapted to their manner of speaking:

> My Children, Onondagas, Mohawks, Oneidas, Cayugas and Senecas, I am comforted to see you arrive here where I have had a fire lit, to see you smoke, and to speak to you. Oh, it is well done, my children, to have followed the orders and commands of your father. Therefore be brave my children. You will hear his word which is full of mildness and peace, a word that will fill all your lodges with joy, and make them happy. For do not think that war is the object of my journey. My spirit is completely filled with peace and it travels with me. Courage therefore my children and rest yourselves.

Then the Count had them presented with ten fathoms of tobacco....

The Indians appeared highly satisfied with the speech that Sieur Le Moyne explained to them, and similarly with the gifts that were made to them at this opening, and which to their custom appearing considerable, led them to hope that subsequently, when Onontio would reveal to them his intentions, he would make them magnificent ones. It was noted that their faces were much altered, and that Torontishati, who is their spokesman and the shrewdest, most intelligent and most influential man among them, from previously being gloomy and thoughtful, had taken on a cheerfulness that was unusual to him. This is a man who has always been an enemy of the French and strong in the interests of the Flemish, which forced Count Frontenac to flatter him in particular and to detain him to dine with him.

Meanwhile Sieur Rendin was working to lay out the fort on the site that the Count had chosen following the plan that he had fixed upon with him; and as soon as they had dined, they ordered men to work at the trench where the stakes were to be planted until such time as they decided on how the troops would be employed in the task, and had the tools fitted with handles. Afterwards he embarked in a canoe to go and inspect the shores of the river and basin, and was delighted to find at the end of the basin a meadow, more than a league in extent as beautiful and regular as any in France, and in its midst to see winding the river which is very wide and capable of carrying barks and ships for more than three leagues.

Therefore, he returned to camp in high spirits seeing that he found all one could wish for, and it seemed that God was blessing his undertaking. But what added to it still more, was to find everyone so impatient to labour and such willingness to advance the works, that he soon hoped to complete them. This ardour that they exhibited led him to change the decision he had taken, to divide all the troops into four brigades and to have them relieved every two hours so that the work might not be interrupted; and he accepted their proposal to share the work between them, each becoming responsible for what would be given to him. This had such good effect that in the evening they began to fell trees with such energy that the officers had difficulty making everyone withdraw to rest and sleep in order to be able to work the next morning.

14th [July]: Scarcely had it dawned on the 14th when all the brigades went to work according to the tasks that had been assigned to them, and all the officers and soldiers bore themselves with so much attachment and eagerness that they almost cleared the side of the fort.

15th [and 16th July]: The work continued with the same vigour, but the rain which fell all morning during the 16th prevented them from working before noon and everyone strove to make up the lost time. The Indians were astonished to see the great clearing of felled trees that had been made and that on one side some were squaring timber, and others bringing stakes, others digging trenches, and that divers works were advancing at the same time. In the evening the chiefs of the Five Nations were given notice that an audience would be held the next day at 8 o'clock in the morning.

17th [July]: Everything being prepared to receive them, they found the Count in the same manner as the first time, and in the speech that he made to them he proposed all the conditions that he wished of them as may be seen by the annexed copy of his oration which was accompanied by magnificent gifts according to Indian custom.

Translated from the French by James Pritchard,
from *Journey of My Lord Count Frontenac to Lake Ontario*

CHARLES SANGSTER

The River and the Lake

CHARLES SANGSTER (1822–1893) was born in the Royal Navy Dockyard on Point Frederick (the site of the Royal Military College) and educated in Kingston. After assorted jobs – at Fort Henry making cartridges for the troops for the 1837 rebellion and a stint writing for the *British Whig* and the *Daily News* – he was employed in the Post Office Department in Ottawa from 1868 to 1886. *The Saint Lawrence and the Saguenay* (1856) and *Hesperus and Other Poems* (1860) were published during his Kingston years.

6

Red walls of granite rise on either hand,
Rugged and smooth; a proud young eagle soars
Above the stately evergreens, that stand
Like watchful sentinels on these God-built towers;
And near yon beds of many-colored flowers
Browse two majestic deer, and at their side
A spotted fawn all innocently cowers;
In the rank brushwood it attempts to hide,
While the strong-antlered stag steps forth with lordly stride.

7

And slakes his thirst, undaunted, at the stream,
Isles of o'erwhelming beauty! surely here
The wild enthusiast might live, and dream
His life away. No Nymphic trains appear,
To charm the pale Ideal Worshipper
Of Beauty; nor Neriads from the deeps below;
Nor hideous Gnomes, to fill the breast with fear:
But crystal streams through endless landscapes flow,
And o'er clustering Isles the softest breezes blow....

11

On, through the lovely Archipelago,
Glides the swift bark. Soft summer matins ring
From every isle. The wild fowl come and go,
Regardless of our presence. On the wing,
And perched upon the boughs, the gay birds sing
Their loves: This is their summer paradise;
From morn till night their joyous caroling
Delights the ear, and through the lucent skies
Ascends the choral hymn in softest symphonies.

12

The Spring is gone – light, genial-hearted Spring!
Whose breath gives odor to the violet,
Crimsons the wild rose, tints the blackbird's wing,
Unfolds the buttercup. Spring that has set
To music the laughter of the rivulet,
Sent warm pulsations through the hearts of hills,
Reclothed the forests, made the valleys wet
With pearly dew, and waked the grave old mills
From their calm sleep, by the loud rippling of the rills.

13

Long years ago the early Voyageurs
Gladdened these wilds with some romantic air;
The moonlight, dancing on their dripping oars,
Showed the slow bateaux passing by with care,
Impelled by rustic crews, as debonair
As ever struck pale Sorrow dumb with song:
Many a drooping spirit longed to share
Their pleasant melodies, that swept among
The echo-haunted woods, in accents clear and strong.

14

See, we have left the Islands far behind,
And pass into a calm, pellucid Lake.
Merrily dance the billows! for the wind
Rises all fresh and healthful in our wake,
Up start large flocks of waterfowl, that shake
The spray from their glossed plumage, as they fly
To seek the shelter of some island brake;
Now like dark clouds they seem against the sky,
So vast the numbers are that pass us swiftly by.

15

Merrily dance the billows! Cheerily leaps
Our fearless bark! – it loves to skim the sea,
The River and the Lake, when o'er them sweeps
The swift unwearied billow fearlessly.
Stretches its spotless sail! – it tightens – see!
How the wind curves the waters all around,
Ploughing into their bosoms fitfully.
Hark to the Tempest's dismal shriek! its bound,
Like to an earthquake, makes the River's depths resound.

Excerpted from *The St. Lawrence and The Saguenay*

THOMAS MOORE

A Canadian Boat Song

THOMAS MOORE (1779–1852), "the national lyrist of Ireland" and friend of the poet Lord Byron, was born in Dublin, the son of a grocer, and educated at Trinity College. A musician as well as a poet, he achieved a large reputation in both Britain and Europe for his lyrics, novels, and biographies. His *voyageur* song, written during a visit to British North America in 1804, became a popular drawing-room ballad.

AS Thomas Moore recounts in a note to this poem, "I wrote these words to an air which our boatmen sung to us frequently. The wind was so unfavourable that they were obliged to row all the way, and we were five days in descending the river from Kingston to Montreal, exposed to an intense sun during the day, and at night forced to take shelter from the dews in any miserable hut upon the banks that would receive us. But the magnificent scenery of the St. Lawrence repays all such difficulties.

"Our voyageurs had good voices, and sung perfectly in tune together. The original words of the air, to which I adapted these stanzas, appeared to be a long, incoherent story, of which I could understand but little, from the barbarous pronunciation of the Canadians. It begins:

> Dans mon chemin j'ai rencontré
> Deux cavaliers très-bien montés;

And the refrain to every verse was,

> A l'embre d'un bois je m'en vais jouer,
> A l'embre d'un bois je m'en vais danser.

I ventured to harmonize this air, and have published it. Without that charm which association gives to every little memorial of scenes or feelings that are past, the melody may, perhaps, be thought common and trifling: but I remember when we have entered, at sunset, upon one of those beautiful lakes, into which the St. Lawrence so grandly and unexpectedly opens, I have heard this simple air with a pleasure which the finest compositions of the first masters have never given me; and now there is not a note of it which does not recall to my memory the dip of our oars in the St. Lawrence. The flight of our boat down the Rapids, and all those new and fanciful impressions to which my heart was alive during the whole of this very interesting voyage.

"The following stanzas are supposed to be sung by those voyageurs who go to the Grand Portage by the Utawas River. For an account of this wonderful undertaking, see Sir Alexander Mackenzie's *General History of the Fur Trade*, prefixed to his journal."

Written on the River St. Lawrence

Et remigem cantus hortatur. – QUINTILIAN

Faintly as tolls the evening chime
Our voices keep tune and our oars keep time.
Soon as the woods on shore look dim,
We'll sing at St. Ann's our parting hymn.
Row, brothers, row, the stream runs fast,
The Rapids are near and the daylight's past.

Why should we yet our sail unfurl?
There is not a breath the blue wave to curl;
But, when the wind blows off the shore,
Oh! sweetly we'll rest our weary oar.
Blow, breezes, blow the stream runs fast,
The Rapids are near and the daylight's past.

Utawas' tide! this trembling moon
Shall see us float over thy surges soon.
Saint of this green isle! hear our prayers,
Oh, grant us cool heavens and favouring airs.
Blow, breezes, blow, the stream runs fast,
The Rapids are near and the daylight's past.

From *The Poetical Works of Thomas Moore*

FRANCES ITANI

The Hungry Year

FRANCES ITANI (1942–), a descendant of Pennsylvania Dutch settlers near Gananoque, was born in Belleville, and as a child returned frequently to the area after her family moved to a rural village in Quebec. She spent a year in Kingston in 1971, one block from Fort Henry. She has published several books of short stories and poems, including *Rentee Bay: Poems from the Bay of Quinte (1785-89)*, a dramatic verse account of "The Hungry Year" suffered by a family of Loyalist settlers, whose names appear in this poem as Emma, Mark, and Bett.

Emma

that first summer we played in Rentee Bay; the fruit
grew wild to the edge of sand. Gooseberries
with the smooth skin, sand cherries; we filled
our caps, ate, filled our caps again
squirted one another with wild sweet juice

we ran along shore Bett and I
holding our skirts high above our knees
whooping and hollering, Mark said
like savages

never guessing how close
we were then
to joy

. . . .

Mark

A year; we've had no news
no sign from father
all the farewells and memories of my
sweet boyhood days are gone
and I am left with the single image
of him
kneeling on skinless knees
before that mob
giving gun-prodded thanks
for their lenity
having walked the twenty miles
in the midst of their jeering
carrying our own fattened goose; then
plucking its bloodtipped feathers
while they waited, triumphant, in a circle
their quick hands nervous over warmed buckets
and when the tar was so thick it dripped
heavy from his thighs
they puffed him in his own goose feathers
strapped him, a leg each side; the rail
burned through his screams his scrotum
they paraded him through streets
left him at the edge of town
having had their fill;
and returned to their homes for supper

he crawled on his belly, like a snake
the twenty miles back
and swore to us from bloodied sheets
he'd drink once more, to his King

. . . .

Mark, Emma, & Bett

I am weary now, of bitterness

. . . .

Emma

we scrub our wretched clothes over rock
making them pale as our skin
Mohawk women stand, stare at us
across the creek
they smear themselves with grease
and paint themselves with ochre
but give us venison
sometimes their prized wild rice
and any quantity of fish, indeed
so plentiful it can be had with a scoop

their laughter rings
as they skim canoes toward the marsh
waggling hands to us
though we've not yet joined them in their games

. . . .

Emma

We have bled our own small pig;
deer have fallen on the snow
wolves fatten on their destruction, while
men perish from want of food

But the children catch a robin
and with roots and green grains, I make
a full kettle of soup

When we have eaten
we pass on the precious potted bones

All along the line this week, our neighbours feast
on robin

Bett

The men go out to hunt
but Mark collapses in the deep snow
and they must carry him
back to the cabin

His arm swings to and fro
as tho t'were but a joke
a moment's pause
but fever rattles in his breast
and multitudes of curls
surround his deathly face

. . . .

All

we commit his flesh to earth
we are swallowed by the blood eye of death
we have importuned the winds
which turn deaf ears
and blow softly by

Emma

if the vision of this loneliness
had been mine before
I'd have stayed in that rebel country
there to make hard swallowed peace
with the new order

the children cling to strength they
cannot see in me but seek
strength I neither feel
nor can create

I stand bereft
lie alone sleepless nights
my daily tasks seem hopeless, like despair

Excerpted from *Rentee Bay: Poems from The Bay of Quinte*

ELIZABETH SIMCOE

Of Musquitoes and Ague

ELIZABETH POSTHUMA SIMCOE (1762–1850) was the posthumous daughter of one of General Wolfe's majors of brigade. She accompanied her husband John Graves Simcoe to Upper Canada when he was appointed its first lieutenant-governor in 1791. Her diary, sketches, and paintings provide an invaluable portrait of the country during the years she spent there.

Sunday July 1st [1792]. We rose very early this Morning in order to take a view of the Mill at Gananowui before we proceeded on our way to Kingston. The scenery about the Mill was so pretty that I was well repaid for the trouble of going. Then we returned to our Large Boat & proceeded. After passing Grande Isle & Isle Cauchois we drew near Kingston which we were aware of before we saw the Houses as we discerned the white waves of Lake Ontario beyond looking like a Sea for the wind blew extremely fresh.

Kingston is 6 leagues from Gananowui, a small Town of about fifty wooden Houses & Merchants' Store Houses. Only one House is built of stone, it belongs to a Merchant. There is a small Garrison here & a harbour for Ships. They fired a salute on our arrival & we went to the House appointed for the Commanding Officer at some distance from the Barracks. It is small, but very airy, & so much cooler than the great House at Montreal that I was very well satisfied with the change. The Queen's Rangers are encamped a 1/4 of a mile beyond our house & the bell Tents have a pretty appearance. The situation of this place is entirely flat, & incapable of being rendered defensible, therefore were its situation more central it would still be unfit for the Seat of Government.

M.2nd. Coll. Simcoe went on board the Onondaga & says we shall find tolerable accommodation in her when we go to Niagara tho he is much disposed to row round Lake Ontario in a Boat, but everybody about us oppose the scheme, as tedious & dangerous.

Probably those who are to be of the party do not like the trouble of such a voyage & I suppose Coll. Simcoe will go at last in a Vessel rather than oppose these Sybarites. Some ladies came to see me, & in the Evening I walked.

T. 3rd. There are Mississaga Indians here they are an unwarlike, idle, drunken, dirty tribe. I observe how extremes meet. These uncivilized People saunter up & down the Town all the day, with the apparent Nonchalance, want of occupation & indifference that seems to possess Bond street Beaux.

7th. I walked this Evening in a wood lately set on fire, by some unextinguished fires being left by some persons who had encamped there; which in dry weather often communicates to the Trees. Perhaps you have no idea of the pleasure of walking in a burning wood, but I found it so great that I think I shall have some woods set on fire for my Evening walks. The smoke arising from it keeps the Musquitoes at a distance & where the fire has caught the hollow trunk of a lofty Tree the flame issuing from the top has a fine effect. In some trees where but a small flame appears it looks like stars as the Evening grows dark, & the flare & smoke interspersed in different Masses of dark woods has a very picturesque appearance a little like Tasso's enchanted wood.

11th. The Indians came to dance before the Gov. highly painted & in their War Costume with little Cloathing. They were near enough to the House for me to hear their singing which sounded like a repetition in different dismal tones of he,' he', he' & intervals a Savage Whoop. They had a skin stretched on sticks imitating a drum which they beat with sticks. Having drank more than usual they continued singing the greatest part of the night. They never quarrel with White People unless insulted by them, but are very quarrelsome amongst themselves, therefore when the Women see them drunk they take their knives & hide them until they become sober.

This Evening I walked thro' a pretty part of the Wood & gathered Capillaire.... I was driven home by the bite of a Musquito thro a leather glove, My arm inflamed so much that after supper I fainted with the pain while playing at chess with Capt. Littlehales.

F.13th. Mrs. Macauley the Garrison Surgeon's Wife drank tea with me. She is a naval officer's daughter & a very agreeable woman.

Scadding caught a beautiful small grass green snake which was quite harmless. After keeping it a day or two he let it go. The way of clearing land in this Country is cutting down all the small wood, pile it & set it on fire. The Heavier Timber is cut thro' the bark 5 feet above the ground. This kills the trees which in time the wind blows down. The stumps decay in the ground in the course of years but appear very ugly for a long time tho the very large leafless white Trees have a singular & sometimes a picturesque effect among the living trees. The settler first builds a log hut covered with bark, & after two or three years raises a neat House by the side of it. This progress of Industry is pleasant to observe.

Sunday 15th July. I went to Church twice. The Clergyman Mr. Stewart [Stuart] is from the U. States. He preached good Sermons with an air of serious earnestness in the cause which made them very impressive.

M.16th. We sailed 1/2 a league this Evening in a pretty boat of Mr. Clarke's, attended by music to Garden Island.

S.21st. There are no rides about Kingston or any pleasant Walks that we have met with. Sailing is therefore our only amusement. Today we were prevented by rain from going to the Mills. It is in the Interest of the People here to have this place considered as the Seat of Gov. Therefore they all dissuade the Gov. from going to Niagara & represent the want of Provisions, Houses etc. at that place, as well as the certainty of having the Ague. However he has determined to Sail for Niagara tomorrow.

Monday 23rd July. At 8 this morning we went on board the Onondaga – Commodore Beaton. We sailed with a light wind. A calm soon succeeded & we anchored 7 miles from Kingston. The men who navigate the Ships on this Lake have little nautical knowledge & never keep a log book. This afternoon we were near aground. The Lake is beautifully transparent, we saw the bottom very plainly....

Sunday March 1st [1795] Kingston. We are very comfortably lodged in the Barracks in Kingston. As there are few Officers here, we have the Mess Room to dine in & a Room over it for the Gov.'s office, & these as well as the Kitchen are detached from our other Three Rooms which is very comfortable. The drawing Room has not a stove in it which is a misfortune, but it is too late in the winter to be of much consequence & we have excellent wood fires. I went to Church today & heard an excellent Sermon by Mr. Stuart.

T.3rd. A thaw. Mr. Frazier who drove my Carriole set out yesterday to return home.

7th. Dined at Mr. Stewart's [Stuart's].

8th. An express from York.

9th. We are desirous of seeing the Bay of Quinté, the ice is as smooth as possible & I am told very pleasant to drive upon, & possibly the change of air may abate the violent cough I still have. We therefore determined to set out today. We called at Mr. Booth's farm 11 miles distant, the next 11 miles brought us to Mr. Macdonell's where we dined & slept.

10th. Set off at 11 & drove 14 miles on this delightful Ice to Mr. Fishers in Hay Bay. He was not at home. We proceeded a farther 15 miles to Mr. Cartwright's Mills on the Appanee [Napanee] River & slept at his House, a romantic spot.

11th. We are now half way up the Bay of Quinté. Had we set out a week sooner we might have gone 60 miles farther for a general thaw is so soon expected that we do not venture. We are now travelling on a Coat of upper Ice formed about a fortnight since & between that & the original ice is 2 feet of water. The rapidity with which a thaw comes on is incredible, from the Ice being excellent in 6 hours it is sometimes inpassable.

We set out at 11 & drove 14 miles to Trumpour's Pt. so named from a Man of that Name who lives there. He was formerly in the 16th Dragoons & lives by selling Horses, his wife gave me some good Dutch cakes as I could not wait to eat the Chickens she was roasting in a kettle without water. This house commands a fine view. We passed a village of Mohawk Indians opposite the Appanee River.

From Trumpour's we went to Mr. Macdonell's & slept there. This Bay is about a mile across thickly inhabited on the North Side. The farms are reckoned the most productive in the Province. This Journey has been of great benefit to my health.

18th. An express went to Niagara. A person lately crossing Lake Champlain passed a large Hole in the Ice & an infant alive lying by the side of it. By tracks it appeared as if a Sleigh had fallen in & it was known that a heavy-laden Sleigh with families in it left the country on the opposite shore the day before, probably the Mother threw the Child out as the Sleigh went down. The Gentlemen carried the Infant to Montreal where a subscription was raised for her Maintenance – a good circumstance this for the commencement of a Heroine's life in a Novel.

April 24th. The Gov. has been so ill since the 21st of March that I have not left his Room since that day. He has had such a cough that some nights he could not lie down but sat in a chair, total loss of appetite & such headaches that he could not bear any person but me to walk across the Room or speak loud. There was no medical advice but that of a Horse Doctor who pretended to be an apothecary. The Gov. out of consideration for the convenience of the staff Surgeon had allowed him to remain at Niagara & his not being made to attend his Duty has caused me a great deal of anxiety to see the Gov. so ill without proper attendance. Capt. Brant's sister prescribed a Root – I believe it is calamus – which really relieved his Cough in a very short time....

26th. I went to Church. It rained. My Umbrella was forgotten & the wet through my sleeves gave me a cold, which perhaps I was the more susceptible of from not having been out of the house so long.

27th. I had a fit of the Ague. The first Boats went down to Montreal.

29th. I had a fit of the Ague.

1st of May. The first Boats arrived from Montreal today. The unusual mild weather occasioned Lake Champlain to freeze very late. Mr. Frobisher's sleigh was lost in crossing it, it contained many bags of dollars & valuable things.

Sunday 3. The Ague again.

M.4th. As I am going away so soon, I am obliged to invite the Ladies to dinner, but I am so ill & weak, I was obliged to sit in the Drawing Room while they went to dinner.

5th. The ague.

6th. Ladies dined here. I walked in the Evening.

7th. Very ill indeed.

8th. Ladies dined here.

11th. I drank tea with Mrs. Stewart & much fatigued by that drive – only a mile.

Excerpted from *Mrs. Simcoe's Diary*

FRANÇOIS-ALEXANDRE-FRÉDÉRIC, DUC DE LA ROCHEFOUCAULD-LIANCOURT

To Beguile Ennui

FRANÇOIS-ALEXANDRE-FRÉDÉRIC, DUC DE LA ROUCHEFOUCAULD-LIANCOURT (1747–1827), was the son of the master of the robes to the King of France. Sympathetic at first to the French Revolution, he fled to England during the Terror in 1792. In 1795 he went to America. His extensive tours through the northern states and Canada led to that massive and invaluable historical document *Voyage dans les États-Unis d'Amerique, fait en 1795*, published in Paris in 1799 in eight volumes.

He had a finger in many philanthropic pies: he established a model farm at Liancourt, founded a school of arts and crafts for the sons of soldiers, and took an interest in the abolition of slavery. He wrote books on taxation, education, prison reform, and poor relief.

THE weather was very warm, and had been so for the last eight or ten days. The mercury in Fahrenheit's thermometer stood, at Naryhall, frequently at ninety-two; but on board the vessel, in the cabin, it was only at sixty-four. It is less the intensity of the heat, than its peculiar nature, which renders it altogether intolerable; it is sultry and close, and more so by night, than by day, when it is sometimes freshened by a breeze, which is not the case in the night; the opening of the windows affords no relief; you do not perspire, but feel oppressed; you respire with difficulty; your sleep is interrupted and heavy; and you rise more fatigued, than when you lay down to rest...

Sunday, the 12th of July. When Ducks' Islands were about twenty miles a-stern of us, the lake grew more narrow, and the number of islands increased. They seemed all to be well wooded, but are not inhabited, and lie nearly all of them along the right bank. On the left is Quenty Bay, which stretches about fifty miles into the country, and the banks of which are said to be cultivated up to a considerable extent. The eye dwells with pleasure, once more, on cultivated ground. The country looks pleasant. The houses lie closer, than in any of the new settled parts of Upper Canada, which we have hitherto traversed. The variegated verdure of the corn-fields embellishes and enriches the prospect, charms the eye, and enchants the mind. In the back-ground stands the city of Kingston, on the bay of the same name, which the French, in imitation of the Indians, called Cadarakwe. It consists of about one hundred and twenty or one hundred and thirty houses. The ground in the immediate vicinity of the city rises with a gentle swell, and forms, from the lake onwards, as it were, an amphitheatre of lands, cleared, but not yet cultivated. None of the buildings are distinguished by a more handsome appearance from the rest. The only structure, more conspicuous than the others, and in front of which the English flag is hoisted, is the barracks, a stone building, surrounded with pallisadoes.

All the houses stand on the northern bank of the bay, which stretches a mile farther into the country. On the southern bank are the buildings belonging to the naval force, the wharfs, and the habitations of all the persons, who belong to that department. The King's ships lie at anchor near these buildings, and consequently have a harbour and road separate from the port for merchantmen. We landed at Port Royal. However *kingly* were the commander and his ship, he took our money. Governor Simcoe expressly desired us not to pay for our passage, as the cutter was a King's ship, and he had amply supplied us with provision. But my friend Dupetitthouars, as well as myself, were so much displeased with the idea, of making this passage at the expense of the King of England, that we ventured to offer our money to Captain Earl. Offers of this kind are seldom refused, nor did ours meet with a denial. Yet, it is but justice to add, that Captain Earl is a worthy man, civil, attentive, constantly on the deck, apparently fond of his profession, and master of his business ....

Kingston, considered as a town, is much inferior to Newark; the number of houses is nearly equal in both. Kingston may contain a few more buildings, but they are neither so large nor so good as at Newark. Many of them are log-houses, and those which consist of joiner's work, are badly constructed and painted. But few new houses are built. No town-hall, no court-house, and no prison have hitherto been constructed. The houses of two or three merchants are conveniently situated for loading and unloading ships; but, in point of structure, these are not better than the rest. Their trade chiefly consists of peltry, which comes across the lake, and in provision from Europe, with which they supply Upper Canada. They act as agents or commissioners of the Montreal Company, who have need of magazines in all places, where their goods must be unshipped.

The trade of Kingston, therefore, is not very considerable. The merchant ships are only three in number, and make but eleven voyages in a year. Kingston is a staple port. It is situated twelve miles above the point of the river, which is considered as the extremity of the lake. Here arrive all the vessels, which sail up the river of St. Lawrence, laden with provision brought in European ships to Quebec...

The district of Kingston supplied, last year, the other parts of Canada with large quantities of pease; the culture of which, introduced but two years ago, proves very productive and successful. In the course of last year, one thousand barrels of salt pork, of two hundred and eight pounds each, were sent from Kingston to Quebec; its price was eighteen dollars per barrel. The whole trade is carried on by merchants, whose profits are the more considerable, as they fix the price of the provision, which they receive from Europe, and either sell in the vicinity, or ship for the remoter parts of Upper Canada, without the least competition, and just as they think proper.

Although the number of cultivators is here greater than in the district of Niagara, yet the vast quantity of land under cultivation is not better managed than thcirs. The difficulty of procuring labourers obstructs agricultural improvements and encourages them to insist on enormous wages...

There is no regular market in Kingston; every one provides himself with fresh meat as well as he can, but frequently it cannot be had on any terms.

For this information I am chiefly indebted to Mr. Steward, curate in Kingston, who cultivates himself seventy acres, part of two thousand acres, which have been granted him as an American loyalist. He is a native of Harrisburg in Pennsylvania, and seems to have zealously embraced the royal cause in the American war. Fifteen hundred pounds sterling, which he had placed in the American funds, have been confiscated. Although he continues warmly attached to the British Monarch, yet he has become more moderate in his political principles; he has preserved some friends who espoused the cause of the Republic, among whom is Bishop White of Philadelphia. Mr. Steward is a man of much general information, mild, open, affable, and universally respected; he is very sanguine in his expectation that the price of land will rise, and that he shall then be enabled to portion out his numerous children. Without being a very skilful farmer, he is perfectly acquainted with the details of agriculture, so that I can place implicit confidence on his statements, the truth of which has also been confirmed by other husbandmen...

The inhabitants of the district of Kingston meddle still less with politics than the people of Newark. No newspaper is printed in the town; that of Newark is the only one published in Upper Canada, which being a mere imperfect extract from the Quebec Gazette, is here taken in by no one. I know but of two persons who receive even the Quebec-paper. As to the interior of the country, no news penetrates into that quarter, a circumstance that excites there very little regret.

In this district are some schools, but they are few in number. The children are instructed in reading and writing, and pay each a dollar a month. One of the masters, superior to the rest in point of knowledge, taught Latin; but he has left the school, without being succeeded by another instructor of the same learning.

There are yet but very few surgeons in this district; they, who assume this appellation, contrive to get well paid for their trouble. Excepting intermittent fevers, which are rather frequent in Kingston, the climate is very healthy. The houses, as has already been observed, are built of wood, for reasons which it is extremely difficult to discern. The town is seated on rocky ground; and not the smallest house can be built without the foundation being excavated in rock, a sort of stone which affords the two-fold advantage of being easily cut, and of growing hard when exposed to the air, without cracking in the frost. The inhabitants allow that, if bricklayers were procured even from Montreal (for there are none in this place), building with stone would be less expensive than with wood. They grant that, in addition to the greater solidity of such buildings, they would afford more warmth in winter, and more coolness in summer, but habit is here, as elsewhere, more powerful than reason. Carpenters' wages amount to sixteen shillings a day; labourers are equally scarce in Newark, and consequently as bad and as dear...

THERE is but one church in Kingston, and this, though very lately built, resembles a barn more than a church.

We had a letter from General Simcoe to the Commanding Officer in Kingston, who, at our arrival, was Captain Parr, of the sixtieth regiment.... He is the son of the aged Governor of Nova

Scotia. At first he seems cold, grave, and reserved; but his countenance brightens on a nearer acquaintance, and grows more open, gay, and cheerful; he soon fell into an easy familiarity of conversation, which was heightened during our dinner. His behaviour was entirely free from ceremony, and indicated that he was not displeased with our society.

This dinner, which he gave to the newly arrived officers, forms for us a remarkable epocha. The ingenuity of the English in devising toasts, which are to be honoured with bumpers, is well known. To decline joining in such a toast would be deemed uncivil; and, although it might be more advisable to submit to this charge, than to contract a sickness, yet such energy of character is seldom displayed on these occasions. Unwilling to oppose the general will, which becomes more imperious in proportion as heads grow warmer, you resort to slight deceptions in the quantity you drink, in hopes thus to avert the impending catastrophe. But this time none of us, whether French or English, had carried the deception far enough, and I was concerned to feel, the remainder of the evening, that I had taken too lively a part in the event of the two detachments relieving each other...

The royal navy is not very formidable in this place; six vessels compose the whole naval force, two of which are small gun-boats, which we saw at Niagara, and which are stationed at York. Two small schooners of twelve guns, viz., the Onondago, in which we took our passage, and the Mohawk, which is just finished; a small yacht of eighty tons, mounting six guns, and lastly the Missasoga, of as many guns as the two schooners, which has lately been taken into dock to be repaired, form the rest of it. All these vessels are built of timber fresh cut down, and not seasoned, and for this reason last never longer than six or eight years. To preserve them even to this time requires a thorough repair; they must be heaved down and caulked, which costs at least from one thousand to one thousand two hundred guineas. The expense for building the largest of them amounts to four thousand guineas. This is an enormous price, and yet it is not so high as on Lake Erie, whither all sorts of naval stores must be sent from Kingston, and where the price of labour is still higher. The timbers of the Missasoga, which was built three years ago, are almost all rotten. It is so easy to make provision of ship-timber for many years to come, as this would require merely the felling of it, and that too at no great distance from the place where it is to be used, that it is difficult to account for this precaution not yet having been adopted. Two gun-boats, which are destined by Governor Simcoe to serve only in time of war, are at present on the stocks; but the carpenters, who work at them, are but eight in number. The extent of the dilapidations and embezzlements, committed at so great a distance from the mother-country, may be easily conceived. In the course of last winter, a judicial enquiry into a charge of this nature was instituted at Kingston. The commissioner of the navy, and the principal ship-wright, it was asserted, had clearly colluded against the King's interest; but interest and protection are as powerful in the New World as in the Old: – for both the commissioner and ship-wright continue in their places…

To beguile *ennui*, and enjoy a few hours longer the society of our friend, Captain Parr, we accompanied him to the distance of six miles from Kingston. His detachment occupied seven vessels, and he had one for himself. The soldiers were without exception as much intoxicated as I ever saw any in the French service. On the day of their departure they were scarcely able to row, which rendered our tour extremely tedious. On our return, wind and current were against us, so that we proceeded very slowly. Canadians rowed our boat, and according to their custom ceased not a moment to sing. One of them sings a song, which the rest repeat, and all row to the tune. The songs are gay and merry, and frequently somewhat more; they are only interrupted by the laugh they occasion. The Canadians, on all their tours on the water, no sooner take hold of the oars, than they begin to sing, from which they never cease until they lay the oars down again. You fancy yourself removed into a province of France; and this illusion is sweet. Our whole day, from six o'clock in the morning until nine at night, was consumed in this tour. So much the better; a day is gone; for although the unwearied politeness of the officers afford us every day in Kingston a comfortable dinner and agreeable society from four to eight o'clock in the evening, yet we cannot but feel much *ennui* in a place, where no sort of amusement, no well-informed man, and no books shorten the long lingering day.

Our situation is extremely unpleasant, and might well render us melancholy, did we give up our mind to irksome reflection…

Excerpted from *Travels in Canada*

SIR GEORGE HEAD

More Noise Than Music

SIR GEORGE HEAD (1782–1855), a British army officer, was sent to Canada in 1814: he travelled widely during his years of service in the country (1814–15, 1816–21). His brother was Sir Francis Bond Head, Governor of Upper Canada during the 1837 Rebellion.

February 15th. – I had now twenty-four miles to proceed to Kingston, where I arrived early in the day. I went to Thibodo's hotel; a large cold, rambling house, the landlord of which was extremely attentive and civil.

February 16th. – As I had proposed to remain a day or two at Kingston, I walked out on the ice to see the ship St. Lawrence, which was here frozen in on all sides, quite hard and fast. Two seventy-fours, a frigate, and some gun-boats, were building in the dock-yard; and the above-named three-decker, mounting 108 guns, two brigs, and a sloop, were in a state of complete equipment. At Kingston, the gigantic features of the river St. Lawrence are particularly striking; for here, at a distance of several hundred miles from the sea, its expanding shores are seen tracing the limits of Lake Ontario. This magnificent fresh-water sea was frozen round the edges to an extent nearly as far as the eye could reach; the waters in the distance appearing like a narrow black line in the horizon. The ship lay close to the town, with which a constant communication prevailed, as the officers and men were living on board just as if she had been at sea. Sleighs of all descriptions were driving round; country vehicles, with things to sell, and others and two ladies, who had driven themselves in a light sleigh drawn by a pony, were holding a conversation under her bows with a gentleman in a cap, which conversation, from its earnestness, seemed to contain warmth enough to thaw the icicles hanging from the cabin windows. Numbers of people were walking, and the snow was so trodden all round the ship, that it was really difficult to believe that a depth of water sufficient to float a three-decker lay under one's feet.

I found, on returning to my inn, that a ball was to be held in the house in the evening, and that my bed-room, moreover, had been determined on as one of the card-rooms. The assembly was held in a large corridor, or wide passage, with doors opening into little rooms on each side; of which latter, mine was one. The company, which was numerous, assembled very early, and soon commenced dancing with high glee. Pulling, romping, turning round and round, &c., being the order of the day, the noise of tongues and feet was "pretty considerable loud." What with the good spirits of the young ladies, and the good humour of the old ones, it was past three o'clock in the morning before the house was clear of its guests, when, the beds having been all taken down for the occasion, I betook myself to a mattress spread for me on the floor.

February 17th. – My landlord gave me for dinner some steaks of a moose-deer, killed in the neighbourhood; the meat was of a fine, wild flavour, although extremely coarse and tough.

February 18th to 22nd. – I left Kingston for York in a two-horse sleigh, which I hired the afternoon, we sailed with a favourable breeze out of the harbour. Before sunset we were quite out of sight of land, and to all appearance as much at sea as if in the middle of the Atlantic. The master of the vessel, as night came on, determined to lay-to until the morning. Had we made the islands called the False Ducks before dark, we should have stood on for Kingston Harbour.

July 7th. – At daylight we proceeded on our voyage, and anchored, at nine o'clock in the morning, at Kingston. I heard that Colonel Phillot of the Royal Artillery was just about to leave Kingston, in a bateau, for Montreal, and it was proposed to me to accompany him; an arrangement which suited me in every way. So, having breakfasted on shore, we were all in the bateau and ready to depart before eleven o'clock. Our bateau was a large flat-bottomed boat pointed at both ends alike, and manned entirely by French Canadians. The wind was favourable, and we had a large sail to assist us; so that we very soon had an opportunity of hearing a genuine Canadian boat-song.

In these melodies there is a vast deal more noise than music, nor of all that I heard these men sing during the voyage, did any bear the slightest resemblance to those I had heard before. The *refrein* of one of our boatmen's ditties I happen to recollect. It is as follows: "Sommes nous au mi – lieu du bois, Sommes nous au ri – vage – e." The above they roared out without mercy, in full chorus, and one at a time sang each verse in solo. The subject treated of the hardihood of the Voyageurs, the troubles and difficulties they encounter, without forgetting their skill and bravery in surmounting them.

Excerpted from *Forest Scenes and Incidents*

JACQUES VIGER

Built with Good Taste

JACQUES VIGER (1787–1858) was born into an influential family in Montreal and distinguished himself in many fields – as a newspaperman, editor, politician, historian, archivist, and collector. He also served in the militia all his life and remained fascinated by things military. He is reported to have had himself "painted in the uniform of a Voltigeur, with Shako, long sabre and Sabretache." His impressions of Kingston appear in his *Reminiscences of the War of 1812–14.*

THE town stands on the site of old Fort Frontenac, a few of whose remains are still to be seen. Indians gave this place the name of Cataracoui, which means 'clay fort' (more properly, perhaps, 'clay bank rising out of the water'). The town is on a point of land. It is built with good taste; the streets lie mostly at right angles, and are straight and wide. On its eastern limits are the barracks and King's storehouses. The barracks, built partly of stone and partly of wood, are two storeys high; they face a large square. A tower, now used as a powder magazine, and a triangular structure near the artillery barracks, are the last vestiges of the French constructions. The remains of an earthwork built by Bradstreet, who captured the fort from the French in 1758, are still to be seen. Two large buildings near the center of the town are used as a military hospital.

Kingston is divided into two portions by a central square, which is used as a parade-ground for the troops. There is also a market-building, and opposite to it is the Anglican church. Both are of wood. To the right of the square are the court-house and cafe (hotel). Both are of stone, two storeys high. The latter is an excellent house in every respect; but the former is built in bad taste. On its ground floor are the kitchen and gaol; the upper flat is divided into two apartments , the largest is used by the Court of Justice. The Sessions sit in October and April annually; one of the apartments is used as a library, consisting of 300 or 400 volumes, the annual subscription to which is twenty shillings.

A teacher of considerable reputation keeps a school which is very well patronized. With aid from the Seminaries and inhabitants of Lower Canada, a (R.C.) church of stone was erected. The interior is still unfinished. It is used, at present, as a public hospital. An old wooden house which was brought from one of the neighbouring lands [Carleton] is now 'The Commandant's House.' It is by no means handsome, but is prettily situated.

The remains of a moat or ditch, also of a glacis constructed by the French, can still be seen in the public square. To the west is Point Mississauga, and still farther west is Point Murray. These two important points have been fortified; batteries have been erected there. The first is faced with heavy square timber. In the rear of the town, and on the right flank, have been erected several redoubts, part of stone and part of wood. They defend the approaches from the north. Other defences have also been made.

The land behind Kingston slopes up gently. To the front is a bay "(the Great River Cataraqui)" running five miles to the north. The government has there magnificent mills. This bay forms a fine harbour, where vessels can be secured most comfortably for wintering. The opposite shore to the east is cut into three points. The two farthest are quite high, but the middle one is, of all others, the loftiest spot in the neighbourhood.

The farthest is Point Hamilton, and is thickly wooded. Off its shore is Cedar Island, which is rocky, and quite recently laid bare of trees. On this island is a telegraph station in view of Snake Island, far out in the lake, and other similar stations. The middle point is Point Henry, which has been cleared of wood, with the object of planting there a camp of observation. It is proposed to erect here extensive fortifications. The nearest point was formerly Point Haldimand, but this has been changed to Point Frederick, or Navy Bay. It is a very level piece of ground, low-lying and well fortified, occupied by the naval buildings, yard, and Admiralty buildings. Between these two points is Navy Bay. Troops are always quartered here in separate and very comfortable quarters. A hulk is moored in the bay between the two points, which is used for hospital purposes. The security of Kingston on the water side depends on the co-operation of the batteries of Point Frederick and Mississauga Point; and the crossfiring from these two points, if well directed, should make the entrance of the harbour an impossibility....

The lands in the immediate neighbourhood are of indifferent quality; they are, however, of far better quality two or three miles away, and are being rapidly settled. The climate is good.

Three miles behind the town flows a creek which has retained the name Petite Cataraqui. It is fairly wide, sluggish and very muddy. It is crossed by the York road; at the end of the bridge a small entrenchment, with embrasures for cannon has been erected....

AFTER spending twenty-one days in the barracks at Kingston, ten days in quarters prepared by us, but not for us, at M. Smith's, and four days in a camp made by us, but once more not for us, on the heights of Kingston, we were ordered by General Prevost, on the 17th of May, to cross over to Point Henry, where we now occupy tents which we again once more put up in a wilderness of stumps, fallen trees, boulders and rocks of all sizes and shapes, sharing our blankets with reptiles of various species, carrying out the precepts of the most self-sacrificing charity towards ten millions insects and crawling abominations!

When we first came to Fort Henry, on the 17th of May, it was covered with stumps, and the ground was full of holes and bumps. The trees had been cut down, but quite recently. With much labour our Voltigeurs succeeded in levelling their camp-ground, the camp consisting of two rows of marquees, facing one broad, central avenue, at the head of which are our Major's quarters, and at the foot a small entrenchment. On a fine day our encampment presents quite a pretty site. The Point is high, and commands the view over the surrounding country. We can here perceive the immense expanse of Lake Ontario; on the distant horizon a few wooded islands; to the right the town and its pretty background; the harbour and its sailing craft. Point Frederick, its fortifications and shipyards, are mapped before us. To the left is Wolfe Island, with extensive forests, dotted here and there with new settlements.

Excerpted from *Reminiscences of the War of 1812–14*

LINUS WILSON MILLER

A Rebel's Tale

LINUS WILSON MILLER (1817–1880) was twenty years old when he left the United States to join the Rebellion of 1837 in Upper Canada led by William Lyon Mackenzie. He was taken prisoner, incarcerated at Fort Henry in Kingston, and condemned to hang. His sentence was commuted to transportation to Van Dieman's Land. In 1845 he was pardoned and returned to the United States where he wrote this account of his adventures.

ON the 23d instant, we were chained and hand-cuffed in pairs, and removed under charge of the sheriff, per steam boat "Traveler," to Fort Henry, Kingston. Our parting with our more unfortunate companions was heartrending in the extreme, as we had little hopes of ever seeing them again in this world; and, with the exception of Beemer, they were all much esteemed....

Arriving in Kingston, we were landed privately, and marched by a back road to Fort Henry, which is by far the most formidable fortification in Upper Canada. After being unshackled, we were turned into a room formerly occupied by Messrs. Parker, Montgomery, and others, and from which they made one of the most wonderful escapes from prison on record. Watson and Parker were re-captured, but the others, fourteen in number, succeeded in gaining the American side of the line....

The best privilege we enjoyed was that of walking in the yard an hour each day. He who has never been a captive can not prize, as we did, the fresh, free air, or the value of an hour's exercise. The physical as well as mental powers suffer alike from inaction, occasioning a morbid sensation, exceedingly detrimental to enjoyment of any kind. This hour was the only opportunity we enjoyed of cultivating an acquaintance with our captive friends in the adjoining room....

A sentry was constantly parading before our windows, and it formed no small part of his duty to look in at his charge every five minutes. But our enemies were the losers by this arrangement, for many a sworn servant of her gracious Majesty here received information with reference to desertion, which was generally improved to the best advantage. We were allowed to write to, and receive letters from our friends, once in two weeks, but all communications were inspected by the sheriff. One or two letters were returned to me, which I had written to my brother, on account of their containing some offensive expressions with reference to our treatment and the government, and thus were we soon taught to praise our enemies, if we wished our friends to know that we were well; and, indeed, I have even found a little fulsome flattery indispensable in this matter. Only say "Mr. So and So, who has us in charge, treats us with the greatest kindness and affability, grants us every indulgence consistent with the faithful discharge of his official duties and is a gentleman of the first respectability," and should you have no money to pay the postage on your letter, Mr. So and So will pay it himself, rather than allow so elegant an epistle to pass unseen into oblivion. We received frequent visits from gentlemen belonging to the British provinces, and occasionally to the States. – They always accompanied sheriff MacDonald, who appeared to feel quite proud of the state prisoners, as we were called, and would generally say something in our praise; but when alone he sometimes gave us a terrible tongue-thrashing, for some trifling indiscretion. He was bitter, cutting, and sarcastic, when he chose to be so, and I am sorry to say it, would swear most vehemently when in a rage. I have ever thought that interest alone made him a supporter of the Government, and that in principle he was with us. Some Tories, who gained admittance under his wing, attempted to abuse and insult our misfortunes; but he told them plainly, in our presence, that while he had charge of us, the Governor himself should not take that liberty. "Place them on an equal footing with yourself," said he to an old Tory, one day, "and you will have no disposition to impose upon them the second time. They are all brave men, and know how to behave themselves, and no man shall take advantage of their defenselessness to insult their feelings."

Soon after our arrival at the Fort we had the misfortune to lose one of our number by death. David Taylor, a young Canadian of mild and gentle demeanor, steady conduct, and good principles, had taken a severe cold at Niagara, where, although removed to the hospital for a day or two, he was much neglected by the doctor, a man who seemed to esteem the life of a rebel captive as of little or no consequence. When we were removed he was quite ill, notwithstanding which, this man ordered him to be shackled, the same as if quite well, and was shamefully harsh and brutal when poor Taylor complained; and I believe that this, together with an almost broken heart, brought on a speedy termination to his earthly sufferings. He never left his bed for an hour after our arrival, but lay in the same room with us, silent, uncomplaining, and fast sinking into the arms of death. Crushed in spirit, his soul seemed to loath a prison life and hasted to be free. The surgeon of the Fort visited him daily, but refused to remove him to the hospital, where proper care might be taken of him, and indeed, gave him little medicine. He too, seemed to care nothing for the life of a prisoner. The sick man, however, wished to remain with us, and we tried hard to supply, as far as possible, the tender care of a mother and sister, whose names were ever and anon on his lips, both in his waking and sleeping hours. "Sister," he would say in his dreams, "dear sister, why, oh! why are you absent from your dying brother?... Mother, dear mother, will you not bless your poor dying son? Will you not say, you forgive him all the trouble and grief he has ever caused you? ... Do, mother, do, dear sister, make my pillow softer; do come and tell me you love me: oh! let me hear those words once more! Oh! the gloomy prison walls – the cells – the chains – how cold and heavy they are on my aching limbs! Will they not take them off even when I'm dying? Must I die in chains? Will they lay my poor body here in this dreadful place, far, far from home and friends? not even a mother, or a sister, to weep when I'm gone! Off, off with the chains! Take me out in the free, fresh air! let me breathe it again, let me look once more upon the sun, and then kill me, for I can't live in prison. There are no chains in heaven! oh no, then I shall be free."

On the 27th instant he appeared to be very low, and it was evident that his end was near.... Hastening to his bedside, I was just in time to see him close his eyes, as we all supposed, forever. He lay about fifteen minutes, apparently quite dead, when, to our great surprise he suddenly revived, and a scene ensued which I can never forget. Within thirty seconds after he was observed to breath again, his eyes opened and his lips began to move, and "Glory – glory – glory! hallelujah! blessed Savior, blessed Jesus! praise Him! O praise the Lord! let the whole earth praise and bless Him!" bust forth, as it were, spontaneously from his tongue.

For several minutes, similar exclamations filled the dying man's mouth, his countenance beaming with inexpressible joy, his eyes and hands raised to heaven, in the attitude of devotion. Around his bed were the careless sinner, the professed infidel, and scoffer at religion, none of whom could refrain from tears. During his whole illness he had never spoken upon the subject of religion except in brief answers to questions put to him by some of his companions. He now addressed us in the following words: "You all thought I was dead, and I thought so, too; for my spirit was free, and I was free, and I was with angels, and with Jesus. Oh, it was a glorious sight, and I would not live upon the earth, if that was heaven. The angels told me I was too willing to die without praising the name of my blessed Savior; that I never had praised Him as I ought...and that I must be raised to show the power of God, and be a witness to you, my dear friends, of his infinite goodness and mercy in pardoning my sins, and in taking from this place of sorrow and suffering to heaven."

Observing one who had nursed him with much care standing aside, deeply affected, he said, "W———, come and shake hands with me: do not weep on my account, but witness the power and goodness of God, who would not allow me to leave you without praising His name, and telling you all what He has done for my soul. Look upon me, friends, and see what a reality, what a blessed reality there is in religion. It fills my soul with bliss and inexpressible joy in this trying hour. Oh! will you not love and serve Him, who has done so much for me? Won't you believe in Him. But I have never praised Him before as I ought; nor did I ever know how very precious He is till now. I have been a great sinner, but He has forgiven me, and is now about to take me home to Himself; and I shall soon be free from bonds and imprisonment. Tell, oh, tell my friends that I die happy, that I love them; that I love the cause of liberty; that I love the Savior. But my time is expired, and I am going! – they come – they come – the angels – bless Jesus – glory – g-l-o-r-y – J-e-s-u-s" – died on his lips, and his happy soul winged its flight, accompanied, doubtless, by angels, to the bosom of its Creator. Thus died David Taylor, aged 26 years.... As I stood by, and closed his eyes, when the last struggle was over, I said in my heart, "Let me die the death of the righteous, and let my last end be like his." His remains were buried without ceremony, in the yard at Kingston, set aside as the resting place of the prisoner; and many a martyr to the cause of liberty has, since then, found a bed by his side, unwept, unhonoured – but blest!...

On the 9th of November, we were much surprised at receiving an order to be in readiness, in an hour's time, for removal to Quebec.... We all felt, that the hasty measures adopted were cruel in the extreme: not one had made any preparation for so long a journey; and but one or two had half clothing enough to guard against the cold weather, or money to purchase such necessaries as the nature of the case demanded; besides, we were not even allowed to write to our friends, chains and hand-cuffs being put on our limbs within a few minutes after we received the notice.... Mrs. Wait was present, encouraging her husband, and indeed all of us, to bear this adversity with becoming fortitude. Woman has been called the weaker sex, from time immemorial; but certain I am, her conduct often proves the saying false. In seasons of distress, when weakness of mind become manifest, then it is that her strength, her fortitude, and enduring constancy, outshine the most dazzling qualities of man. Those who have experienced or witnessed her ministrations under such circumstances, can best appreciate her inestimable worth....

We were marched to the wharf in our chains, a distance of nearly half a mile, placed among the horses belonging to a troop of cavalry, on the middle deck of the steamer "Cobourg," where we had but just room enough to stand upright.... No time was lost in getting under way, and as we glided swiftly down the St. Lawrence, although sensible that every moment was increasing the distance between me and home, and friends, yet I saw nothing, and felt nothing, but the irons, and cold, piercing winds, and I wished for nothing so much as death. Never had I felt cold so intensely before.... But for a blanket and pea-jacket, served out to each man, I verily believe I should have frozen to death.... During the night, some of our number lay down, in a pile, among the horses, which, with the hand-cuffs, chains, and manure, formed a very interesting group. It was a night of dreadful misery to all of us....

Excerpted from *Notes of an Exile to Van Dieman's Land*

WALTER HENRY

Of Black Bass and Asiatic Cholera

WALTER HENRY (1791–1860) was born in Ireland and educated there and in England. An army surgeon during the Peninsular and Nepalese wars and the 1837 Rebellion, he was well known for his advanced views on hygiene and the treatment of cholera. He was stationed in Kingston from 1831–1833; in 1852 he returned to Canada as Inspector-General of Hospitals and later retired to Belleville.

KINGSTON, finely situated on a rising ground at the north eastern and lower extremity of Lake Ontario, and at the upper end of the extraordinary Rideau Canal, is a town possessing great local advantages from this favourable position, and from the deep water of the harbour, which is sufficient for the largest ships. From these physical reasons – to say nothing of the strength of the military defences of Fort Henry, or the excellent character of its inhabitants, Kingston must always be a place of note; and by and bye, when the wild land in the back Townships around it is brought into cultivation, the shores of the beautiful Bay of Quinté made the resort of emigrants, as they ought to be, and the impediments to the navigation of the Trent removed – this loyal and respectable town must participate largely in the general prosperity of the neighbourhood.

The bridge is a substantial wooden one, six hundred yards in length; spanning the neck of the Bay, with a draw-arch for craft passing up to the Rideau. The sail to the first batch of locks, commands a prospect of finely wooded banks, of moderate elevation; and on each side patches of cultivated land and good farm houses appear in rich and luxuriant relief. This riant aspect is strongly contrasted with the gloom and melancholy of the view on entering the Canal. The black stumps of the half-burned trees sticking out of the drowned land – the solitude of the literally "dismal swamp" – the shallow, inky, and fetid water, with its unhealthy associations, are utterly disagreeable to the eye, and excite the most distasteful and unpleasing ideas: and it must be confessed that however advantageous to the Province this additional internal communication and artery of trade may be, the inundated shores of the Rideau add nothing to its beauty…

Our regiment occupied three points here – the Téte du Pont Barracks, Fort Henry and Point Frederick. For the first month or two we were very healthy, but as the summer advanced the malaria from the Rideau swamps began to act on the men; and we had a good deal of intermittent fever, generally of a mild description, and that yielded readily to medicine.

After a few weeks, when we had looked about us a little, and reconnoitred our position, we began to bethink us that Lake Ontario was celebrated for its fish; and to take measures of hostility against the black bass, which we heard highly spoken of, as affording lively sport on the line and making a capital dish at table. So I bought a skiff, prepared minnow tackle, struck the top-gallants of my salmon-rods; and, one fine day in June, crossed over to Garden Island, sitting in the stern of my pretty little craft, whilst my servant plied a tiny pair of oars.

I had a rod and line at each side, at right angles with the skiff, and another line astern. Having attached a minnow and a gaudy fly to each, I commenced trolling along, with the stern line rolled up as far as was necessary, on a stick in my pocket. We had not gone a hundred yards when one reel spun away merrily, and there was a bass of a couple of pounds on the minnow-hook, leaping out of the water most vivaciously. Before I had secured this gentleman I felt a tug at my pocket, and discovered than another about the same size was fast on the stern-hook. I caught him also; and thus we went on, amusingly enough, for three or four hours; and returned in the evening with three dozen of good bass, a few of which were four pounds weight.

The bass is an excellent fish – firm, white and sweet at table, and very lively on the hook; leaping out of the water like a salmon. They are good either boiled or fried – at breakfast or dinner, and make an admirable curry. During our stay on the shores of Lake Ontario, I caught some thousands of them, and ate them constantly without satiety…

THE question whether the pestilence, which under the name of Asiatic Cholera, had spread through the British Islands in 1831 and 32, would be able to force its way across the broad barrier of the Atlantic, was mooted in this remote Province with much interest, some apprehension and a great difference of opinion. The generality of my professional brethren, with myself, thought the ocean was too vast to be passed; and that the new world would continue happily exempt from the plague that was devastating the old.

Unfortunately these sanguine hopes and speculations turned out unfounded. The cholera crossed the Atlantic, and poured over Canada and all North America, like a destroying flood. Indeed the mortality attending it was proportionately much greater than in the mother country, or any part of Europe; and at Montreal the disease was, for the population, four or five times more deadly than at Paris.

On the 8th of June, the pestilence made its first appearance in Quebec, having been apparently imported with a ship full of emigrants from Ireland. It proceeded up the river to Montreal, where it burst out like a volcano on the 11th. Its course was capricious and uncertain; some intermediate villages being ravaged, and others passed over altogether. At Prescott, two deaths occurred on the 15th, and on the 17th it reached Kingston.

The Director General of the Medical Department, Sir James McGrigor, mindful of the maxim, *"venienti occurrite morbo,"* had providently issued orders to his officers early in the year respecting the proper steps to be taken in preparing, as well as possible, for the approaching mischief; which my friend, Dr. Skey, at the head of the department here, was indefatigable in enforcing; with the addition of such local directions as his perfect acquaintance with these Provinces, and long general experience elsewhere, might suggest. I have not the slightest doubt but that many lives were saved in the Canadas, by the preventive measures then taken throughout this command.

As soon as it was known that malignant cholera had really appeared in Quebec, it was plain enough that it would find its way to the shores of Lake Ontario. My old friend, Colonel Nicol, was our Commandant at Kingston; and I well knew what fearless energy might be expected from him in the midst of any epidemic, however deadly. We first had the barracks and hospitals most carefully cleaned and whitewashed: the duties and fatigues of the soldiers were lightened as much as possible, and they were daily inspected with great care by their medical officers. The canteen was placed under vigilant supervision, and preparations were made to isolate the barracks, and to remove the married soldiers resident in the town, with their families, to a camp on the other side of the bay.

Although the cholera raged in the town for the next fortnight, we had no case in the regiment till the 4th July, when two grenadiers were attacked with frightful spasms – I was sent for on the instant – bled them both largely, and they recovered. Ten other men of the regiment were taken ill, and treated in the same way: the agonizing cramps yielded to the early and copious bleeding, as to a charm, and they also all recovered.

Encouraged by the result of these, and several similar instances amongst the poor people of the town, I began vainly to imagine that this plan of treatment would be generally successful; and wrote confidently to this effect to Dr. Skey: but I was soon to be undeceived. Three men and a woman, of the 66th, were attacked the same night. I saw them immediately; and the symptoms being the same to all appearance, they were bled like the others, and all died within twelve hours of the first attack. The spot which their barrack at Point Frederick occupied, was a promontory near the dock-yard, the air of which was vitiated by the neighbourhood of the rotting ships. The company quartered there was removed to camp on the hill the next morning, and had no more cholera.

The fact is, I believe that we had two different diseases, confounded together under the common name of cholera, to contend with: one of these maladies having very much the character of tetanus, or locked-jaw. This genus was marked by early, severe and universal spasms, affecting every muscle, and causing great torture. This appeared to be easily curable, and the early bleeding in this peculiar and sthenic type wrought miracles, when judiciously and fearlessly employed. In the other more dangerous form, when the malady stole on more quietly, the patients sank early into hopeless debility, and here medicine was of very little avail.

We all heard wonderful accounts of the effects of transfusion of saline fluid into the veins, and Dr. Sampson, the principal practitioner in Kingston, and a man of talent, was determined, as well as myself, to give it a fair trial.

We used it in twenty bad cases, but unsuccessfully in all – though the first effect in every instance was the apparent restoration of the powers of life; and in one remarkable case of a poor emigrant from Yorkshire, life was protracted seven days by constant pumping. Here the man almost instantaneously recovered voice, strength, colour, and appetite; and Sampson and myself, seeing this miraculous change, almost believed we had discovered the new elixir of life in the humble shape of salt and water.

The appearance of Kingston during the epidemic was most melancholy – "While the long funerals blacken all the way."

Nothing was seen in the streets but these melancholy processions. No business was done, for the country people kept aloof from the infected town. The yellow flag was hoisted near the market place on the beach, and intercourse with the Steamboats put under Quarantine regulations. The conduct of the inhabitants was admirable, and reflected great credit on this good little town. The Medical men and the Clergy of all persuasions, vied with each other in the fearless discharge of their respective dangerous duties; and the exertions of all classes were judicious, manly and energetic: for the genuine English spirit showed itself, as usual, undaunted in the midst of peril, and rising above it.

We had thirty-six cases of bad cholera – besides a host of choleroid complaints, in the regiment. Of these we lost five men and two women. No child suffered.

During the prevalence of the disease it seemed to me that a number of errors in diet were generally entertained and acted on in our little community. Because unripe fruit, or excess in its use does mischief, all fruit was now proscribed by common opinion; and vegetables of every description were placed under the same ban, so that the gardeners saw their finest productions rotting unsaleable. This was folly; for the stomach was more likely to suffer than to benefit from the want of its accustomed pabulum of mixed animal and vegetable substances. It was proper to live temperately – to avoid supper eating, or eating late in the day – as eight-tenths of the attacks came on in the night – to eschew excesses of all kinds – but, above all to be fearless and place confidence in Providence.

If, amidst so much distress, ludicrous ideas could be entertained, there was enough to excite them on this subject of abstinence from vegetables. Huge Irishmen who had sucked in the national root with their mother's milk, and lived on it all their lives, now shrank from a potato as poison. I heard a respectable and intelligent gentleman confess that he was tempted by the attractive appearance of a dish of green pease, and ate *one* pea, but he felt uncomfortable afterwards, and was sure it had disagreed with him.

The disease ceased entirely, and the usual intercourse was restored between the Garrison and the Town in the middle of October.

Excerpted from *Trifles from My Port-folio*

CHARLES DAWSON SHANLY

First Impressions

CHARLES DAWSON SHANLY (1811–1875), born and educated in Ireland, studied art, then considered a career as a writer in London, but came with his family to Upper Canada in 1836. He was briefly editor of the comic magazine *Punch in Canada*, to which he contributed unsigned poems, satire, and cartoons. In 1857 he moved to New York and began writing for the *Atlantic Monthly* and the *New York Leader*. He retained his deep interest in painting and some of his sketches are in the McCord Museum in Montreal. In this poem (taken from the Shanly Family Scrapbook c. 1830–1850 in Queen's University Archives) Shanly commemorates the naming of Kingston as the capital of the Province of Canada.

First Impressions

First Impressions, Kingston March, 1842
Capital city! young metropolis
Of this wide wooden land, thy rugged way
A medley strange presents, a queer display
Thy thoro'fare O Regiopolis!
Elderly females, dogs and horned cattle,
And swine for filthy offals "doing battle",
And men on crutches scramble to and fro.
"Go it ye cripples!" Hark! they cry of "fire!"
The quarrier's warning cry before a "blow;"
Down down the miners on their faces go,
Like hawks "upon their quarry stooping" low,
Bang! there it goes–"like bricks" the folks retire;
I'm blowed if I dont run! Upon my soul
Kingston thou art indeed a blasted hole.

From *Shanly Family Scrapbook*

CHARLES DICKENS

The Seat of Government

CHARLES DICKENS (1812–1870) was already famous in North America when Washington Irving invited him to visit the United States. In 1842 Dickens and his wife spent several months touring the United States and Canada. His *American Notes* published the same year was highly controversial. The Dickenses spent only three days in Kingston before joyfully departing for Montreal.

THE time of leaving Toronto for Kingston is noon. By eight o'clock next morning the traveller is at the end of his journey, which is performed by steamboat upon Lake Ontario, calling at Port Hope and Cobourg, the latter a cheerful, thriving little town. Vast quantities of flour form the chief item in the freight of these vessels. We had no fewer than one thousand and eighty barrels on board between Cobourg and Kingston.

The latter place, which is now the seat of government in Canada, is a very poor town, rendered still poorer in the appearance of its market-place by the ravages of a recent fire. Indeed, it may be said of Kingston, that one half of it appears to be burnt down, and the other half not to be built up. The Government House is neither elegant nor commodious, yet it is almost the only house of any importance in the neighbourhood.

There is an admirable jail here, well and wisely governed, and excellently regulated in every respect. The men were employed as shoemakers, ropemakers, Blacksmiths, tailors, carpenters, and stonecutters; and in building a new prison, which was pretty far advanced towards completion. The female prisoners were occupied in needlework. Among them was a beautiful girl of twenty, who had been there nearly three years. She acted as bearer of secret despatches for the self-styled Patriots on Navy Island during the Canadian Insurrection: sometimes dressing as a girl, and carrying them in her stays; sometimes attiring herself as a boy, and secreting them in the lining of her hat. In the latter character she always rode as a boy would, which was nothing to her, for she could govern any horse that any man could ride, and could drive four-in-hand with the best whip in those parts. Setting forth on one of her patriotic missions, she appropriated to herself the first horse she could lay her hands on; and this offence had brought her where I saw her. She had quite a lovely face, though, as the reader may suppose from this sketch of her history, there was a lurking devil in her bright eye, which looked out pretty sharply from between her prison bars.

There is a bomb-proof fort here of great strength, which occupies a bold position, and is capable, doubtless, of doing good service; though the town is much too close upon the frontier to be long held, I should imagine, for its present purpose in troubled times. There is also a small navy-yard, where a couple of Government steamboats were building, and getting on vigorously....

Excerpted from *American Notes*

WALT WHITMAN

A Miracle of Sunset

WALT WHITMAN (1819–1892) was born in Long Island, New York. At eleven, he became an office boy, and was later a printer, a schoolteacher, and a magazine and newspaper editor before publishing the first edition of *Leaves of Grass* in 1855. In the early 1890s he travelled to Canada to spend time with his good friend and first biographer, Dr. R.M. Bucke, a psychiatrist from London, Ontario and the author of *Cosmic Consciousness*. Bucke guided Whitman to Kingston where he introduced him to Dr. Metcalf, warden at Rockwood Institute, Kingston's first asylum.

July 27. A Day and Night on Lake Ontario. Steamboat middling good-sized and comfortable, carrying shore freight and summer passengers. Quite a voyage [Toronto to Kingston], the whole length of Lake Ontario; very enjoyable day, clear, breezy, and cool enough for me to wrap my blanket around me as I pace the upper deck. For the first sixty or seventy miles we keep near the Canadian shore – of course no land in sight the other side; stop at Port Hope, Coburg, etc., and then stretch out toward the mid-waters of the lake.

I pace the deck or sit till pretty late, wrapt in my blanket, enjoying all, – the coolness, darkness, – and then to my berth awhile.

July 27 [28]. Rose soon after three to come out on deck and enjoy a magnificent night-show before dawn. Overhead the moon at her half, and waning half, with lustrous Jupiter and Saturn, made a trio-cluster close together in the purest of skies – with the groups of Pleiades and Hyades following a little to the east. The lights off on the islands and rocks, the splashing waters, the many shadowy shores and passages through them in the crystal atmosphere, the dawn-streaks of faint red and yellow in the east, made a good hour for me. We landed on Kingston wharf just at sunrise.

July 28. To-day Dr. M[etcalf] took me in his steam yacht a long, lively, varied voyage down among the Lakes of the Thousand Islands. We went swiftly on east of Kingston, through cuts, channels, lagoons(?) and out across lakes; numbers of islands always in sight; often, as we steamed by, some almost grazing us; rocks and cedars; occasionally a camping party on the shores, perhaps fishing; a little sea-swell on the water; on our return evening deepened, bringing a miracle of sunset.

I could have gone on thus for days over the savage-tame beautiful element. We had some good music (one of Verdi's compositions) from the band of B battery as we hauled in shore, anchored, and listened in the twilight (to the slapping rocking gurgle of our boat). Late when we reached home.

July 29. This forenoon a long ride through the streets of Kingston and so out into the country and the lake-shore road. Kingston is a military station (B battery), shows quite a fort, and half a dozen old martello towers (like big conical-topt pound cakes). It is a pretty town of fifteen thousand inhabitants.

[In the back of the Canada diary is the following, evidently a first draft or memorandum for a letter to some one.]

Aug 1. I write this in the most beautiful extensive region of lakes and islands one can probably see on earth. Have been here several days; came down, leisurely cruising around, in a handsome little steam-yacht which I am living on half the time. The lakes are very extensive (over 1000 square miles) and the islands numberless ... here and there dotted with summer villas.

[same date] Sunday noon. Still among the Thousand Islands. This is about the centre of them, stretching twenty-five miles to the east and the same distance west. The beauty of the spot all through the day, the sunlit waters, the fanning breeze, the rocky and cedar-bronzed islets, the larger islands with fields and farms, the white-winged yachts and shooting row-boats, and over all the blue sky arching copious – make a sane, calm, eternal picture, to eyes, senses, and my soul.

Evening. An unusual show of boats gaily darting over the waters in every direction; not a poor model among them, and many of exquisite beauty and grace and speed. It is a precious experience, one of these long midsummer twilights in these waters and this atmosphere. Land of pure air! Land of unnumbered lakes! Land of the islets and the woods!

Lakes of Thousand Islands, Aug 2. Early morning; a steady southwest wind; the fresh peculiar atmosphere of the hour and place worth coming a thousand miles to get. O'er the waters the gray rocks and dark-green cedars of a score of big and little islands around me; the added splendor of sunrise. As I sit, the sound of slapping water, to me most musical of sounds.

One peculiarity as you go about among the islands, or stop at them, is the entire absence of horses and wagons. Plenty of small boats, however, and always very handsome ones. Even the women row and sail skiffs. Often the men here build their boats themselves.

Forenoon. A run of three hours (some thirty miles) through the islands and lakes in the Princess Louise to Kingston. Saw the whole scene, with its sylvan rocky and aquatic loveliness, to fine advantage. Such amplitude – room enough here for the summer recreation of all North America.

Excerpted from *Walt Whitman's Diary In Canada, 1904*

RUPERT BROOKE

Something Ominous and Unnatural

RUPERT BROOKE (1887–1915) was the archetypal Georgian poet, whose collected poems appeared after his death in Scyros. He travelled for a year in America and the South Seas just before the First World War, and his lively *Letters from America* was published in 1916 with an introduction by Henry James.

MEN have lived contentedly on this land and died where they were born, and so given it a certain sanctity. Away north the wild begins, and is only now being brought into civilization, inhabited, made productive, explored, and exploited. But this country has seen the generations pass, and won something of that repose and security which countries acquire from the sight.

The wise traveller from Ottawa to Toronto catches a boat at Prescott, and puffs judicially between two nations up the St Lawrence and across Lake Ontario. We were a cosmopolitan, middle-class bunch (it is the one distinction between the Canadian and American languages that Canadians tend to say 'bunch' but Americans 'crowd'), out to enjoy the scenery. For this stretch of the river is notoriously picturesque, containing the Thousand Isles. The Thousand Isles vary from six inches to hundreds of yards in diameter. Each, if big enough, has been bought by a rich man – generally an American – who has built a castle on it. So the whole isn't much more beautiful than Golder's Green. We picked our way carefully between the islands. The Americans on board sat in rows saying "That house was built by Mr ———. Made his money in biscuits. Cost three hundred thousand dollars, e-recting that building. Yessir." The Canadians sat looking out the other way, and said, "In nineteen-ten this land was worth twenty thousand an acre; now it's worth forty-five thousand. Next year..." and their eyes grew solemn as the eyes of men who think deep and holy thoughts. But the English sat quite still, looking straight in front of them, thinking of nothing at all, and hoping that nobody would speak to them.

So we fared; until, well on in the afternoon, we came to the entrance of Lake Ontario.

There is something ominous and unnatural about these great lakes. The sweet flow of a river, and the unfriendly restless vitality of the sea, men may know and love. And the little lakes we have in Europe are but as fresh-water streams that have married and settled down, alive and healthy and comprehensible. Rivers (except the Saguenay) are human. The sea, very properly, will not be allowed in heaven. It has no soul. It is unvintageable, cruel, treacherous, what you will. But, in the end – while we have it with us – it is all right; even though that all-rightness result but, as with France, from the recognition of an age-long feud and an irremediable lack of sympathy. But these monstrous lakes, which ape the ocean, are not proper to fresh water or salt. They have souls, perceptibly, and wicked ones.

We steamed out, that day, over a flat, stationary mass of water, smooth with the smoothness of metal or polished stone or one's finger-nail. There was a slight haze everywhere. The lake was a terrible dead-silver colour, the gleam of its surface shot with flecks of blue and a vapoury enamel-green. It was like a gigantic silver shield. Its glint was inexplicably sinister and dead, like the glint of glasses worn by a blind man. In front the steely mist hid the horizon, so that the occasional rock or little island and the one ship in sight seemed hung in air. They were reflected to a preternatural length in the glassy floor. Our boat appeared to leave no wake; those strange waters closed up foamlessly behind her. But our black smoke hung, away back on the trail, in a thick, clearly-bounded cloud, becalmed in the hot, windless air, very close over the water, like an evil soul after death that cannot win dissolution. Behind us and to the right lay the low, woody shores of Southern Ontario and Prince Edward Peninsula, long dark lines of green, stretching thinner and thinner, interminably, into the distance....

Excerpted from *Letters from America*

GAIL FOX

My Beautiful City

GAIL FOX (1942–) was born in Connecticut and graduated in music and history from Cornell University. She did graduate work in Toronto before moving to Kingston in 1966 with her husband Michael. For several years she edited *Quarry Magazine* within the Queen's University English Department. She now lives in Fredericton, New Brunswick. Her publications include *Dangerous Season, The Royal Collector of Dreams, Houses of God*, and *End of Innocence: Selected Poems 1988.*

Love Poem

I

Kingston,
harbour from which my chaos retreated:
let me confess
that you are my beautiful city,
my point in mortality,
and that I can never give you
what you have given me.

II

In Kingston, everything turns upon its relationship to the lake, the canal, the St. Lawrence. Birds of Kingston are, more often than not, gulls and their calls can be heard even on Princess Street, where the traffic is thickest and people most oblivious. The best thing to do in Kingston is to walk, always nearing water, always smelling the clean wind off the water.

Sometimes Michael likes to walk with me.

Down through the university to McDonald Park and then along the waterfront. At night the dying elms assume a new life and I tell Michael how Gramps used to teach me about the red lights that elms give off in the darkness, their secret method of communicating to anyone willing to listen. And Michael tells me that his mother, Ruby, knows almost every tree in North America. For years, she has saved pieces of their bark and leaves to touch and remember. And then, we are at the beach and Michael starts skipping stones, poising them delicately in his hands and then gracefully guiding them into the dark lake. His stones always skip six or eight times no matter what their shape. He has such fine control. The stones are in his power and hit the lake with the precision of a memory.

And when I remember you, Michael,

you are skipping stones
  on the shores of Kingston town,
and it is dark
  and we are informed with each other
    as the soaring stones
  know air and darkness,
and finally,
    the depth and sliding dreams
  of Lake Ontario.

III

In winter I dream all night and all day and sometimes, Michael is with me and we dream together, for a Kingston winter allows for long months of dreaming, long months of projecting upon the whiteness everything that will ever be important, everything that surfaces from our galactic spaces, our inner seas. Today I dream this of Michael:

You are alone
in forests

the snow is quiet
there are trees

there is nothing
like emptiness

anywhere

you walk
with no words
even shadows
are more than darkness

skin floats
on the bones of stars

your dream
returns

over and over

IV

Some nights, alone, the snow is raw with stars, they bleed across the white like inhuman wounds, they rock upon the frozen water, they moan. On these dark nights, I am a stranger here, a traveller of space and darkness, bound to nothing. Yet the darkness is almost more than I can handle; those cars passing, I think, are Kingston cars and will never know my name.

And some nights, Michael, some long Kingston nights, the snow I stumble on would taste especially good in your mouth, and your hands would be my hands ...

From *End of Innocence: Selected Poems 1988*

ALLAN BROWN

Lakeshore

ALLAN BROWN (1934–) came to Kingston from Vancouver in 1970 to attend Queen's and lived here until 1992 when he moved back to British Columbia. He was literary editor of *Quarry Magazine* from 1982 to 1984, and taught creative writing at St. Lawrence College. He has published many books of poetry, including *The Burden of Jonah ben Amittai, The Almond Tree*, and *Winter Journey*.

Lakeshore, Kingston

Squirrels feed eagerly
among the yellow leaves.
Lakeshore again and
the gulls turning.
The branches of the tree
are invisible
with the sun behind them;
the branches of the tree
show clearly
in front of the sun
reflected in water.

The blue clouds darken.
The small grass.
The sun seems
a part of this sky.
The branches of the tree
move slowly.
The sound of the water.

From *This Stranger Wood*

JEAN-JACQUES HAMM

Madcap Wind

JEAN-JACQUES HAMM (1936–) was born and educated in Alsace. "Being used to bilingualism," he immigrated to Canada and teaches at Queen's University. He has written plays, short stories, and a novel and has published two volumes of poetry, a volume of experimental texts, and scholarly works on Stendhal.

Public Garden

grey seagulls
the scent of a woman
one catches in passing
a chip-wagon
public toilets
massed beds of flowers
children on the sand
trees young once more
maples or beeches
chestnuts or oaks
some stands of spruce
a jogger or two
and the madcap wind
secret, insinuating
the whimsy of beings
the deep desires
and the rapture of dreams

Translated by Mary-Alice Thompson,
from *Entre Zorn et Saint-Laurent: Poemes*

ERIC FOLSOM

Old Hymns

ERIC FOLSOM (1951–), originally from New England, attended university in Montreal and Halifax where he met the Cape Bretoner who was to become his wife. When she was accepted into graduate school at Queen's University, he followed and "we both sort of never left. Why should we?" He now edits *Next Exit* and is an associate editor of *Quarry Magazine*.

Graveyard Where the Trillium Grows

I

Limbs
of Dutch elm diseased trees
gather in river eroded eddys.

Family trees, taut,
brought home smallpox
to the limestone farm,
Pittsburgh, C.W.

Their children, aged
fourteen, nine, and so on
in close order to the grave.

They were emigrants
from across the sea,
            men of Argyll,
            women of Northampton.

They will return by the river that brought them,
            when the dates are washed clean
            from the stone, by the rain.

II

The river Saint Lawrence
            gouges,
pulling pioneer dust
            and sand downstream,
a portable hillside,
a graveyard moving to the sea,
            moving...

YOUR BONES!

                        (A thigh?
                        or upper arm?   No.
                        Shin bone,
                        and thin, long
                        bones of foot
                        protruding from the bank
                        where the graves wash
                            away.)
Your bones,
knobbed end sticking sideways out of gravel,
waiting for next rain
                        to fall,
waiting to tumble with unheard sound
                        into the river,
                        another exit.

Your very bones.

III

My pen is in here, somewhere,
fell out of my shirt pocket
into trailing vines of purple wildflowers,
on its way, also, to the sea
with everything and everyone
from Pittsburgh Township,
formerly Argyll,
formerly buried.

Old hymns
gather at the river.

From *Quarry Magazine*

TOM MARSHALL

Ghost Stones

TOM MARSHALL (1938–1993) was born in Niagara Falls and came to Queen's University as a student in 1957. He recounts that he passed his "industrious undergraduate years without really taking in the beauty of the Kingston setting." He taught English at Queen's and was the author of several acclaimed books of poetry, fiction, and criticism, including *Dance of the Particles*, *Adele at the End of the Day*, *Goddess Disclosing*, and *Multiple Exposures/Promised Lands: Essays on Canadian Poetry and Fiction*.

Robert Frost in Kingston

I wonder what he made
of the city's walls?
That most Canadian
of Yankee bards? He was not
an imperialist even if
we were colonials.

The limestone walls, the lake,
the open country
whose stone is gathered here
into city. Did he see
miniature domes and spires? Is he here
still? (As I shall be?)

Did he perhaps walk
on the March lake
as I have written
(without evidence) that
Macdonald did? Did he see
domes and towers and spires?

I cannot know. But it seems
appropriate that he should be
a presence. A watchful, "craggy" ghost among
the ghost stones that are first
transparent in spring sunshine
then invisible, opening to cosmic fire.

From *Dance of the Particles*

This poem appeared in *Dance of the Particles* with the following footnote: "In January 1921 Robert Frost, the reigning American poet at that time, was invited to visit Queen's and become the first poet-in-residence to occupy such an office in any Canadian university . . . (*Canadian Notes and Queries*, No. 20, 1978). During his visit the poet spent an afternoon with a 'small group of local versifiers' and also helped to judge a poetry competition. According to Lawrence Thompson's biography of Frost, he came either for one week (text) or for two weeks (footnote) in March. He was, as far as I know, the last as well as the first poet-in-residence at Queen's."

Symphony in Stone

Preface

PHYSICALLY Kingston is one of the most beautiful cities on the continent and its architecture has attracted artists and writers alike. But even before the city was built, people and animals must have stood "in stillness facing the lake."

The building materials of the city were conveniently at hand. Wayne Clifford, writing about gathering stone at the river, recalls Father Louis Hennepin nearly three centuries earlier, noting that it was "naturally polished by the shock of the water." The fabric dictated the shape of the city too, for as the poet Bronwen Wallace has written, "limestone just naturally piles itself into forts/and prisons, churches, universities, mansions." The walls and monuments of the city are an inescapable (sometimes literally) part of the landscape.

Who does not admire the great courthouse and City Hall – quite a few according to the historian Arthur Lower – the two cathedrals, the forts, the gracious old houses, so lovingly restored? Again, the scenery inspires the writers: to romantic raptures in the case of Katherine Hale and Agnes Maule Machar, to comedy in Robertson Davies and Sharon Abron Drache.

Some of the monuments are old and hidden – the stone steps from the original Fort Frontenac; a few are new – the sculpture *Time* on the waterfront must be the setting for almost more wedding pictures than the grand house Summerhill. The lion in the park is to be found on many a page.

There is a darker side. It is hardly surprising to find that imprisonment is a frequent theme for Kingston writers when there are nine prisons in and around the city. Fort Henry, too, was used as a prison after the Rebellion of 1837 and during the Second World War, and this section contains accounts of escape attempts in both those periods. For writers like Don Bailey, prison can be a place from which we emerge chastened and changed, a true penitentiary. For Michael Ondaatje, and the earlier "Putzi," it is a challenge to the inmates' ingenuity. Again, a contrast, with

Susanna Moodie admiring the warm and comfortable, although not very elegant dress of the male convicts, and the small unhappy child in Don Bailey's poems, condemned to be imprisoned long before his actual captivity, hoping that "Pain is only a bad sad story," praying "to the stars for a happy ending."

So these are some of the images this limestone city has evoked – and some of the stories and reflections the city has inspired, this "symphony in stone."

There are also plenty of less obvious and literal prisons, requiring just as much determination and ingenuity to escape. Poverty, ignorance, and fear are powerful prisons, sometimes escaped only in death.

WAYNE CLIFFORD

Set Out of Measure

WAYNE CLIFFORD (1944–) has lived in Kingston since 1970 and considers the city "one of the four centres of human habitation I've come across that seems to retain some portion of civic spirit; the other three are Amsterdam, Barcelona and Paleohora, Crete." On his return from graduate school in the United States, he built a stone wall for a cottage on the St. Lawrence. "The poem [in this book] grew out of what my hands did." He is the author of several collections of poetry, *Glass Passages, An Ache in the Ear, 1966–1976*, and *Man in a Window.*

Building the Stone Wall

I

The thot of a wall
builds its stones against
the river or constrains
the terrier, stupid, goes
for the neighbours' heels.

But the thot splits seas'
histories, an energy equal
to water or the terrier's
containment. Purpose
for a wall isn't real

weight to the hands, tho
the slop of mortar is
the wall learning to make
itself thru the muscle.
The thot of a wall is not

a heart circulating what
current flows, but September's
when the river's lowest. Shoals
grow out of shallow bottom
and weedcrusted limestone

slabs show to pick and sort.
The wall will allow no space
at all to the terrier's yap
altho the thot of a willow
sprouting next year by it

will uproot stones
the terrier's bones.

2

In the dry grass, two quarriers.

Heat.   Starling.   Coffee.

The older, the other, stone cut squat
like a lazy man,

                    shift in the grass
as ease is also an occurrence of energy.

But a man waking to strike back sleep,
arm raised against the light, isn't
blind to heat. Convinced of the lungs

and heart, feels flame in gut and muscle.
Burning of body for body's sake, taught
luck. Not the hand's lack, taut
after labour, to call one from the other
strike sparks on stone or sleep in
a burning man. Not only

the form of the hand
(thumb and index) gathers
what's difficult, what ought

if a man's life equal the hard
in him, but a grain between split
and chisel, strength in the rock
the maul a force as anger.

Father and son, one talks, the heat
transparent off the coffee. Starling.

Flags on edge on spruce rails
stay by their weight, scoring the wood
a fine dust from cutting.

'Flagging's twenty-seven a hundred square feet.'

Closure. A tight-lipped man.
There is the clap shut of a tin lunchbox
discusses everything.

3

The dangers of stone are

arhythmic; the faulted rock
gives out.

                Only what continues
is part, whole and exact.
You were speaking of

what,
        how limestone
faces are exact, or
if they are.

Under the cliff's lip
river, fragments
of the stone covered

with slime, disappearing.

Out of step, as we
walked back, uneven outbreaks
of rock throwing
the foot off

the impulse
of height reduced to actual
measure.

That made of stone
surrounds us, this town's houses
its streets
cut square, set

or set out of measure
from an exactness of mind.

Now not speaking, you
grow to them and disappear.

4

Rather than pry it out with bar
and pick, I gather from the river.

In sneakers and gloves, fumble
the large pieces under water
before I bear the ache, arms
and belly tight. As the puzzle grows

wall on its side, incomplete
the eye refines a sense of fit.
The pattern fills in. Where it
will not, an iron edge set right

splits, simple thru the distance
the wrist and shoulder hold the blow
that a man equal his motion.

An institution to splinter rock between
the hands, two curves, up and down, grows
weightless falling or numb with force.

The apposition, left or right, that
the blow howled at my anatomy
in all its stones.

5

The river lifts
a water limb
onto the land

collects rain and
thaw, connects
caress the water
bathes us in. Ships

in enervation find
its current pliant.

A man rests in his arms'
limber, slung jacket full of wind

like pulse ripples skin
at the throat, shirt open, shouts

his distance, push into
inaudible resistance
shock at the bow, waves

anyway, an open mouth
and arm up, white
sleeveless shirt, the inner
arm whiter.

The river an arm
grasps rock, fills
the wake as the man
pulls on his jacket
in the wind.

6

Indispensable to the desired form
is a dispensation in the stone,
where the edge fell, that same line
blood, in the palm. Less a fulcrum

between the event and its energy
than a sharp pain, the edge of joy
two-sided in the mind. A workman
in his fingers if both hands reach

ten. In the sake of the rock is
the sought shape, caught between pain
or pain, except that pleasure can
still bear its elemental gain.

A man working that familiar
moaning in it. No breathing
in the stone. Sensation hadn't yet
been uncovered. Counting backward

from one began zero. Pain's numb
to memory, delight if unendurable.
Life, even, isn't. The order's there
one stone at a time that fits.

As anger in the shape of a man
struggling with the rock, to escape,
the stone coiling, said: It is so and no
more. Further maims. Therefore an end.

7

After a winter
the wall's unfallen.
Floodwater covers
its lowest third.

Frail larvae
flail over capstone
and algae waves green
again where I'd
scraped it off.

The terrier harries
the narrow beach
snaps at short waves
filling his muzzle
with froth.

From *An Ache in the Ear*

LOUIS HENNEPIN

Naturally Polished

LOUIS HENNEPIN (1640–1705) was a Belgian-born Recollet, explorer, and historian who was sent to Quebec as a missionary in 1675. The following year he was sent to Fort Frontenac; in 1678 he went with La Salle to explore the Niagara River and the Illinois. (His drawing of Niagara Falls is considered the earliest-known view.) In 1681 he returned to Europe to write a wildly successful narrative of his travels, *A New Discovery of a Vast Country in America*. His work went through more than forty-six editions in his day.

A Description of Fort Catarokouy, call'd since Fort Frontenac.

This Fort is situated a Hundred Leagues from Quebec (the Capital City of Canada) up the River St. Laurence Southwards. It is built near to the Place where the Lake Ontario (which is as much as to say, the pretty Lake) discharges it self. It was surrounded with a Rampart, great Stakes and Palisado's, and four Bastions, by the Order of Count Frontenac, Governor-General of Canada. They found it necessary to build this Fort for a Bulwark against the Excursions of the Iroquese, and to interrupt the Trade of Skins that these Savages maintain with the Inhabitants of New York, and the Hollanders, who have settled a new Colony there; for they furnish the Savages with Com-modities at cheaper Rates than the French of Canada...

This Fort, which at first was only surrounded with Stakes, Palisado's and earthen Ramparts, has been enlarg'd since the commencement of my Mission into these Countries, to the circumference of Three hundred and sixty Toises (each of these being six Foot in length) and is now adorn'd with Free-Stone, which they find naturally polish'd by the shock of Water upon the brink of the Lake Ontario or Frontenac. They wrought at this Fort with so much diligence and expedition, that in two Years time it was advanc'd to this perfection, by the Care and Conduct of Sieur-Cavelier de la Sallé, who was a Norman born;

a Man of great Conduct and profound Policy. He oft-times pretended to me, that he was a Parisian by Birth, thinking thereby to engage Father Luke Buisset before-Mention'd, and me, to put more confidence in him: For he had quickly observ'd from our ordinary Conversation, that the Flemins, and several other Nations, are prone to be jealous of the Normans. I am sensible that there are Men of Honour and Probity in Normandy, as well as elsewhere; but nevertheless it is certain, that other Nations are generally more free, and less sly and intriguing, than the Inhabitants of that Province of France.

This Fort Frontenac lies to the Northward of this Lake, near to its Mouth, where it discharges it self; and is situated in a Peninsula, of which the Isthmus is digg'd into a Ditch. On the other side, it has partly the Brink of the Lake surrounding it, partly a pretty fort of a natural Mould, where all manner of Ships may ride safely.

The Situation of this Fort is so advantageous that they can easily prevent the Sallies and Returns of the Iroquese; and in the space of Twenty four Hours, can wage War with them in the Heart of their own Country. This is easily compass'd by the help of their Barques, of which I saw Three all deck'd and mounted, at my last departure thence. With these Barques, in a very little time, they can convey themselves to the South-side of the Lake, and pillage (if it be needful) the Country of the Tsonnotouans, who are the most numerous of all the Provinces of the Iroquese. They manure a great deal of Ground for sowing their Indian Corn in, of which they reap ordinarily in one Harvest as much as serves 'em for two Years: Then they put it into Caves digg'd in the Earth, and cover'd after such a manner, that no Rain can come at it.

The Ground which lies along the Brink of this Lake is very fertile: In the space of two Years and a half that I resided there in discharge of my Mission, they cultivated more than a hundred Acres of it. Both the Indian and European Corn, Pulse, Pot-Herbs, Gourds, and Water-Melons, throve very well. It is true indeed, that at first the Corn was much spoil'd by Grasshoppers; but this is a thing that happens in all the Parts of Canada at the first cultivating the Ground, by reason of Extream Humidity of all that Country. The first Planters we sent thither, bred up Poultry there, and transported with them Horned Beasts, which multiply'd there extreamly. They have stately Trees, fit for building of Houses or Ships. Their Winter is by three Months shorter than at Canada. In fine, we have all the reason to hope, that e're long, a considerable Colony will be settled in that Place. When I undertook my great Voyage, I left there about Fifteen or Sixteen Families together, with Father Luke Buisset a Recollet, with whom I had us'd to administer the Sacraments in the Chapel of that Fort.

While the Brink of the Lake was frozen, I walk'd upon the Ice to an Iroquese Village, call'd Ganneouse, near to Kente about nine Leagues off the Fort, in company of the Sieur de la Sallé above-mention'd. These Savages presented us with the Flesh of Elks and Porcupines, which we fed upon. After having discours'd them some time, we return'd, bringing with us a considerable number of the Natives, in order to form a little Village of about Forty Cottages to be inhabited by them, lying betwixt the Fort and our House of Mission. These Barbarians turn'd up the Ground for sowing of Indian Corn and Pulse, of which we gave them some for their Gardens. We likewise taught them, contrary to their usual custom of eating, to feed upon Soupe, made with Pulse and Herbs, as we did.

Father Luke and I made one Remark upon their Language, that they pronounc'd no Labial Letters, such as B, P, M, F. We had the Apostilock Creed, the Lord's Prayer, and our ordinary Litany, translated into the Iroquese Language, which we caus'd them to get by heart, and repeat to their Children; and forc'd their Children to pronounce as we did, by inculcating to them the Labial Letters, and obliging 'em to frequent converse with the Children of the Europeans that inhabited the Fort; so that they mutually taught one another their Mother-Languages; which serv'd likewise to entertain a good Correspondence with the Iroquese.

These Barbarians stay'd always with us, except when they went a hunting; which was the thing we were much concern'd about: for when they went for five or six Months ravaging through their vast huge Forests, and sometimes Two hundred Leagues from their ordinary abode, they took their whole Family along with them. And thus they liv'd together, feeding upon the Flesh of wild Beasts they kill'd with Fire-Arms they us'd to receive of the Europeans, in exchange of their Skins: And it was impossible for any Missionary to follow them into these wild Desarts; so that their Children being absent all the season of Hunting, forgot what we had instill'd into them at Fort Frontenac...

Excerpted from *A New Discovery of a Vast Country in America*

KATHERINE HALE

Houses of Romance

KATHERINE HALE (pseud.) AMELIA BEERS GARVIN (1878–1956) was a well-known journalist in her time. She was born in Galt and married the editor and publisher John W. Garvin in 1912. She produced several volumes of poetry, legends, and books about historic Canadian houses.

THERE'S a flash of crimson about Kingston. At any moment you may see a Gentleman Cadet with his cape upon his arm and his cane in his hand. Motors rush through the prim streets, but the stamp, stamp of horses, the champ, champ of bridles, the clamp of soldiers, suits Kingston best – and a ship at the end of the street.

I go about and wonder who lives here and there, for the atmosphere awakens interest and curiosity. Old French families, British officers, men of letters and politicians have dwelt in this ancient seigneurie of Cataraqui, and traces of them persist.

Alwington House, lovely as I saw it set in a mid-summer garden, was built by the fourth Baron Le Moyne, which links it with the ancestral fortress castle at Longueuil and with Alwington Manor on the Saint John River.

This Le Moyne was a Grant. His father, a Scotch captain, married Carolina de Longueuil. She became a baroness in her own right at her father's death. In 1841, Alwington was the residence of three Governors-General. To two of them, it was an ill-fated house. Near its gates, Lord Sydenham's horse swerved, and he died as a result of the fall. Sir Charles Bagot, who succeeded him, also died at Alwington. He was followed by Sir Charles Metcalfe, who resided there until the seat of Government was moved to Montreal.

The Longueuil estate was really on Wolfe Island, which lies like a gold-green shoal at the point where the St. Lawrence flows out of Lake Ontario. This island was an Indian haunt centuries ago. Dark faces had peered out at stray white men who came up and down the river, long before Frontenac arrived at the wooden fort on the Cataraqui. France and England both craved its fertile meadowlands, hence Wolfe's name for an old French holding.

Carolina Grant, Baroness de Longueuil, lived here for years in a small house which now is used as a summer cottage. Her daughter, who had married an Irish clergyman of a literary turn, the Rev. Antisel Allan, built Ardath, a lovely limestone house, going almost sheer down to the water. People remember it in its zenith as "a dream of beauty." There were terraced gardens and roses in summer, and great hearth fires in winter where men of letters travelling this way always received a welcome. The son of the house was a well-known novelist, Grant Allan.

On Rideau Street East, stands the house in which Sir John A. Macdonald spent most of his boyhood; and nearly opposite, across the river, is the little abode once occupied by Molly Brant, the sister of the Mohawk Chief. And there is a house where Tom Moore boarded, and where Charles Sangster lived; but these are not easy to find. " The little, loyal rectory " of the Stuarts is linked with the story of Dundurn, linked with the manor house of the de Gaspés at St. Jean Port Joli, and with many families who are vital to the life of Canada.

In 1870 the late Sir Richard Cartwright built a pretty summer residence on the site of an old grant given to his grandfather by George III for service to the state. It is a rocky point jutting into the St. Lawrence, but in spite of its arid soil it is well wooded. Hundreds of men were employed by Sir Richard to turn it into a small estate.

Miss A. M. Going, of Kingston, relates the story of "one of the oldest cab drivers", who told a member of the Cartwright family that when he was young he often took Sir Richard down to see how the work was progressing, and once saw the workmen roasting a sheep whole for their dinner.

Here are lake views and tall pine trees, and a screen of maples from which the house takes its name. It is a place which so successfully evades the passerby that it might be called Hidden House.

And about ten miles from Kingston, motorists travelling westward on the old Indian Trail, which skirts the northern shore of the Bay of Quinte to the Carrying Place, must pass one of the most interesting of the Loyalist houses to be seen in Ontario – The White House, the home of the Fairfield family for five generations. There is something of the south about the lovely old place, white painted, vine-hung, not at all venerable in appearance despite the fact that it is the first two-storey house and the oldest of its size in Ontario still retained by the family who built it.

The Fairfields, of English descent, came up from Vermont with the Michael Grass expedition of Loyalists. They brought with them negro slaves, and lived in log huts until they could build the "big house." Months were spent in its erection, for it was intended to resist time and weather. Its thick brick walls, the deep basement and huge chimneys were protected by wood. The wide centre hall, and winding staircase with banisters of black walnut and mahogany, the hard oak floors and windows set just in the right places – all speak of care and comfort and beauty. And when at last, in 1793, the house was completed, records show that "from far and near came the United Empire Loyalists over the corduroy roads, or blazing a trail through the unbroken forest" to a house warming, where wine flowed like water and great roasts were cooked before the huge fireplace which took an eight foot back log. The log was placed with a chain fastened to a team of oxen outside the window. They pulled it slowly while men guided the log across the floor to is place at the back of the hearth.

Excerpted from *Canadian Houses of Romance*

A.R.M. LOWER

Symphony in Stone

ARTHUR REGINALD MARSDEN LOWER (1889–1988) is one of Canada's major, most controversial, and eminently quotable historians. Born in Barrie, Ontario, he was educated at the University of Toronto and Harvard, served in the Royal Naval Volunteer Reserve in the First World War, taught in Winnipeg, and came to Kingston in 1947 as Douglas Professor of History. He wrote many books, forthright newspaper articles on both local and national affairs, and a sprightly autobiography, *My First Seventy-Five Years.*

KINGSTON is unique. It may be compared with Halifax and Quebec, but it is not as crowded as Quebec and not quite as slummy as Halifax. And some sections of it preserve the eighteenth century better than either of the others. Its market square has two sides (though one of them is disfigured by the pseudo-Greek temple of a bank) which the architect must find sheer delight. One of these is composed of the city hall (built 1843), the most dignified city hall in Canada. The satisfaction which the citizens of Kingston take in it, their pride in their past, and their acumen in discerning what makes their city attractive are illustrated by the way in which in the eighteen-eighties the battery park out in front of it was turned into a railway freight yard. Men of our own generation have "shamed the boast that they are wiser than their sires" by tearing off the great hand-cut entrance pillars and grinding them up for road-metal. In a genuinely civilized country those responsible for such a deed would have been regarded as criminals: it seems accident, not intelligence, which has secured us any public amenities we happen to have in Canada.

Kingston has not only the remains of its city hall, but also its court-house and its Anglican cathedral, all in the same pre-Gothic, semi-classical style. There is also a pair of federal buildings close by, with a little park between them, the whole making a pleasing *ensemble.* King Street, which runs off the city-hall square, has many examples of the attractive old stone residences which are only now, a century and a half after their building, becoming appreciated. To take a walk through some of the old streets of this town is a delight, and there is hardly a man among its old inhabitants who would not tear them all down tomorrow. The town has many buildings which exemplify not only Upper Canada's 'eighteenth century,' but also its transition to the 'nineteenth,' such as the two churches which were built just about at the half-century mark, the Roman Catholic St. Mary's Cathedral and the Methodist Sydenham Street. Of these, St. Mary's is the more impressive in sheer bulk, and it is a better example of the revived Gothic than its counterpart in Montreal. It has not, however, the grace of Sydenham Street, which, while not 'medieval' in its shape and seating arrangements, scores through an effective arrangement of spire and roof. Both these churches, particularly Sydenham, and the town as a whole, triumph over mere period by the beauty of their stonework.

If Canadians were Americans, with comparable pride, Kingston, which Bruce Hutchison has described as "a symphony in stone," might get treatment similar to that which Williamsburg, Virginia, has received and, as it were, be 'put under glass' (as has been done with nearby Fort Henry) for the delight of the future and the strengthening of Canadian social bonds. No such danger, however, seems to confront it.

Excerpted from *Canadians in the Making: A Social History of Canada*

ROBERTSON DAVIES

Beyond the Powers of Gush

ROBERTSON DAVIES (1913–), the son of the owner of the Kingston *Whig-Standard*, was educated in Canada and at Oxford. He has been an actor, literary editor of *Saturday Night*, editor and publisher of *The Peterborough Examiner*, and for twenty years Master of Massey College in the University of Toronto. He has won many awards and his later novels are admired internationally, but Kingstonians find his early comic novels about "Salterton" and "Waverley University" essential and entertaining reading: *Tempest-Tost* (1951), *Leaven of Malice* (1954), and *A Mixture of Frailties* (1958). In interviews he has said "Kingston is magical" and that the city's "introversion makes for great depth."

IN her daydreams Freddy sometimes fancied that her native city would be known to history chiefly as her birthplace, and this as much as anything shows the extent of her ambition. Salterton had seen more of history than most Canadian cities, and its tranquillity was not easily disturbed. Like Quebec and Halifax, it is a city which provides unusual opportunities for gush, for it has abundant superficial charm. But the real character of Salterton is beneath the surface, and beyond the powers of gush to disclose.

People who do not know Salterton repeat a number of half-truths about it. They call it dreamy and old-world; they say that it is at anchor in the stream of time. They say that it is still regretful for those few years when it appeared that Salterton would be the capital of Canada. They say that it is the place where Anglican clergymen go when they die. And, sooner or later, they speak of it as "quaint."

It is not hard to discover why the word "quaint" is so often applied to Salterton by the unthinking or the imperceptive; people or cities who follow their own bent without much regard for what the world thinks are frequently so described; there is an implied patronage about the word. But the people who call Salterton "quaint" are not the real Saltertonians, who know that there is nothing quaint – in the sense of the word which means wilfully eccentric – about the place. Salterton is itself. It seems quaint to those whose own personalities are not strongly marked and whose intellects are infrequently replenished.

Though not a large place it is truly describable as a city. That word is now used of any large settlement, and Salterton is big enough to qualify; but a city used to be the seat of a bishop, and Salterton was a city in that sense long before it became one in the latter. It is, indeed, the seat of two bishoprics, one Anglican and one Roman Catholic. As one approaches it from the water the two cathedrals, which are in appearance so strongly characteristic of the faiths they embody, seem to admonish the city. The Catholic cathedral points a vehement and ornate Gothic finger toward Heaven; the Anglican cathedral has a dome which, with offhand Anglican suavity, does the same thing. St. Michael's cries, "Look aloft and pray!": St. Nicholas' says, "If I may trouble you, it might be as well to lift your eyes in this direction." The manner is different; the import is the same.

In the environs of the cathedrals the things of this world are not neglected. Salterton is an excellent commercial city, and far enough from other large centres of trade to have gained, and kept, a good opinion of itself. To name all its industries here would be merely dull, but they are many and important. However, they do not completely dominate the city and engross the attention of its people, as industries are apt to do in less favoured places. One of the happy things about Salterton is that it is possible to work well and profitably there without having to carry one's work into the remotest crannies of social life. To the outsiders, who call Salterton "quaint," this sometimes looks like snobbishness. But the Saltertonians do not care. They know that a little snobbery, like a little politeness, oils the wheels of daily life. Salterton enjoys a satisfying consciousness of past glories and, in a modest way, makes its own rules.

More than is usual in Canada, Salterton's physical appearance reveals its spirit. As well as its two cathedrals it has a handsome Court House (with a deceptive appearance of a dome but not, perhaps, a true dome) and one of His Majesty's largest and most forbidding prisons (with an unmistakable dome). And it is the seat of Waverley University. To say that the architecture of Waverley revealed its spirit would be a gross libel upon a centre of learning which has dignity and, in its high moments, nobility. The university had the misfortune to do most of its building during the long Victorian period when architects strove like Titans to reverse all laws of seemliness and probability and when what had been done in England was repeated, clumsily and a quarter of a century later, in Canada. Its buildings are of two kinds: in the first the builders have disregarded the character of the local stone and permitted themselves an orgy of campaniles, baroque staircases, Norman arches, Moorish peepholes and bits of grisly Scottish *chinoiserie* and *bondieuserie*, if such terms may be allowed; in the second kind the local stone has so intimidated the builders that they have erected durable stone warehouses, suitable perhaps for the study of the sciences but markedly unfriendly toward humanism. The sons and daughters of Waverley love their Alma Mater as the disciples of Socrates loved their master, for a beauty of wisdom which luckily transcends mere physical appearance.

At an earlier date than the establishment of Waverley four houses of real beauty were built in Salterton by the eccentric Prebendary Bedlam, one of those Englishmen who sought to build a bigger and better England in the colonies. By a lucky chance one of these, known as Old Bedlam, is upon the present university grounds, and houses the Provost of Waverley.

While upon this theme it may be as well to state that, among the good architecture of Salterton, there is much that is mediocre and some which is downright bad. The untutored fancy of evangelical religion has raised many a wart upon that fair face. Commerce, too, has blotched it. But upon the whole the effect is pleasing and, in some quarters of the town, genuinely beautiful. There are stone houses in Salterton, large and small, which show a justness of proportion, and an intelligent consideration of the material used, which are not surpassed anywhere in Canada. These houses appear to have faces – intelligent, well-bred faces; the knack of building houses which have faces, as opposed to grimaces, is retained by few builders.

It was in one of these, though not the best, that Freddy lived with her sister Griselda and her father, George Alexander Webster. The house was called St. Agnes' and it was very nearly a genuine Bedlamite dwelling. But when St. Agnes' was three-quarters finished Prebendary Bedlam had run out of money, and had not completed his plan. He had not died bankrupt or in poverty, for in his day it was almost impossible for a dignitary of the Church of England to descend to such vulgarities, but it had been an uncommonly narrow squeak. After his death the house had been completed, but not according to the original plans, by an owner whose taste had not been as pure as that of Bedlam, whose mania for building had been guided by a genuine knowledge of what can be done with stone and plaster. In a later stage St. Agnes' had suffered a fire, and some re-building had been done around 1900 in the taste of that era. Since that time St. Agnes' had been little altered. George Alexander Webster had made it a little more comfortable inside; the basement kitchen had been replaced by a modern one, and arrangements had been made to heat the house in winter by a system which did not combine all the draughtiness of England with the bitter cold of Canada, but otherwise he had not touched it.

His contribution to the place was made in the grounds. St. Agnes' stood in ten or twelve acres of its own, and Webster's taste for gardening had brought them to a pitch which would surely have delighted Prebendary Bedlam. Under the owner's direction, and with the sure hand of Tom to assist, the gardens had become beautiful, and as always happens with beautiful things, many people wanted them...

Excerpted from *Tempest-Tost*

SHARON ABRON DRACHE

A Limestone Mikveh

SHARON ABRON DRACHE (1943–) is the author of three works of fiction, *The Mikveh Man*, *Ritual Slaughter*, and *The Golden Ghetto*. For several years she lived in Kingston where she raised her family before moving to Ottawa.

IN one of the oldest cities in Canada, considered for many historical reasons a city of firsts, lived Rabbi Meir and his wife, Bertha. The couple had been the spiritual leaders of Kingston's only Jewish congregation for almost twenty-five years. Indeed, the Jews were very proud of what they thought was tangible proof of their stability.

Despite the fact that the majority were not observant, their synagogue had always been called 'orthodox'. As Boris Wolinsky, the president once said, "I may not be religious myself, but when I go to *shul*, I want to feel like I'm in a *shul*, not a church. If I wanted a church, there arc lots in Kingston!"...

"Do you know what I really want, dear Bertha?"

"What Meir?"

"A *mikveh*."

"A *mikveh*? You're *meshuggah*! Who will use it? I'm too old and there are not three women in Kingston who are observant enough to visit the ritual bath."

"No, the women won't use it, but what about me? I could go with my *minyan* and a few of the university students before *Shabbos* and other holidays. Who can tell how many might follow? Remember my ancestor, the Ba'al Shem Tov? (Meir's cousin was married to the BeSHT's great-great-grandchild.) In Podalia, where the Hasidic leader lived, the *mikveh* became a custom for men."

"But this is Kingston. You can't turn those *apikorsim* into Hasidim."

"Who knows, Bertha?" he continued, full of enthusiasm.

"This will not be an ordinary *mikveh.* I plan to call my cousin to make the arrangements."

"Which cousin is this?" Meir had cousins who did all kinds of religion-affiliated jobs, from synagogue beadles, to scribes, to ritual slaughters.

"Cousin Kalman from the Bronx. Not only is he a rabbi, he's also a Mikveh Man. He will make a *mikveh* that will do Kingston proud."...

AT the Sabbath table, Cousin Kalman spoke about his family in the Bronx. "We're so fortunate, Rose and I. The children and grandchildren live practically next door and only five blocks from *Bes Yankov.*"

Meir inquired after Uncle Nachum, the most devout member of the family, a descendant from the *Datschlaver* dynasty of Polish Hasidim. They spoke of mutual friends, Benjamin Leipsig and Judah Weisberg, for they were the two others, who like Meir, left a big Jewish community to bring enlightenment to the Diaspora – for Meir, Montreal was Jerusalem.

Benjamin was a rabbi in Miami where the women wore sleeveless dresses to *shul.* Judah was in Detroit at an equally *treyfe* synagogue where they operated the bronze doors of their Holy Ark by remote control.

"Tell me, how are you two?" asked Kalman. "How do you manage here?"

"Uncle Benjamin's family is in Datschlav, just north of Montreal," Meir assured him. "Over two hundred families now. One day, they hope to have a separate town. They'll close the stores on *Shabbos* and other Jewish holidays.

"But, since Uncle Benjamin died two years ago, we haven't seen the relatives," confessed Meir. "To tell you the truth, they make me uncomfortable. They think Bertha and I are black sheep for living in Kingston."

"Take a look at them and you see who the black sheep are," Bertha sighed, smoothing her *shantung* skirt.

Kalman changed the subject, "How's Danny?" (Danny was the Levys' only child.)

In a stream of praise Bertha rambled. "You know he and his wife Miriam went to Israel in '67. After the war, they settled on Kibbutz Uriah, near Tel Aviv. Danny still paints. Several galleries carry his work, and Miriam, she sings in a Jaffe nightclub... And

Moshe and Micah?" Bertha answered her own question." My grandchildren have ambitions – Moshe wants to be a teacher and Micah, *veysmir*, a mime! He idolizes Marcel Marceau."

"How old are the boys?" Kalman interrupted.

"Moshe is seven, Micah, six. Let me show you a picture." Bertha scurried to the living room mantle, returning with a gold framed photo. Proudly, she held the photograph under Kalman's nose.

"Beautiful – already they have plans, but the years pass and the plans change," said Kalman, thinking of the path his own life had taken. First as a beadle in his father's *shul*, then rabbi, and now Mikveh Man! As a child he was a poor student but his teachers always took special interest in him because he had an extraordinary sense of the supernatural.

He would amuse them and his family and friends with endless stories about his Voices. One went like this:

> On the occasion of my Bar Mitzvah, My Voices appeared just as I was about to recite the weekly portion. They brought me a pair of golden wings, similar to the ones they wore. Standing before the Holy Ark, my body trembling, I feared I might crush their delicate present. My father asked: "Why are you shivering, Kalman?" Of course I didn't tell him a thing. Not then.
>
> At home that evening, as soon as I counted three stars in the sky, I tried on my gossamer wings and flew about our garden.

After Kalman told this tale, he always related the following: "Every ten years, on the anniversary of my Bar Mitzvah, My Voices returned with another gift. On my twenty-third birthday I received three coral eggs. To this day, when I rub them, I cause unusual events to come about. At thirty-three, My Voices brought me two translucent turquoise eyes through which I am able to see all the good and evil in the world, simultaneously. At forty-three, I received a silver wand, capable of turning back time, and at fifty-three (nine years ago), My Dear Voices gave me a shovel!"

Such was the eccentric nature of Cousin Kalman. After chanting the final benedictions at supper, Meir could resist no longer. "Tell me exactly how you plan to make our *mikveh*?"

Kalman hesitated, "On *Shabbos*?"

"I don't mind," Meir shrugged.

"Very well," reaching into his vest pocket, he handed Meir a photograph. "You and Bertha, take a good look – do you recognize the church?"

"It's the oldest in Kingston. Built in the mid 1800's, I believe."

"That's where we'll find our *mikveh*!" Kalman nodded.

"What?"

"It's made of limestone."

"Dear Cousin," Rabbi Meir insisted, "we can't find a *mikveh* in a church. Even if we could, how could we use it? A *mikveh* in a church is no *mikveh*."

It was then that Kalman wondered if he should go upstairs to fetch his red plaid valise. He could display his Voices' gifts, show how he could accomplish the impossible.

But, alas, he knew the wings would be rusty, the eggs faded to pink, the eyes dull blue, and the wand murky gray. Every Sabbath his gifts lost their powers. Even the shovel was deceptive. From sundown on Friday until Sabbath's end, this ordinary spade became a jeweled sceptre.

"Don't worry," Kalman said, "we won't leave the *mikveh* in the church. After we find it, we'll carry it away."

"And how do you propose to find it?"

"By digging for it, naturally."

"Kalman, we love you and we have great faith in your abilities, but we cannot agree to such a plan. The community thought I was crazy when I asked for a *mikveh*. If I tell them we have to dig for it in a church, they'll probably fire me."

"They want to honor you, not fire you," Kalman reminded. "Let me explain: the original church font was unusually large. In those days, they still performed baptism by immersion. Surely you have heard of the unceasing efforts of the local bishop with the Indians in the 1800s – he used to baptize two or three at a time in that font."

"Wait a minute," Meir interrupted. But Kalman paid no attention.

"That font has lain buried in the courtyard between the rector's house and the cathedral for years. And don't look so worried. The church has another font, much smaller than the old one, since today they baptize by pouring, and sprinkling. I assure you they'll never want the old font back." Kalman's eyes gleamed. "They won't even know it's gone, will they?"

"How do you know?" Bertha inquired. But Kalman remained

tight-lipped, got up, and went into the living room. She followed with his cup of tea and a plate with thick slices of honey cake.

"Bertha makes the best cake," Kalman said.

"The best," Meir agreed.

While they drank tea, they began chuckling and soon they were laughing so hard, tears came to Meir's eyes. "So Kingston will finally have a *mikveh* – when do we start digging, Kalman?"

"Immediately after *Shabbos*, we'll assemble at the *shul* – around nine. I hope to get to the church by ten. With luck, we'll hit the *mikveh* by three in the morning."

"I guess I'll have to tell the congregation tomorrow morning during services. I fear they won't agree to your plan."

"Don't tell them, until the last minute," Bertha suggested, totally caught up in the adventure. "Tell them you heard there's buried treasure in the churchyard and we Jews ought to dig it up and give it to the city."

Meir's eyes shone. "Part of what you say is true, a *mikveh* is a treasure." But he wondered why he clung to the old ways, as he summoned his strength: "I'm going to tell them the truth. I'll tell them we're digging for the *mikveh* in a churchyard."

"They'll hit the *shul* roof," Bertha said.

THE next day, following service, Meir still had not made his announcement. He watched his congregation trickle out of the sanctuary while his loyal *minyan* stood around, chatting with Kalman. Rabbi Levy invited them to his study for a glass of whiskey, toasting: "Here's to the success of the Mikveh Man." The quorum drank. Everyone, in a slightly inebriated state, pledged support.

Meir didn't waste a minute. "Be back here tonight by nine. Bring your shovels."

It's difficult to describe what the line of men looked like parading with Kalman through the town. The solemnity of the occasion called for complete silence, each trooper with a shovel on his shoulders, on what Kalman called *the mikveh march*. He, however, did not carry his. Instead, he schlepped his red plaid valise.

The men dug and dug, resting briefly at one-hour intervals. At three in the morning, there was still no sign of the font, and the *minyan* was tired and disbelieving. Panic-stricken, Joe Lithwick cried out: "The priest gets here at six-thirty. If he catches us and this hole, we risk being shoveled into it."

"We'll just dig for one more hour," Kalman announced. "I'm sure we'll reach the font by four."

By the fourth stroke of the clock tower, one quarter of the churchyard had been dug up. Max was sweating. "We'll have to get this dirt back before dawn," he said to Kalman.

"Don't worry – I personally will take care of the dirt, after we find the font."

Throughout the entire evening, Kalman hadn't participated. Instead, he sat on his suitcase, giving orders, where to dig, where to pile. Occasionally, he got up and poked at the hill of dirt beside the hole. Max said, "I suppose you're looking for the font. Surely, we should have found it by now, Kalman?"

But the little man from the Bronx only shrugged.

At five, the sun began to rise and the quorum was silent with fear. They threw down their shovels, refusing to dig deeper. Kalman paced the perimeter of the opening in the earth.

Before the astounded *minyan*, he opened his red plaid valise and took out his golden wings. He fastened them securely to his black, baggy jacket arms, leaped smoothly into the air, and flew about the churchyard, landing at the end of the hole near his suitcase. He carefully pulled out his three coral eggs, which he immediately winged to the bottom; then he flew back up, collecting his translucent turquoise eyes, which he positioned on top of the heap of dirt, so they could act as a telescope. He soared slowly over the opening in the earth, waving his wand, while the men stood by in a state of shock.

Kalman urged each of them to hold his wand over the hole and also to gaze through the two turquoise eyes. Reluctantly, they did as he asked. He took his ordinary shovel and covered the three coral eggs with exactly six shovels full of church dirt. Instantly and miraculously, everyone present thought he could see the font, big enough for the immersion of several people, adequate for a real *mikveh*, shining in the early morning sun.

IF I told you the men lifted the font out of the hole and that they carried to it their *shul* on their shoulders, marching back over the same route they had taken to the church, you wouldn't believe me.

If I told you that Kalman transported the font singlehanded on his golden wings, back to the synagogue, you wouldn't believe me either.

But if I remind you that Kingston is a city of historical firsts, perhaps you'll concede that the first *mikveh* in town may have been created by a rabbi from the Bronx, in honor of the occasion of the twenty-fifth anniversary of the hiring of Rabbi Meir and his wife, Bertha, the first rabbinical couple to stay in Kingston for more than three years, in fact, twenty-five!

Excerpted from *The Mikveh Man*

AGNES MAULE MACHAR

A Canadian Weimar

AGNES MAULE MACHAR (1837–1927) was the daughter of Dr. John Machar, Minister at St. Andrew's Presbyterian Church in 1827 and Principal of Queen's in 1846. She wrote *The Story of Old Kingston*, the first full-length history of the city, and published countless literary articles, novels, a volume of lyrics, and historical tales for children.

BUT if Kingston seems not to have been predestined for a busy manufacturing centre, it has, as we have seen, attractions of its own, which are not less valuable assets, all things considered, than those which pertain to busy mills and bustling ports. Its advantages of situation; its quiet, tree-embowered streets, with their vistas of verdure; the broad cincture of blue water almost surrounding the gentle hill-slope that looks down on wide lake and winding river; its parks and open spaces; its tranquil halls of learning, and its tasteful churches, all promote its attractiveness as a residential city, in addition to the scholastic and academic advantages that make it an almost ideal university town.

As a summer resort, Kingston has also manifold charms – offering, from its facilities of water communication, a central point for pleasant excursions in various directions. Making Kingston his headquarters, the tourist may explore the pleasant pastoral scenery of the Bay of Quinté, with its early historical associations, – the waterfront of the old "Midland District;" may thread his way in steamer, skiff, canoe, sailing yacht or motor launch amid the mazes of the Thousand Islands; may direct his wandering course through the locks and picturesque windings of the Rideau Canal, or may penetrate by rail into the remoter wilds of the rugged County of Frontenac, stretching its mineral-bearing rocks to the banks of the foaming Madawaska. This region has already become an important mining one, and it is likely to become more so in the future as its natural riches become further developed, an end which will be promoted by two new smelting works (for iron and zinc) which are about to be established at Kingston. The townships bordering on Kingston and Pittsburg Townships – Storrington and Loughborough – contain many lovely bits of scenery about the pretty inland lakes abounding in that region, and are already becoming a favourite haunt of the holiday roamer. Wolfe and Amherst Islands (the latter originally named the Isle of Tanty, or Tonti, from La Salle's faithful lieutenant), as well as some smaller islands between them, can also supply pleasant summer quarters, cooled by the lake breezes. But the most popular summer resort of the Kingstonians is the Township of Pittsburg, on the opposite side of the Cataraqui River and bridge, with its pretty village of Barriefield, named after an early Commodore, which looks across at the old city, of which it enjoys a magnificent sunset view, and up at the grey Fort Henry crowning the adjoining hill, now only fit for a barracks, and happily not required for any other purpose; in token of which the masonry of its river wall is fast crumbling away. Just beyond the Fort hill, and opposite to the still picturesque Cedar Island, with its now roofless Martello tower, lies the charming summer home of our veteran statesman, Sir Richard Cartwright; and all along the shore of the St. Lawrence, for five or six miles below, are scattered summer cottages or little camps or settlements, in which many citizens find holiday repose and change of scene from city sights and sounds. Some ten or twelve miles farther down, the Thousand Islands open their alluring labyrinths, and the number and variety of the summer abodes interspersed amid the bosky isles suggest a happy modern Arcady.

With such an environment as has here been very imperfectly outlined, Kingston may well be called "beautiful for situation," and her aesthetic advantages may yet be found to outweigh the more tangible material ones she has missed. May we not predict for our old Canadian town the enviable destiny of becoming, perchance, in the future a Canadian Weimar, the home of philosophers and sages, where the Arts and Muses may find a congenial abode, "far from the madding crowd," and the thought-dispersing distractions of a too conventional and ambitious modern life? Such a destiny, with its idealizing and uplifting influences, would be worthy of her comparative antiquity, her traditions, and the character of her founders.

Excerpted from *The Story of Old Kingston*

KATE STERNS

Between Madness and Sanity

KATE STERNS (1961–) was born in Toronto and grew up in Kingston. In 1984 she moved to England where, after a brief career in theatre as a stage manager, she began writing fiction. In 1992, she published *Thinking About Magritte* to critical acclaim.

THE city, although small, boasted: five prisons, three hospitals, one mental institution and one university. Inhabitants of the place grew up thinking it natural one way or another to enclose and protect people. Nobody escaped attention. All of these buildings were made of the grey, dimpled limestone after which the city was named. Recorded in the history books was a fire which had left the infant city in ruins. It was then they began to construct out of limestone instead of wood. The stone was plentiful and readily quarried. One of the properties of limestone is that it splits easily along its plane of weakness. On occasion absent-minded prison wardens and university professors wandered into the wrong institution, mistaking one for the other. People sailing along the lake glided past the prisons and argued about the cruelty of the correctional system, not realizing that beyond the walls a class in quantum physics was taking place.

The north end of Limestone consisted of a series of haphazard streets, all with the uneven look of a line drawn freehand. They were late additions to the city and unplanned. Towards the end of the nineteenth century an overflow of immigrants and dock-workers, one group attracted to Limestone's prosperity and the other chiefly responsible for creating it, had made them necessary. They used up available space the way spilled water claims a table-top. For most of the immigrants this neighbourhood was no more than a whistle-stop. They moved on quickly to other cities or at least to a better neighbourhood, south of Divide Street, which acted according to its name and split the city down the middle. After a time trains replaced ships as a cheaper and faster means of transport. Limestone began to lose its advantage as a harbour city and the dockers found themselves out of work, consigned to history. Over the next seventy years the north end of the city adopted the grim, concentrated visage of its few remaining tenants. More and more street corners played host to women and children whose husbands and fathers had found temporary accommodation in one of the local prisons. Visitors to Limestone never ventured north of Divide Street except by mistake. Maps of the city grew fuzzy around the edges as if a problem undefined was a problem solved.

Members of Limestone's city council were faced with the daily embarrassment of having to step over drunks and homeless children on their way to work. So a resolution was passed. With the intention of making the streets as clear as their consciences the council magnanimously voted to purchase several of what were, by now, tumbledown houses and donate them to the neighbourhood's indigent population. One of these was No. 22 Colbourne Street, where the Midnight Cowboy had grown up and still lived. The house comprised several stories, most of them untrue. What there was of metal rusted and was never replaced. Plastic sheeting covered several of the windows. The fragile properties of glass were treated with amused contempt by the occupants. On one side was a Chinese laundry and on the other a blind alley. Across the street, visible from Cowboy's second-floor window, was a shoe repair shop, recently gone bust, over which lived Limestone's only prostitute. On slow nights she chatted with Cowboy, but he knew that now was her busy season with one convention after another booked into the Holiday Inn. Reserve prostitutes had been bused in from neighbouring towns for the duration and installed in the less luxurious surroundings of the Plaza Hotel.

– Next week it's chiropractors, Cowboy, she'd yelled earlier, arching her back. Thank God!

Now a light, red and shiny as the inside of an eyelid, winked seductively at a man whose fly was open before he was halfway up the stairs. Before the prostitute had time to produce the American Express/Mastercard/Visa forms, the man had flung himself spreadeagled onto the bed. Thinking that for once this might be the real thing formalities were overlooked. The lovers moved in graceful arcs no wider than a belly dancer's hips. They slurped and sucked greedily and the woman wondered why, in the movies, love makes no sound....

THE architect of the Limestone Psychiatric Hospital was often accused of making symbolic gestures. Mr Atkinson was only thirty-five when, in 1920, the first stone was laid but he maintained the attire of a Victorian gentleman.

– This is a disgraceful era, he complained. I'm here against my will.

Faced with a battery of raised eyebrows at the city council meeting, the mayor pointed out that genius always demands generous leeway.

The proposed location for the new asylum was a prime piece of waterfront property, slightly diminished in value due to its proximity to the men's penitentiary. The *Limestone Gazette* insinuated that the property had been donated to the city by the wealthy family of a prominent politician, now broken under the strain of public life, in exchange for a room in the asylum. Every morning dozens of convicts who were to engage in the actual construction were transported to the site under the watchful eyes of their keepers. Regulations stipulated that work was to be carried out in absolute silence although the phrase "Look out!" was occasionally permitted, more for the safety of the keepers than the prisoners. Mr Atkinson found the atmosphere so oppressive that he developed the habit of wandering among the men under the guise of inspecting sewage pipes and cornices, distributing notes hastily scribbled from one prisoner to another. By this means love affairs flourished, political debates raged and rumours were circulated. One of these involved the news that the asylum, on account of the politician, was to hire a French chef. Bearing this in mind, several of the prisoners did everything in their power to recommend themselves as potential patients. One man persistently mistook a dead chicken for a hammer, while another staged impromptu performances of *Swan Lake*.

– These lunatics will ruin the asylum, giggled Mr Atkinson.

When the building was completed the critics (no one asked the certifiably insane) were delighted. They spent weeks unearthing clues they imagined Mr Atkinson had left for them in his design. For example, although the hospital was constructed almost entirely of limestone there were one or two fissures where wood and brick had been allowed to take hold.

– Might this not represent, they slyly commented, the cracked minds of the patients?

On hearing this, the architect kissed his parrot (named Chat Lunatique) and lamented.

– Why, he wondered, do all critics smell of ashes and gin?

In addition, the path leading from the main building, set in the centre of a great estate, was long and winding.

Surely, the critics claimed, this is a metaphor for the arduous journey between madness and sanity.

Throughout his long life the architect vigorously denied these charges ...

Excerpted from *Thinking About Magritte*

SUSANNA MOODIE

Within the Massy Walls

SUSANNA MOODIE (1803–1885) was born in Suffolk into a highly literary family. In 1832 she immigrated with her husband, settling first near Cobourg, an experience vividly if crankily portrayed in *Roughing it in the Bush*. In 1839 the family moved to Belleville. *Life in the Clearings* chronicles this more agreeable period.

SO much has been written about the city of Kingston, so lately the seat of government, and so remarkable for its fortifications, and the importance it ever must be to the colony as a military depôt and place of defence, that it is not my intention to enter into a minute description of it here...

It is about three years ago that I paid a visit with my husband to the Penitentiary, and went over every part of it. I must own that I felt a greater curiosity to see the convicts than the prison which contained them, and my wishes were completely gratified, as my husband was detained for several hours on business, and I had a long interval of leisure to examine the workshops, where the convicts were employed at their different trades, their sleeping cells, chapel, and places of punishment. The silence system is maintained here, no conversation being allowed between the prisoners. I was surprised at the neatness, cleanliness, order, and regularity of all the arrangements in the vast building, and still more astonished that forty or fifty strong active looking men, unfettered, with the free use of their limbs, could be controlled by one person, who sat on a tall chair as overseer of each ward. In several instances, particularly in the tailoring and shoemaking department, the overseers were small delicate-looking men; but such is the force of habit, and the want of moral courage which generally accompanies guilt, that a word or a look from these men was sufficient to keep them at work.

The dress of the male convicts was warm and comfortable, though certainly not very elegant, consisting (for it was late in the fall) of a thick woollen jacket, one side of it being brown, the other yellow, with trowsers to correspond, a shirt of coarse factory cotton, but very clean, and good stout shoes, and warm knitted woollen socks. The letters P.P. for "Provincial Penitentiary," are sewed in coloured cloth upon the dark side of the jacket. Their hair is cut very short to the head, and they wear a cloth cap of the same colours that compose their dress.

The cells are narrow, just wide enough to contain a small bed, a stool, and a wash-bowl, and the prisoners are divided from each other by thick stone walls. They are locked in every night at six o'clock, and their cell is so constructed, that one of the keepers can always look in upon the convict without his being aware of the scrutiny. The bedding was scrupulously clean, and I saw a plain Bible in each cell.

There is a sort of machine resembling a stone coffin, in which mutinous convicts are confined for a given time. They stand in an upright position; and as there are air-holes for breathing, the look and name of the thing is more dreadful than the punishment, which cannot be the least painful. I asked the gentleman who showed us over the building, what country sent the most prisoners to the "Penitentiary?" He smiled, and told me to "guess." I did so, but was wrong.

"No," said he, "we have more French Canadians and men of colour. Then Irish, English, and run-a-way loafers from the States. Of the Scotch we have very few; but they are very bad – the most ungovernable, sullen, and disobedient. When a Scotchman is bad enough to be brought here, he is like Jeremiah's bad figs – only fit for the gallows."

Mr. Moodie's bailiffs had taken down a young fellow, about twenty years of age, who had been convicted at the assizes for stealing curious coins from a person who had brought them out to this country as old family relics. The evidence was more circumstantial than positive, and many persons believed the lad innocent.

He had kept up his spirits bravely on the voyage, and was treated with great kindness by the men who had him in custody; but when once within the massy walls of the huge building, his courage seemed to forsake him all at once. We passed him as he sat on the bench, while the barber was cutting his hair and shaving off his whiskers. His handsome suit had been removed – he was in the party-coloured dress before described. There was in his face an expression of great anguish, and tears were rolling in quick succession down his cheeks. Poor fellow! I should hardly have known him again, so completely was he humbled by his present position.

Mr. M———y told me that they had some men in the "Penitentiary" who had returned three different times to it, and had grown so attached to their prison that they preferred being there, well clothed and well fed, to gaining a precarious living elsewhere.

Executions in Canada are so rare, even for murder, that many atrocious criminals are found within these walls – men and women – who could not possibly have escaped the gallows in England.

At twelve o'clock I followed Mr. M——— to the great hall, to see the prisoners dine. The meal consisted of excellent soups, with a portion of the meat which had been boiled in it, potatoes, and brown bread, all very clean and good of their kind. I took a plate of the soup and a piece of the bread, and enjoyed both greatly.

I could not help thinking, while watching these men in their comfortable dresses, taking their wholesome, well-cooked meal, how much better they were fed and lodged than thousands of honest industrious men, who had to maintain large families upon a crust of bread, in the great manufacturing cities at home...

There was one man among these dark, fierce-looking criminals, who, from his proud carriage and bearing, particularly arrested my attention. I pointed him out to Mr. ———. "That man has the appearance of an educated person. He looks as if he had been a gentleman."

"You are right," was his reply. "He was a gentleman, the son of a district judge, and brought up to the law. A clever man too; but these walls do not contain a worse in every respect. He was put in here for arson, and an attempt to murder. Many a poor man has been hung with half his guilt."

"There are two men near him," I said, "who have not the appearance of criminals at all. What have they done?"

"They are not felons, but two soldiers put in here for a week for disorderly conduct."

"What a shame," I cried, "to degrade them in this manner! What good can it do?"

"Oh," said he, laughing; "it will make them desert to the States the moment they get out."

"And those two little boys; what are they here for?"

"For murder!" whispered he.

I almost sprang from my seat; it appeared too dreadful to be true.

"Yes," he continued. "That child to the right is in for shooting his sister. The other, to the left, for killing a boy of his own age with a hoe, and burying him under the roots of a fallen tree. Both of these boys come from the neighbourhood of Peterboro'. Your district, by the bye, sends fewer convicts to the 'Penitentiary' than any part of the Upper Province."

It was with great pleasure I heard him say this. During a residence of thirteen years at Belleville, there has not been one execution. The county of Hastings is still unstained with the blood of a criminal. There is so little robbery committed in this part of the country, that the thought of thieves or housebreakers never for a moment disturbs our rest. This is not the case in Hamilton and Toronto, where daring acts of housebreaking are of frequent occurrence...

Excerpted from *Life in the Clearings*

OSCAR RYAN AND OTHERS

Just Like a Castle in a Fairy Tale

OSCAR RYAN (1904–) wrote booklets, poems, and stage pieces and, for two decades, theatre reviews for *The Canadian Tribune*. His biography of the Communist leader Tim Buck was published in 1975. *Eight Men Speak* was written by a collective; all the authors were members of the Workers' Experimental Theatre.

ACT I. – SCENE I

The scene is the lovely and expensive "landscaped" garden of the Warden of the Penitentiary, Major Stone. To the right of the stage can be seen part of the Warden's house. Steps lead from the door to the house on to a terrace on which is arranged attractive garden furniture – two or three easy chairs and a small wicker table. The table bears the necessary utensils for the "cocktail" hour. Steps lead down from this terrace to the garden (front stage) where more expensive garden furniture is scattered around, also another small table bearing glasses, cocktail shaker, etc.

It is the late afternoon of a beautiful Fall day in the early part of October, the air warm, but invigorating. The whole setting gives the impression of uncramped freedom and luxury. Back stage, and to the left, in comparison with the luxurious garden and glimpse of the Warden's house, can be seen the wall and turrets of Kingston penitentiary, grim and foreboding, and the silhouette of a guard, rifle in hand, standing on duty.

As the curtain rises, a TORCHSINGER, standing on the terrace, sings the last few bars of "Give me Liberty or Give me Love." She is a blond siren, expensively dressed, and though evidently paid by the Stones to entertain at their week-end party, is quite at ease in the company in which she finds herself. She flirts openly with the SUPERINTENDENT of the Penitentiaries, who is seated at the table on the terrace, a little to her right, and it is quite evident that the Superintendent is by no means indifferent to her charms.

In the garden below, MRS. BERKELEY, a sleek adventuress from England, who is visiting the Stones, leans against the garden seat and listens with rapt expression to the song. Other people's husbands are her meat and at the moment MAJOR STONE, warden of the Penitentiary, is evidently entangled in her snares. The Major is a military man, every inch of him, and quite willing, at the least provocation, to go into a long discourse on the trials of a warden of the penitentiary. Although his superior, the Superintendent for the most part allows the Warden to carry the conversation – perhaps out of politeness or more likely because he is more engrossed with his fair companion, the Torchsinger. MRS. STONE, white haired and matronly, acts as the perfect hostess, although occasionally showing that she is by no means pleased by the very open infatuation of her husband, the Warden, for Mrs. Berkeley. Mrs. Stone is seated at the table (front stage) also listening to the Torchsinger. The ladies are all in dinner gowns, the men in dinner jackets. From the cocktail hour in the garden, it is evidently their intention to adjourn to the house for dinner.

As the song ceases there is loud applause and enthusiastic chattering. The Superintendent jumps up and escorts Torchsinger to a chair at the table on the terrace.

MRS. BERKELEY: England would go wild over you.

SUPERINTENDENT: A toast! (*all raise glasses*)

SUPERINTENDENT: – to the lovely lady with the loveliest voice! (*all drink*)

TORCHSINGER (*the only one who has no glass*): Am I an orphan?

SUPERINTENDENT (*flustered and embarrassed*): Please kick me! I'm a scoundrel. I'll never forgive myself. (*Busies himself with drinks*)

MRS. STONE: Let's do it properly then, and have a new toast.

SUPERINTENDENT: And new drinks! (*gallantly hands Torchsinger a glass*)

MAJOR (*who has been also pouring new drinks, now hands glasses to Mrs. Stone and Mrs. Berkeley*): A toast – to the adorable lady, with the adorable voice! (*all drink again, chattering*)

MRS. BERKELEY: Do sing for us again won't you?

MAJOR: S-s-sh.... Here comes the minister. (*assumes comic-tragic posture*) We're lost!

(*The Major crosses stage to meet the* REV. SILAS SCRYMGEOUR. *He is tall, scrawny and cadaverous looking, evidently of the Anglican faith. He carries a large black umbrella under his arm and his black hat in his hand. He is inclined to titter and simper.*)

MAJOR (*jokingly*): O – I hope you won't mind, Mr. Scrymgeour. No harm, of course. Just a little light refreshment. Not a habit, of course. But – er – sit down. (*Offers Scrymgeour chair. Scrymgeour, however, remains standing.*) Perhaps you'd like some ginger ale. I'll fetch a bottle for you.
(Major goes into the house.)

SCRYMGEOUR (*tittering*): Oh, I'm a very broadminded man of the cloth, though I do disapprove of excessive – er – use of – er – stimulants, that is – er – where it's more apt to do harm – that is – er – among the lower classes. (*accepts glass from Major who has meanwhile returned with ginger ale*)

MRS BERKELEY (*gushing*): Your sermon was thrilling, Mr. Scrymgeour!

MRS. STONE: Really enlightening!

SUPERINTENDENT: Quite first rate, reverend!

MAJOR (*flourishing ginger ale bottle*): Inspiring sir, downright inspiring!

SCRYMGEOUR (*smiling modestly*): I – er

MAJOR (*again offering chair*): Have a seat. (*he returns to right stage where Mrs. Berkeley is reclining on garden seat*)

MRS. STONE: Yes, do.

SCRYMGEOUR (*seated*): My sermon –

MRS. BERKELEY: Do you think them all out beforehand?

SCRYMGEOUR: As a rule I do, but this time it came in a flash as I walked down near the brook last night.

MRS. BERKELEY: Ah, brooks! I adore brooks. – Do you know (*turning to the Major who is leaning over back of garden seat*) you have the most delightful place out here in Kingston. So much like the English countryside. Meadows, rivers, crisp autumn air! And that old pile of rocks (*points to walls of penitentiary at left*) just like a castle in a fairy tale. (*turning to Mrs. Stone*) But aren't you ever frightened that some of these convicts will escape and attack you here?

MRS. STONE (*smiling*): Oh, they're pretty secure behind those walls.

MAJOR: And if any man ever did manage to break out of his cell he'd be popped pretty soon by one of those guns (*pointing*) up there in the tower.

MRS. BERKELEY (*shuddering*): What a frightful lot of queer creatures you must have in there.

SCRYMGEOUR: There are some fine men though, like Mr. Cavanaugh. He's a stockbroker you know from Toronto. He shouldn't be in but for an indiscretion or two.

MRS. BERKELEY: Indeed, how interesting. Poor man! Having to be in there with that pack of criminals.

MAJOR (*generously*): Well, they're not exactly in *there*. They're out at Collins Bay, preferred class, you know.

SUPERINTENDENT (*hastily correcting what might be an error on the part of his subordinate*): But we treat them all alike.

TORCHSINGER: Say, you've got eight reds here, haven't you?

MRS. STONE: They're very dangerous, too. They were going to start a revolution and had to be locked up.

MAJOR (*sitting on garden seat*): They were guilty of violence!

MRS. BERKELEY: Violence!

SCRYMGEOUR (*in a horrified tone*): Yes, they went around the country making speeches and organizing soviets.

MRS. STONE: They're against the government, my dear.

MRS. BERKELEY: How frightful! Why weren't they shot?

MAJOR: Oh, this is a democratic country, Mrs. Berkeley, so we gave them five years.

MRS. BERKELEY: Do they give you much trouble?

MAJOR: They don't get a chance to. Besides we've watched them pretty closely day and night since they came in. Though we do have more bother with them than with the others (*gets up and starts pacing back and forth*).

MRS. BERKELEY: Really?

MAJOR: It's not so much them, as their friends outside. Every day we get resolutions, telegrams, protest letters and that sort of thing from all kinds of societies, unions, meetings. Trouble-makers! They're always kicking, always accusing us of discriminating against their wretched communist convicts. (*The Major by this time has worked himself into quite a frenzy*) If we censor a letter, there's a howl of protest. If our guard tries to stop their visitors from discussing red affairs, they go off and write to the Minister of Justice (*he drops into garden seat and looks to Mrs. Berkeley for sympathy*).

(*Meanwhile, on the terrace, the Superintendent seems quite content to allow the Warden to talk "shop" alone, and is engaged in an open flirtation with the Torchsinger.*)

SCRYMGEOUR (*to Mrs. Berkeley*): And they want books to be sent in (*righteously*). As if the prison library isn't good enough.

MRS. STONE: As if Sir Walter Scott and Rudyard Kipling aren't good enough literature for a bunch of reds.

SUPERINTENDENT (*tearing himself away from Torchsinger for a moment*): This man Ewen, a Scotsman mind you, wanted a German grammar book. Imagine anyone wanting to learn to jabber in Hun.

(Torchsinger hands him her glass to be refilled.)

MRS. BERKELEY (*horrified*): The Traitor!

MAJOR: Some people think I've got a soft job. There's one outfit though that seems to be out to make it hard for me.

MRS. STONE (*brightly, she is determined to break up the affair between Mrs. Berkeley and the Major*): You mean that Labor Defense League?

MAJOR: Uh-huh. Even if they only suspect something they start raising the roof, putting all kinds of fool ideas into the minds of the public. (*His indignation carries him away. He gets up and starts pacing up and down behind garden seat.*) These eight reds must be pretty precious to them. The public! The public's butting in entirely too much into prison administration, into things that don't concern them. (*Mrs. Berkeley meanwhile is gazing languidly up at him. Her attitude seems to say, "You big, wonderful man"*) Convicts aren't in prison to be pampered, they're here to be punished, and that's my business. (*He looks down and catches the adoring gaze of Mrs. Berkeley, and is immediately her devoted slave. He picks up wrap on back of seat and places it round her shoulders.*) Getting too chilly for you, Mrs. Berkeley?

MRS. BERKELEY (*affectedly*): I think it's lovely sitting out here.

MAJOR (*sits down beside her and opens cigarette case*): Cigarette?

(*Up on the terrace, the Superintendent offers Torchsinger a cigarette and lights it for her. Suddenly remembers Mr. Scrymgeour and passes case to him. Scrymgeour pushes case away with both hands, and with great dignity. The Major, meanwhile is lighting Mrs. Berkeley's cigarette and his own, a sharp cough from his wife reminds him that he has entirely overlooked her. He jumps to his feet and offers his case.)* –

MRS. STONE (*very coldly*): No, thanks.

MAJOR (*getting back to his favorite subject with apparent relish*): Prison administration –

MRS. STONE (*leaning over and tapping him on the sleeve with her lorgnette*): Now, George, let's not talk shop any more. I'm sure Mrs. Berkeley and Mr. Scrymgeour will be bored to death. (*She turns sweetly to Mrs. Berkeley and in an over-polite voice continues*) My dear, why not stay with us for a fortnight. See something of the countryside, meet some of the people.

SCRYMGEOUR: Very fine old families! (*nods happily*)

MAJOR (*very quickly*): Yes, do!
(*Mrs. Stone looks at him suspiciously, coughs, and taps with her foot. Major looks very embarrassed.*)

MRS. BERKELEY (*pretends to be unaware of this byplay*): So sorry, I've got to be back home the day after tomorrow. Thank you though. (*She ogles Major*) I'll miss this place. So much room to roam around in. (*gushes*) So perfectly picturesque.

MAJOR (*his ardour a little squelched*): Uh-huh. Weather's pretty even. Though I do remember eight years ago it rained and stormed something fierce. Pretty near couldn't leave the house. Almost like prisoners ourselves (*laughs*) two whole days.

MRS. STONE (*remembering her duties as hostess, takes bottle of ginger ale from table and crosses stage to Scrymgeour*): Have some more ginger ale, Mr. Scrymgeour?

SCRYMGEOUR (*accepting glass of ginger ale*): Thank you so much (*sanctimoniously*). But don't let me interfere with your recreation.

TORCHSINGER: Gee, reverend, you sure are broadminded. (*She turns to Superintendent, seizes him by the hand and pulls him to his feet.*) Let's dance, if it's O.K. with the reverend.

SCRYMGEOUR: Go right ahead, brothers and sisters (*giggling*). So long as it isn't one of those new-fangled heathenish tangoes.

(*Orchestra strikes up a waltz. The Torchsinger and Superintendent dance on terrace, and, after a few revolutions of the dance, find themselves off stage right. The Major dances front stage with Mrs. Berkeley. Scrymgeour drinks his ginger ale, while Mrs. Stone arranges glasses on table. The dancing continues for a few seconds and is interrupted by the entrance of the Deputy Warden and Guard X, left stage rear. They are both in the uniform of the guards of the penitentiary.* THE DEPUTY WARDEN *appears to be an average man with a military training.* GUARD X *is rather dumb. He is a man who follows his orders to a letter – in fact, a paid bully. He follows a little behind his superior officer.*)

DEPUTY (*to Major, who has stopped dancing*): Pardon the intrusion sir, could we speak with you for a moment?

MAJOR: Excuse me, ladies. Excuse me, gentlemen. (*Bows to Mrs. Berkeley, who goes over to right of stage to join Mrs. Stone. The Superintendent and Torchsinger have already left. Mrs. Stone and Mrs. Berkeley disappear into the house, chatting. Scrymgeour finds himself alone on the terrace. He surreptitiously pours himself a cocktail, drinks it, and follows the two women. Major to Deputy Warden*): Yes, what is it, Deputy?

DEPUTY: I think you'd better hear what Guard X here just reported to me, sir.

MAJOR (*turning to Guard X*): Well, my man.

GUARD X (*saluting briskly*): Well, sir, I've just had a tip off from convict Donald that the convicts are planning to start trouble in a few days. It's over the cigarette paper business, sir, and the other usual complaints.

MAJOR (*a little impatiently*): Yes, yes, I've heard them for years.

GUARD X (*disappointed*): Really looks like trouble this time, sir.

MAJOR: You'd better station extra guards and cancel afternoons off for two weeks, Deputy. I'll be down to the office right after dinner. (*Turns to Guard X.*) See what you can pump from Donald. Get all the information, mind you. Promise him an extra shot of dope next week. We'll give it to him if he gives us anything worth while. (*Pauses and thinks for a moment or two.*) Must be the men in the stone shed, I suppose?

GUARD X: Yes, sir.

MAJOR (*as if he has just discovered Guard X there*): That'll be all, Guard. Report at my office at nine in the morning.

GUARD X: Very good, sir. (*Salutes and exits left stage.*)

MAJOR (*thoughtfully*): It's been coming for years, Deputy. We've got to act at once. With this trouble coming on top of the fuss those labor people outside are making, we'll be in a fine mess.

DEPUTY (*taking a step forward, very confidentially*): Well, what about Tim Buck, sir?

MAJOR (*sharply*): Buck, what about Buck?

DEPUTY (*coming still closer and putting hand on Major's arm*): He and those other agitators convicted of advocating force and violence. (*He is very proud of this idea of his and continues quite gleefully.*) Tim Buck, agitator, plots convict uprising. How'll that be?

MAJOR (*turning thought over in his mind*): Tim Buck, riot leader. (*Brightly as if he has found a way out*) Not bad, not bad, Deputy. Maybe that'll settle him and his red horde. (*sneeringly*) Asking for German grammar books!

(*As he speaks his last line the Major turns towards the house. He half salutes the Deputy in dismissal. The Deputy returns it smartly and also turns to leave. Both are in motion as the* CURTAIN *falls.*)

Excerpted from *Eight Men Speak*

DON BAILEY

Song of the Prisoner

DON BAILEY (1942–) was placed in an orphanage at two and went on his own at thirteen. He spent time in jail and married twice before he was twenty. Committing bank robberies led to his being sentenced to twelve and a half years in Kingston Penitentiary. While there he began to write, encouraged by David Helwig. His books include *In The Belly of the Whale*, *Swim for Your Life*, and *Homeless Heart*, which won the Canadian Authors' Association Silver Medal for Poetry in 1989. He now works with his wife Daile Unruh as a film producer and editor; together they have produced films for Vision TV and have compiled *Canadian Christmas Stories in Prose and Verse* as well as *Great Canadian Murder and Mystery Stories.*

Etchings

I

There are no pictures, but etchings remain in my
mind. An old lady, my grandmother, is pushing me
in a swing. I can hear the cries of the other
children in the playground as she propels me
higher and higher. I remember the fear,
fingers wrapped into tight wet fists clutching the
swing's chain as I soar above the branches
towards the sun.

I close my eyes and feel joy in the dark, as if I'm
floating on a cloud of my own dreams. I am
marching along beside my father, with him teaching
me to whistle and the two of us are brave together
beyond belief. It's just a dream because I've never
met the man. He's a soldier in the war, fighting
somewhere to save us all from an enemy who
measures victory by the depth of our despair.

But I am happy. Swinging over streets I try to spot
moving cars. Gas is rationed. Only trucks making
deliveries of critical material are allowed on the
roads. Dairy products and meat are scarce. Sugar is
a sweet memory. But the legion still serves rum.
My mother waits there for word from the front.
Her vigil is long. I lie awake nights waiting to hear
her stumble up the stairs, speaking in code.

I am a child of three, fond of fairy tales, listening
to the soothing voice of my grandmother tell the
story of a young cement finisher. He has a wife
and two children. But no work. So he joins the
army. For the steady pay cheque. And they teach
him how to shoot a rifle. But the hero is a
reluctant killer. In the dark of night he chokes
on a bullet from his own gun. Bang!

2

When I am five a social worker takes my brother
and me from the orphanage and drives us to our new
home. But Teddy cries too much. He doesn't believe
me when I say our mother is dead, our father is
missing and grandmother is too old to look after
us. He cries and wets his pants. Our new mother
has bad nerves. She can't stand his stink.
Whimpering my brother is whisked away.

Sometimes still, so many years later I dream of
him and remember the two of us that last day
standing in the darkness of the garage. I hear the
crunch of cinders under my feet as I hold him
in my arms and we move together as if dancing to a
tune I am humming. It is a song from the war and
I am sure that my father taught me to whistle the
melody before I knew the words. A song of love.

When I am seven I learn that my brother has died
in a mishap at the orphanage. The social worker
describes how he climbed up to the top of the
toilet cubicle, stood on the wooden ledge, and tied

a rope made from bed sheets to the water pipe. The other end was fastened into a noose and put around his neck. Then he slipped and dangled for an hour behind the locked shit house door.

But I am learning. Pain is only a bad, sad story, and at night I sneak out of the house and lie on my back in the wet grass. I pray to the stars for happy endings and imagine my father dancing on the moon, his voice floating down to me, singing all the popular songs that I've memorized from the radio. He encourages me to hum along and sometimes gives me a solo chorus.

3

I'm a stupid kid lost in my own world of day dreams. At nine I've managed to hang in with the same family for four years. My social worker is proud of me and gives me credit for being good. Adaptable but not adoptable. A joke between us. She picks me up one day a week and takes me to the hospital where naked I march up and down a runway in front of a bunch of doctors.

My heart has a hole in it. One of the valves has a leak. My spine is crooked and a man with a rubber hammer who likes to thump my knees suggests a brace. The room is cold and I stand there with my little dick and dinky balls shrivelled up, listening to them discuss my health, wondering quietly how crickets got into my bones. For a while I imagine I am an orphanage for the world's homeless crickets.

But it's really rickets. I liked the crickets better. I tell my social worker this but she doesn't smile. She stops the car and begins to cry, leaning against me so I get to cop my first feel of a woman's breast. But her soft nearness frightens me. Her embrace is sympathetic. I don't want to be part of her sorrow. Her weakness angers me. I open the door and run. But she catches me.

I am taken to a shrink. He asks me about death and if I know I'm dying. He makes me play a game using a diagram of a baseball diamond. He asks me to imagine being at bat and hitting the ball. Where will it land, he asks. And I reply, nowhere. I'll hit the ball in such a way that it'll float forever. Just above everybody's head. The crowd will roar for someone to grab it but no one can reach that high.

...

Growing Up

I stole my first car when I was thirteen. It was Christmas Eve. I saw an old man with a pile of wrapped gifts in front of Eatons putting his key in the lock, and I knocked him down and booted him in the balls. An older boy who didn't think I'd have the nerve joined in and broke the man's jaw with one kick. I grabbed the man's wallet while my friend jumped behind the wheel. I was too young to drive. Nobody tried to stop us. The Sally Ann Santa Claus continued to ring his bell for donations. The carollers never dropped a note and the shoppers hurried by while we left this guy all bloody in the snow.

The same night I broke into the printing plant and destroyed the old, off-set press. My dad had modernized and didn't use it anyway. My friend drove us up to his family's cottage which we set on fire to keep warm. We stood in the snow listening to the liquor bottles we hadn't taken explode, both of us a little drunk and laughing and pointing at each new colour that appeared in the red flames, and both of us marvelling at how quiet the night was. Getting so crazy or scared that we started singing popular songs we learned from the radio and trying not to think about the drive back.

We ran a road block. The cops gave chase and we skidded into a snow bank. I hit my head on the dash, but my friend sailed through the windshield, the glass cutting an artery in his throat so deeply that he bled to death before the ambulance arrived.

Prison

My third day in the reformatory a big guy with a flat nose came up to me on the buller gang and said he'd take care of me if I'd bend over for him in the shower. It wasn't meant as a joke. Everybody looked at me, wheel barrows that carried the dirt from one mound to another were put down. Inmates leaned against their shovels and the guards snickered. Everyone likes a little entertainment. I smiled at the guy and then swung my spade so that the sharp edge caught him across the cheek. I heard the bone break and then he screamed. I whacked him twice across the knees so he'd go down and then using the flat of the shovel on his face I kept swinging until it was hard to tell his features from the wet mud on thc ground. No one interfered.

My sentence was increased and I was transferred to a more secure prison. For the next nine years nobody bugged me.

Song of the Prisoner

I wrote my dad and told him I was sorry for everything, especially the off-set press. I know he prized it. I asked him about his banjo playing, had he learned any new songs. I asked him to forgive me. I told him I was taking correspondence courses and, when I got out I'd get a job and pay him back for all his kindness. I knew I wasn't his kid. He didn't have to take me in. If it hadn't been for the stupid war he'd never have met me. I told him I wished I'd been a better son. Even a pretend one.

Thirty eight letters I sent. No replies. I watch the birds in the branches of the trees beyond the barred windows. They seem to stare at me and their beaks move but I hear no sound. Their songs exist only in my memory. Sometimes I can recall the trill of a meadow lark, the chirping of a sparrow, the demanding caw of a crow. And some days the smell of cigarette smoke mingles in my mind with the sharp odour of printer's ink.

But then one day an envelope arrives. Inside is a business card. My name and address are clearly printed on it along with a kind of slogan in bold type:

LOVE IS JUST LIFE'S CONSOLATION PRIZE

I laugh so hard, the guard comes running in panic, but by then I'm humming the line. Before they put me in the hole I'm singing it at the top of my lungs.

The Keeper

He is the perfect friend. Because he has the keys to my life, he never lies. He says it's a shame that people like me can't sign a paper so I can stay in prison until I die. He cites the statistics that prove that eighty-five percent of hard cases like me spend their lives in and out of jails anyway. Why not sign the pledge. Get it over with. Listen to those big gates slam behind you only once. To prolong the possibility of freedom is to suffer. His philosophy is to put those in pain out of their misery.

He visits me when his shift is finished. He has a fold up golf chair he puts in front of my cell. He could go home but is more interested in helping me improve myself. He claims his wife of thirty years is a hopeless case, caught up in bingoes and church socials. So he sits down outside the bars and has me read for twenty minutes from the books he brings. Dickens is his favorite, particularly *David Copperfield*. The Keeper claims I read with great passion and clear comprehension of the subject.

He has taught me to play chess and he carries a small board and wooden box with the pieces in his pocket. It is a game he claims that teaches a man to be on his guard. And he illustrates by discussing his mandatory retirement date that comes up in less than six months. By threatening legal action he has convinced the authorities to extend his tenure at least one more year. His opinions swagger across a continent of subjects and some nights we talk so late he sleeps in a spare cell.

On the subject of love he has a humourous saying: *love conquers all* – that and a gold American Express card.

Endnote

This morning the Keeper was found dead. Gone in his sleep. He died in the house his wife called home. I will miss him. As I miss the others. But I know he did not abandon me. He journeyed on alone to the land of dreams he could not live.

I have learned one small thing in these years of rage.

In my imagination I see a young boy step forward, his lip trembling, his arm pointed towards the sky. He is my son, my brother, my father. The Keeper. Even me. Like fragile birds, we are all weeping at our failure to fly. The wind seems more welcoming than the earth. We dream of taking wing and drifting home.

But home is in our hearts, my son, my brother, my father, my Keeper, and even me. Dear hearts, our hearts, are where we imagine them.

Only I can abandon my own heart.

Excerpted from *Homeless Heart: Persona Poems*

MICHAEL ONDAATJE

Blue Tin Roof

MICHAEL ONDAATJE (1943–) was born in Sri Lanka and came to Canada in 1962. He received a Master of Arts degree from Queen's in 1967 and now teaches at Glendon College in Toronto. He spent many summers at a farm north of Kingston near Verona with his former wife Kim Ondaatje. He is Canada's only three-time winner of the Governor General's Award – in 1971 for *The Collected Works of Billy the Kid*, in 1979 for *There's a Trick with a Knife I'm Learning To Do*, and in 1992 for *The English Patient*, which co-won the prestigious Booker Award and won the Trillium Award. His novel *In the Skin of a Lion* includes a portrayal of Kingston life, while many of his poems are set in the Kingston region.

THERE was a blue tin jail roof. They were painting the Kingston Penitentiary roof blue up to the sky so that after a while the three men working on it became uncertain of clear boundaries. As if they could climb up further, beyond the tin, into that ocean above the roof.

By noon, after four hours, they felt they could walk on the blue air. The prisoners Buck and Lewis and Caravaggio knew this was a trick, a humiliation of the senses. Why an intentional blue roof? They could not move without thinking twice where a surface stopped. There were times when Patrick Lewis, government paintbrush in hand, froze. Taking a seemingly innocent step he would fall through the air and die. They were fifty yards from the ground. The paint pails were joined by rope – one on each slope – so two men could move across the long roof symmetrically. They sat on the crest of the roof during their breaks eating sandwiches, not coming down all day. They leaned the heels of their hands into the wet paint as they worked. They would scratch their noses and realize they became partly invisible. If they painted long enough they would be eradicated, blue birds in a blue sky. Patrick Lewis understood this, painting a bug that would not move away alive onto the blue metal.

Demarcation, said the prisoner named Caravaggio. *That is all we need to remember.*

And that was how he escaped – a long double belt strapped under his shoulders attaching him to the cupola so he could hang with his arms free, splayed out, while Buck and Patrick painted him, covering his hands and boots and hair with blue. They daubed his clothes and then, laying a strip of handkerchief over his eyes, painted his face blue, so he was gone – to the guards who looked up and saw nothing there.

WHEN the search had died down, and the lights-out whistle had gone off, Caravaggio still remained as he was, unable to see what he knew would be a sliver of new moon that gave off little light. A thief's moon. He could hear Lake Ontario in this new silence after the wind died. The flutter of sailboats. A clatter of owl claw on the tin roof. He began to move in his cocoon of dry paint – at first unable to break free of the stiffness which encased him, feeling his clothes crack as he bent his arm to remove the handkerchief. He saw nothing but the night. He unhooked the belt. Uncoiling the rope hidden around the cupola, he let himself down off the roof.

He ran through the township of Bath with the white rectangle over his eyes, looking for a hardware store he could break into. He was an exotic creature who had to escape from his blue skin before daylight. But there was not one hardware or paint shop. He broke into a clothing store and in the darkness stripped and dressed in whatever would fit him from the racks. In the rooms above the store he could hear jazz on the radio, the music a compass for him. His hands felt a mirror but he would not turn on the light. He took gloves. He jumped onto a slow milk-train and climbed onto the roof. It was raining. He removed his belt, tied himself on safely, and slept.

In Trenton he untied himself and rolled off down the embankment just as the train began to move again. He was still blue, unable to see what he looked like. He undressed and laid his clothes out on the grass so he could see them in the daylight in a human shape. He knew nothing about the town of Trenton except that it was three hours from Toronto by train. He slept again. In the late afternoon, walking in the woods that skirted the industrial section, he saw REDICK'S SASH AND DOOR FACTORY. He groomed himself as well as he could and stepped out of the trees – a green sweater, black trousers, blue boots, and a blue head.

There was a kid sitting on a pile of lumber behind the store who saw him the moment he stepped into the clearing. The boy didn't move at all, just regarded him as he walked, trying to look casual, the long twenty-five yards to the store. Caravaggio crouched in front of the boy.

– What's your name?
– Alfred.
– Will you go in there, Al, and see if you can find me some turpentine?
– Are you from the movie company?
– The movie? He nodded.

The kid ran off and returned a few minutes later, still alone. That was good.

– Your dad own this place?
– No, I just like it here. All the doors propped outside, where they don't belong – things where they shouldn't be.

While the boy spoke Caravaggio tore off the tail of his shirt.

– There is another place in town where you can see outboard motors and car engines hanging off branches.
– Yeah? Al, can you help me get this off my face and hair?
– Sure.

They sat in the late afternoon sunlight by the doors, the boy dipping the shirt-tail into the tin and wiping the colour off Caravaggio's face. The two of them talked quietly about the other place where the engines hung from the trees. When Caravaggio unbuttoned his shirt the boy saw the terrible scars across his neck and gasped. It looked to him as if some giant bird had left claw marks from trying to lift off the man's head. Caravaggio told him to forget the movie, he was not an actor, he was from prison. "I'm Caravaggio – the painter," he laughed. The boy promised never to say anything.

They decided that his hair should be cut off, so the boy went back into the store and came back giggling and shrugging with some rose shears. Soon Caravaggio looked almost bald, certainly unrecognizable. When the owner of Redick's Door Factory was busy, Caravaggio used the bathroom, soaping and washing the turpentine off his face. He saw his neck for the first time in a mirror, scarred from the prison attack three months earlier.

In the yard the boy wrote out his name on a piece of paper. From his pocket he took out an old maple-syrup spile with the year 1882 on it, and he wrapped the paper around it. When the man came back, cleaned up, the boy handed it to him. The man said, "I don't have anything to give you now." The kid grinned, very happy. "I know," he said. "Remember my name."

HE was running, his boots disappearing into grey bush. Away from Lake Ontario, travelling north where he knew he could find some unopened cottage to stay quietly for a few days. Landscape for Caravaggio was never calm. A tree bending with difficulty, a flower thrashed by wind, a cloud turning black, a cone falling – everything moved anguished at separate speeds. When he ran he saw it all. The eye splintering into fifteen sentries, watching every approach.

He ran with the Trent canal system on his right, passing the red lock buildings and their concrete platforms over the water. Every few miles he would stop and watch the glassy waters turn chaotic on the other side of the sluice gate, then he was off again. In two days he was as far north as Bobcaygeon. He slept that night among the lumber at the Boyd Sawmill and one evening later he was racing down a road. It was dusk. He has slept out three nights now. The last of the blue paint at his wrist.

The first cottages showed too many signs of life, the canoes already hauled out. He retreated back up their driveways. He came to a cottage with a glassed-in porch and green shutters, painted gables, and a double-pitch roof. If the owners arrived he could swing out of the second-floor window and walk along the roof. Caravaggio looked at architecture with a perception common to thieves who saw cupboards as having weak backs, who knew fences were easier to go through than over.

He stood breathing heavily in the dusk, looking up at the cottage, tired of running, having eaten only bits of chocolate the boy had given him. *Al.* Behind him the landscape was darkening down fast. He was inside the cottage in ten seconds.

He walked around the rooms, excited, his hand trailing off the sofa top, noticed the magazines stacked on a shelf. He turned left into a kitchen and used a knife to saw open a can. Darkness. He wanted no lights on tonight. He dug the knife into the can and gulped down beans, too hungry and tired for a spoon. Then he went upstairs and ripped two blankets off a bed and spread them out in the upstairs hall beside the window which led to the roof.

He hated the hours of sleep. He was a man who thrived and worked in available light. At night his wife would sleep in his embrace but the room around him continued to be alive, his body porous to every noise, his stare painting out darkness. He would sleep as insecurely as a thief does, which is why they are always tired.

HE *climbs into black water. A temperature of blood, he sees and feels no horizon, no edge to the liquid he is in. The night air is forensic. An animal slips into the water.*

This river is not deep, he can walk across it. His boots, laces tied to each other, are hanging around his neck. He doesn't want them wet but he goes deeper and he feels them filling, the extra weight of water in them now. The floor of the river feels secure. Mud. Sticks. A bridge a hundred yards south of him made of concrete and wood. A tug at his boot beside the collar-bone.

As Caravaggio sleeps, his head thrown back, witnessing a familiar nightmare, three men enter his prison cell in silence. The men enter and Patrick in the cell opposite on the next level up watches them and all language dries up. As they raise their hands over Caravaggio, Patrick breaks into a square-dance call – *"Allemand left your corners all"* – screaming it absurdly as warning up into the stone darkness. The three men turn to the sudden noise and Caravaggio is on his feet struggling out of his nightmare.

The men twist his grey sheet into a rope and wind it around his eyes and nose. Caravaggio can just breathe, he can just hear their blows as if delayed against the side of his head. They swing him tied up in the sheet until he is caught in the arms of another. Then another blow. Patrick's voice continuing to shout out, the other cells alive now and banging too. *"Birdie fly out and the crow fly in, crow fly out and give birdie a spin."* His father's language emerging from somewhere in his past, now a soundtrack for murder.

The animal from the nightmare bares its teeth. Caravaggio swerves and its mouth rips open the boot to the right of his neck. Water is released. He feels himself becoming lighter. Being swung from side to side, no vision, no odour, he is ten years old and tilting wildly in a tree. A wall or an arms hits him. "Fucking wop! Fucking dago!" *"Honour your partner, dip and dive."* His hands are up squabbling with this water creature – sacrificing the hands to protect the body. The inside of his heart feels bloodless. He swallows dry breath. He needs more than anything to get on his knees and lap up water from a saucer.

Three men who have evolved smug and without race slash out. "Hello wop." And the man's kick into his stomach lets free the singer again as if a Wurlitzer were nudged, fast and flat tones weaving through a two-step as the men begin to beat the blindfolded Caravaggio. What allies with Caravaggio is only the singer, otherwise his mind is still caught underwater. Then they let him go.

He stands there still blindfolded, his hands out. The caller in the cell opposite quietens knowing Caravaggio needs to listen within the silence for any clue as to where the men are. They are dumb beasts. He could steal the teeth out of their mouths. Everyone watches but him, eyes covered, hands out.

The homemade filed-down razor teeth swing in an arc to his throat, to the right of the ripped-open boot. He droops back against the limestone wall. The other leather boot releases its cup-like hold on the water as if a lung gives up. A vacuum of silence.

He realizes the men have gone. The witness, the caller from the upper level, begins to talk quietly to him. "They have cut your neck. Do you understand! They have cut your neck. You must staunch it till someone comes." Then Patrick screams into the limestone darkness for help.

Caravaggio finds the bed. He gets to his knees on the mattress – head and elbows propping up his bruised body so nothing touches the pain. The blood flows along his chin into his mouth. He feels as if he has eaten the animal that attacked him and he spits out everything he can, old saliva, blood, spits again and again. Everything is escaping. His left hand touches his neck and it is not there.

Excerpted from *In the Skin of a Lion*

JOHN MONTGOMERY

A Hole Sufficiently Large

JOHN MONTGOMERY (1788–1879) was an ancestor of Tom Marshall who has written a poem about him. He was born in Gagetown, New Brunswick, but settled in York. His Yonge Street tavern became a meeting place for William Lyon Mackenzie and his followers who were plotting a rebellion. Montgomery was arrested, tried for treason, found guilty, and sentenced to be hanged, later to be banished. He claimed to have been convicted on perjured evidence and in a remarkable prophecy said: "When you, Sir, and the jury shall have died and perished in hell's flames, John Montgomery will yet be living on Yonge Street." He was sent to Fort Henry, but escaped to the United States. He returned to Canada in 1843 under the Amnesty Act and did indeed survive judge, jurors, witnesses, and prosecutors.

Account of an Escape from Fort Henry

WE were taken from town to Fort Henry in the Sir Robert Peel, in charge of Sheriff Jarvis and a guard of negroes. Seven of us were allowed to occupy the cabin, the rest were placed on deck under guard. Several of us proposed to seize the vessel, and Anderson and myself, being chained together, were deputed to go on deck and watch the signal when we were to seize the man at the helm. We watched until in sight of the harbor, when no signal being given, we went below, and found that the idea had been abandoned. On landing, we were immediately sent to Fort Henry, where our irons were knocked off. Next morning Dr. Shellen, Mr. Hodge, and the American prisoners, were marched off to Quebec. Having managed to secrete my money, to the amount of $75 in bills, and my watch, in my boots, we were enabled to make up a purse of $30 for those about to leave us, as otherwise they would have been destitute.

We had been but a small time in the fort, when, through information given by a person kindly affected towards me, we learned that there was a possibility of our being enabled to effect our escape. This information we did not at first pay much attention to; but after Lord Durham had, on his arrival from Quebec, twice visited the fort, each time refusing our prayer for an interview, and when we had been told that any complaint should be in the form of a petition, we sent one down to Quebec and received for answer a simple acknowledgement of its receipt, by Lord Durham, accompanied with an assurance that it would be forwarded to Sir George Arthur, in whom Lord Durham had the greatest confidence. We felt that it was useless to look for mercy, and that we might at least make a venture. Accordingly we organized a committee to investigate into the correctness of the information received, and, hearing the former account substantiated, we began to make our arrangements.

We had learned that a portion of the wall in our room, although four and half feet thick, had been completed only a short time, and the mortar was not yet dry. Behind this wall was an oak door, leading to a subterranean passage which opened into a gun room; and as the shutters which covered the port holes hung on chains, we could easily let ourselves down by means of ropes made of our sheets into the sally port of a depth of ten feet; and by the same means were enabled to get on level ground. Our sole implements of labour consisted of a piece of iron ten inches in length, and a disk nail. Having obtained half a cord of wood, we piled it up in the middle of the floor, as if for the purpose of airing our bed-clothes, but in reality to hide the stone and mortar which we took from the hole.... We, at length, went boldly to work; the unusual noise at first attracted the sentry, who came up to the window where I was reading the Bible, and asked the cause of it. I answered by pointing to two men, who, apparently for their amusement, but in reality to deaden the strokes on the wall, were, with shovel and tongs, beating the stove with all their might, and eliciting thereby roars of laughter from their companions: while I earnestly requested them to stop such trifling, and think of their apparently serious position.... We commenced on Tuesday and it was Sunday ere we had made a hole sufficiently large enough to enable us to go through. As the keeper had been married the Thursday before, we begged him to take his wife to church, and allow us to refrain from our usual airing. This he was very glad to do...

When the guard beat the evening tattoo and descended from the ramparts, we commenced our escape. We reached the sally port in safety: but here I had the misfortune to fall into the pit and break my leg. One of my companions descended and took my hand, and we were pulled up by the rest.... It was a fearful night of storm and lightning, but we decided to take down towards the river, and when daylight came to take the woods. We had resolved to divide into parties for greater safety. We therefore divided our biscuits equally among fourteen men, Brophy, Morden, Chase and myself, decided to make for Cape Vincent, agreeing to meet the others at Watertown, should we not be retaken.

We traveled a considerable distance on Monday, and in the evening tried to get a boat. My leg having become greatly inflamed, and as I found it impossible to proceed, it was decided that we should rest in the woods and try, by application of cold water, to reduce the inflammation. This was done; we remained for some time; at length, having got a boat, I was helped down to it, and about midnight we started in the direction of Kingston, and then crossed to Long Island, in order to escape a government vessel sent in search of us.

We landed on Long Island, and pulled our boat up into the woods, but finding ourselves near people known to be unfriendly, we decided to cross the island and ascertain our chances of escape from the other side. We were obliged to carry our boat; which was very difficult to do with my broken leg, but I carried paddles and other articles. With great pain, and in a state of exhaustion, we at length succeeded in launching our boat and proceeded to what we felt sure was the mainland. On arriving here we knelt down and thanked God for our safety, and earnestly prayed for that of our companions.

Excerpted from *The Life and Times of Wm. Lyon Mackenzie*

JAMES A. ROY

An Orchestrated Escape

JAMES ALEXANDER ROY (1884–1973) came to Kingston from Scotland in 1920 after a colourful career in the First World War. He was a member of the English Department at Queen's for thirty years. A collection of his poems, *Christ in the Strand*, was published in 1922. Among other works he wrote biographies of Cowper and Joseph Howe and an "Appreciation" of his friend J. M. Barrie. "His farewell salute to Canada" on his retirement to Edinburgh, *Kingston: the King's Town*, remains an invaluable source of information about the city.

FORT HENRY was opened to accommodate civilians interned under the Defence of Canada Regulations. These prisoners were later transferred to permanent internment camps at Petawawa and Kananaskis. After standing empty for a time, while it was being overhauled, the Fort was opened again in July 1940, to accommodate civilian internees and enemy merchant seamen from the United Kingdom who had been picked up from Reykjavik to Lagos. The sailors spent most of their time playing "soccer" against teams from other ships. Elderly captains walked up and down in carpet slippers, on a strip of ground corresponding to the length of the bridge of their ship.

In October the civilian internees were removed, and on November 5 German officers, some of high rank, and various non-military personages of importance began to arrive. The best known of these was "Putzi" Hanfstaengel, quondam friend of Goebbels and a favourite musician of Hitler's, who figured in an amusing episode. Before a concert which he had arranged, he asked the Commandant if he might have a copy of the *Pickwick Papers*, which he said he wanted to read again. It struck the Commandant that the request was a somewhat unusual one, and before saying either yes or no, he consulted one or two persons who had some acquaintance with the literature of the Victorians. One pundit said that he could not stand the book himself but that Dickens had once been in Kingston and had visited the penitentiary, and that was very probably the reason why "Putzi" wanted to read the *Pickwick Papers*. He no doubt wished to make some sort of comparison; perhaps he had a Ph.D. thesis in mind. Whereupon "Putzi" got the book and retired to his quarters presumably to read it. On the following evening the concert took place. A player-piano had been ordered from a local music store and there was an admirable array of talent. "Putzi" was at his brilliant best, and every one of the P.O.W.'s, as he left the barrack-room concert hall, thanked the Commandant and said what a splendid evening it had been. Then the piano movers loaded the player-piano on a lorry, drove slowly through the gateway of the Fort past the sentinels there, deposited their burden at the music store and went their separate ways. The young lady clerk smiled when one of the men remarked that the player-piano seemed to him to be heavier than it had been earlier in the evening: he must be getting old, she suggested, as she locked the door behind him. She was staying behind for a few minutes, she explained.

Meanwhile at Fort Henry the P.O.W.'s had fallen in for roll call – and one of their number was missing. Search was made for him everywhere, sentries were questioned, search parties were sent out to flush the neighbouring scrub, without result. The prisoner seemed to have vanished into thin air. Then suddenly the Commandant had an inspiration, an odd alliteration jingled through his brain – '"Putzi", *Pickwick Papers*, player-piano.' In a trice a patrol of Military Police was roaring across the La Salle Causeway and "sounding through the town." Their lorry drew up in front of the music store just in time to conclude an amusing little comedy that was played there. The young lady had been busy making her entries when she was alarmed to see the player-piano begin to shimmy. She watched it in alarm, then, pulling herself together, she went across to investigate and found, in the space where the bellows should have been, a slim young German Luftwaffe officer who had locked himself in and was unable to get out. She released him and the German was in the act of apologizing for his unexpected presence when the patrol arrived and led their captive quietly back into camp.

"Putzi's" reason for wishing to read the *Pickwick Papers* is contained in Chapter XLV of that work. Mr. Pickwick had gone to the Fleet prison rather than pay the damages and costs of his action to Messrs. Dodson and Fogg, and Weller Senior had this bright idea for getting the old gentleman out.

"Sammy," whispered Mr. Wheller, looking cautiously round: "my duty to your gov'ner, and tell him if he thinks better o' this here bis'ness, to comminicate with me. Me and a cab-net-maker has dewised a plan for gettin' him out. A pianner, Samivel, a pianner," said Mr. Weller, striking his son on the chest with the back of his hand, and falling back a step or two.

"Wot do you mean?"

"A pianner forty, Samivel," rejoined Mr. Weller, in a still more mysterious manner, "as he can have on hire; vun as von't play, Sammy."

ON November 23, 1941, German officers were removed in accordance with a special agreement reached with the German government that combatant prisoners of war should not be interned in fortress buildings...

Excerpted from *Kingston: The King's Town*

WATSON KIRKCONNELL

Still as a Sepulchre

WATSON KIRKCONNELL (1895–1977) was born in Port Hope and educated at Queen's. After serving in the First World War he studied music in Toronto and then at Oxford. He taught English and classics in Winnipeg, was head of the English Department at McMaster, and in 1948 became President of Acadia University. A founding member of the Canadian Authors' Association, he published more than 150 books and booklets. This poem appeared in *Queen's Quarterly* in 1922.

Fort Henry Revisited

October moonlight floods the barren hill
With mellow magic, and the silvery way
Gleams whiter, winding up to walls of grey
Old stone that slumber on the summit, still
As a sepulchre by antique tribes designed,
Save as the hollow ramparts breathe faint groans.
A far dog howls, and on the rotting stones
Dead grasses whisper to the sighing wind.
Strange shadows form and vanish on the wall:
Wraiths of departed sentries, peering; gaunt,
Uneasy captives seeking flight; and all
The restless visions with which fancy teems,
Vague as the wistful memories that haunt
The crumbling ruins of our childhood dreams.

From *Queen's Quarterly*

Neighbours

Preface

THE real life of any city is its people – talking, dancing, fishing, walking, quarrelling, drinking, gossiping. Not only does Kingston have its full share of characters – independent-minded descendants of Loyalists, literati preoccupied with good coffee and bad poems, academics, trendy or impeccably absentminded – it has the good luck to have witty and perceptive writers and artists to immortalize them.

In a small community such as this, we tend to bump into each other – on the way to market, library, harbour, or Tai Chi. Who has not met a friend or acquaintance and paused to enjoy a conversation before hurrying on? We assemble at sail-pasts and buskers' festivals, flea markets and shopping malls; at Santa Claus and football parades where cheerleaders, Queen's bands, and Highland dancers stride by, splendidly colourful (and warm) in their sweaters and kilts. We get caught in Kingston's version of a traffic jam (five cars) and meet, more bleakly, when visiting friends or family in hospital.

Kingston loves a local character who "makes good" in the larger world; the newspapers have always delighted in charting the careers of former residents, most notably Sir John A. Macdonald, its most famous and beloved almost-native son, whose statue in City Park oversees all. But it is in such mundane occupations as going to the grocery store or talking to the neighbours over the back fence that we build the true life of the community.

And here the writers respond to this wonderfully mixed community. Bronwen Wallace describes her disconcerting neighbours. Steven Heighton's late afternoon stroll is certainly on the wrong side of "Divide" Street, an area blissfully unrecognized by nineteenth-century Lucretia Gildersleeve, the type of dear old lady gently skewered in S.F. Wise's perceptive essay, to whom the north side of Princess Street was as unfamiliar as Albania.

After the frolic portrayed during the long Victorian afternoon in the poetry of Charles Mair and Evan MacColl, it is dismaying to encounter the generally bleaker view of twentieth-century Kingston writers as almost unbearably presented in Fred Euringer's *Centennial Portrait* or Judith Thompson's *The Crackwalker* – or the stupefying dullness of Gerard Bessette's "Narcotown" with the invisible walls that (used to) enclose the ambitious faculty wife. But this sombre approach is offset by "the realistic note of thanks" extended by the German scholar and poet Ernst Loeb. And even if Agnes Maule Machar's genteel dream of a Canadian Weimar has not yet been achieved, there is hope for Elizabeth Greene's painter, delineating the market. We can revel in Carol Shields' gentle satire of small literary presses, Diane Schoemperlen's lively portrait of an emergent writer, Al Purdy's quarrelling and Seymour Mayne's dancing poets. George Whalley, desperately ill in hospital but spying a millimetre of green, and the dying Ellen in Matt Cohen's novel, with her transcendent vision of "bright and shimmering shapes moving like burning shadows in the air." Echoing and expanding on the exaltation of the young rebel in Linus Miller. Surely we must agree with Sir John A.'s conclusion in Tom Marshall's poem, "something might be made of this wood."

BRONWEN WALLACE

Neighbours

BRONWEN WALLACE (1945–1989) was rapidly becoming a distinctive voice for a warm and outreaching feminism before her tragically early death. She lived and worked in Kingston as a volunteer at Interval House, a home for battered women, and also taught creative writing at Queen's and St. Lawrence College. In 1984 she won the Pat Lowther Award for Poetry. Her publications include *Signs of a Former Tenant, Common Magic, The Stubborn Particulars of Grace, People You'd Trust Your Life To,* and *Arguments with the World.*

Neighbours

(for Lorna Crozier, who asked)

Though don't think you're the only one.
Everybody does.

"So you're from Kingston. The prison town. Well,
what's it like down there, with all those
criminals?"

Sometimes I tell them
Clifford Olson is my next door neighbour,
he and the other rapists and baby killers,
their lives down to a few square feet,
a narrow hour in the exercise yard
a block from here at Kingston Pen.

Sometimes I describe
the time I went to P4W
to teach a writing class
where the first woman I met
with her red hair in rollers, a red flowered
housecoat on and those slippers with the pom-poms

also red, red toenails and finger nails
looked like everybody's aunt from the Big City
who is always more interesting than your mother,
though the truth is she'd chopped her husband up
with an axe.

Another way to answer your question
is to talk the geology, history
and architecture of this city, built on rock
and out of it; about whether limestone
just naturally piles itself into forts
and prisons, churches, universities, mansions
for the rich or whether the people who settled
couldn't see anything else in it
but their need to wall something in
or out. I could introduce you
to the man whose backyard touches mine.
A retired guard, he'll tell you
things are worse than ever, prisons
run like luxury hotels by asshole politicians,
con-lovers, like the lawyers and social workers
who've never seen the ranges where the guards work;
how can they know? somebody knifes you
and they act like it's your fault
for being a screw in the first place.
He stuck it out for the pay and the pension,
the house, university for his kids. Not bad,
for a guy who never finished highschool
though now he's got this lung disease
and the doctor says it doesn't look good.
Stooped on the back porch, grey and wheezing,
he coughs up forty years of smoke and anger,
one statistic among many, like the guys
on the inside, who tried a different way out.

A while ago, some one
broke into a friend's house
and beat her unconscious.
For no reason. She came up
from a deep sleep and he was already
there, his hands at her throat.

The police were amazed
when she came to. They showed her
pictures and pictures of young white males.

Is this him? Is this him?
More amazing, she refused to lay charges,
though all she'll say is that she doesn't feel
prisons are the answer. Her face, when she speaks
is calm, repaired now, though I think I can see
ragged places in the darks of her eyes
that he tore there, for good.

Some days, when the cries of other victims
rise from the day's headlines,
I think what she says
is the biggest pile of crap
I've ever had to listen to.
Others, I hear in it
the sound that flows through those who've come back
from a few hours dying, a current that runs
beneath their descriptions of white light
and someone there to guide you into it,
a parent or a friend, someone from before.

This is when I remember
how the layers of limestone match
the fluctuations of an ancient ocean,
just as the fields outside the city
ride the wider movements
of the rocks that formed the continent.
I remember how the streets here
follow the meeting of lake and river
so that you never end up
where you think you're going to.

Some days, when the guy at the back
comes out to say hello, his look
is the one my dad's face had
after his heart attack, that big man
suddenly lying there, embarrassed to suffer
what so many others have already had to.

In his grey face, something opens,
softly. Like those colours
that tint the skin of limestone
when you really look at it.

Some days, I drive home
through fields July's brought little to
but the common yellows of hawkweed, mustard;
colours, I read somewhere, that insects see
as ultra-violet, a luminescent landscape
we can't use, though the city
rises from it, scared and hopeful,
like a friend I haven't seen in years
who wants to show me in her walk
or how she's done her hair
another way of wearing
everything I thought I'd recognize.

From *The Stubborn Particulars of Grace*

STEVEN HEIGHTON

Silhouettes Resolve and Vanish

STEVEN HEIGHTON (1961–) is the author of *Stalin's Carnival*, which won the Air Canada Award and the League of Canadian Poets Gerald Lampert Award. He has also published *Foreign Ghosts* and *Flight Paths of the Emperor*, which was nominated for a Trillium Award. A graduate of Queen's University, he lives in Kingston and edits *Quarry Magazine*.

Walker

Sometimes walking home in late afternoon
the look of a lane catching the light will catch
your eye and you might pause at the head
of the lane and looking down it watch
shadows crawl into nooks and tin pails or the tint
of spent sun on a red brick garage
and maybe a boy kicking shards of grit or a clenched
can over hot gravel. You might walk up that lane
by gaping factories, yards rusting and gates, flies
floating like dust from old carpets until
you stop in a path of sun, then, turning
take it between buildings.
In the shadows there
as white shirts and tattered
sheets beat at the light
breeze, a tended dooryard will appear
to your left. Unexpected
you will pause a minute or so then
go to the door and knock as the air
of late August insinuates
something, hear the clink of cutlery and vague
voices from kitchen windows where half-
remembered silhouettes resolve and vanish, in the eaves
the scream and flutter of birds
in the neighboring street an engine starting
and somewhere the slam of a door, shut.

From *The New Quarterly*

JAMES RUSSELL

The Indian Captive

JAMES RUSSELL (dates unknown) is probably a pseudonym, perhaps for the father of lost Matilda Milford, whose sufferings are so feelingly described in his book. At any rate, he claims that his romantic story is true. Mr. Milford lived near "Three Rivers," where the book was published. He was a comfortable merchant in eighteenth-century Quebec, and his daughter, possessor of a marvellous picture book, became one of a number of celebrated Indian captives.

AT length an idea occurred to Mr. W. which he immediately communicated to his wife. It was as follows: – He belonged to Albany, in the State of New-York, where he had a younger brother, whom he intended to write to, and request him to pay him a visit, when he would make known to him proposals which would, in all probability, ultimately turn out to his advantage. These were, to make over to his brother his house, shop, merchandise, &c. for such sum as they might agree upon, and take his bill for the amount, payable at his convenience; and as he himself had never been called upon to swear allegiance to either the British or American Governments (being so far from the seat of war) there was nothing to prevent him from removing to the British territories, particularly as he was still partial to that constitution; taking his ready money (which was ample for a re-establishment in business) with him, and removing to Kingston, in Upper-Canada, being the place which he preferred...

On their arrival at Kingston, they were necessitated to be contented with a very ordinary domicile, all the principal lodgings being occupied by the British troops.

Though Mr. W. was perfectly in circumstances to have spent the remainder of his life in comfort and even elegance, independent of any business whatever; he, however, like most other men who have all their lives been accustomed to the busy scenes of commerce, declined to remain inactive, particularly as he could not be said to have much passed the meridian of life, and was very desirous of again entering into business; but as he had now come to a strange place, he did not wish to be too precipitate in settling himself, but preferred rather to look around him a little, in order to acquire some local knowledge; and, if possible, find out an advantageous situation for business. With this view, he was one market day sauntering through the town, carefully noting the various business-thoroughfares, when he happened to step into a respectable looking store, and entered into conversation with its owner (a Mr. Johnston) on the nature and extent of the business of the place, when, in the course of conversation, Mr. J. happened to mention that he intended to withdraw from business as soon as he could, in consequence of a considerable legacy having been left him by a near relative in Scotland. It instantly occurred to Mr. W. that if he could effect a reasonable arrangement with Mr. J. it might be a good opportunity for his commencing business, as the house was in a most eligible situation, and had long been occupied as a Store. He accordingly communicated to Mr. J. his intention of beginning business, and proposed making a purchase of his whole property, to which he found Mr. J. in no way averse; but as Mr. W. was a man who, however henpecked the world might think him, would not take any step of such moment as the present without the concurrence of his partner in life, he informed Mr. J. that Mrs. W. and himself would call next day for the purpose of inspecting the premises; and in the event of their liking them, of which he said he had scarcely a doubt from the little he had seen of them, and if Mr. J. was reasonable in his demands, they would in all probability come to an agreement.

The following day Mr. and Mrs W. accompanied by Matilda, went to Mr. Johnston's store and found him busy in attending to a number of Officers, and their Ladies. Several of the former on observing Matilda, eyed her with such intense regard, as quite disconcerted her and also Mrs. W. who felt in the keenest manner for poor Matilda, and their confusion being observed by Mr. J. he requested them to walk into the parlour, an invitation they gladly accepted of; for both Mrs. W. and Matilda were but poorly calculated for encountering the insolent stare of those military men, who, when they have obtained His Majesty's Commission and mounted a sword and the other accompaniments of that profession, seem to think (for so they certainly act) that they are at once commissioned to outrage all the common decencies of life; instead of keeping in view the noble and exalted duties which so peculiarly belong to the glorious profession of arms, for such the profession is, and no one is fit to have a commission, nor will he ever do honour to it unless he is a knight-errant at heart. Should this ever meet the eye of any Gentlemen in the army, let them not feel offended, for it is by no means intended to reflect on the whole of them – many of whom are indeed an honour to their dignified station, but it is impossible to deny that many others who having been useless, or perhaps a nuisance, in the place or vicinity where they were born, obtain a commission through some rotten interest or for money perhaps but indifferently obtained, act according to their origin, and only disgrace their profession, and make the unthinking throw odious reflections on their more noble comrades in arms.

When Mr. J. found a little leisure, he conducted Mr. and Mrs. W. through the different apartments of the house, and over the premises generally, with all of which they were pleased; and an inventory of the goods in the store having been taken, a bargain was soon concluded, for they were both honest and reasonable men, the one well disposed to sell, and the other equally willing and able to purchase; and in such a case there is no need for wasting previous time in that jew-like higgling but too prevalent in this country, and which indicates the strongest disposition on both sides to cheat as far as they possibly can. A notarial deed was speedily made out, the money paid, and Mr. W. at once took possession of his new establishment...

MR. W. having retained Mr. J.'s principal clerk, on account of his local knowledge, as well as his general good character, and being himself a man long habituated to business, and in every way well qualified for it, the custom of the shop, which had long been good, rather increased than diminished. Among the Military Officers, there was a very sensible increase, the cause of which Mr. and Mrs. W. were at no loss to divine; and they again became very uneasy on Matilda's account, but were careful to conceal their apprehensions from her and every one else; but resolved to watch over her with a jealous eye, as their knowledge of the world warned them of the necessity, of so doing...

Numerous were the invitations which they received to Balls, &c. all with the view, as they suspected, of bringing Matilda on the carpet, but they found means to politely evade them. The only friendly intimacy which they formed was with an American family, who were, like themselves, Loyalist, and resided about a mile above Kingston, on the bank of the St. Lawrence. There was in this family a young lady, about the age of Matilda, who, though handsome and well accomplished, was yet in every respect inferior to her. A strong intimacy soon took place between these young ladies, and they sought each other's company as much as they could; and this was the more natural, as they both led rather secluded lives. Several Military Officers were very assiduous in their attentions to Matilda (particularly one by the name of Fitzgibbon) when they had an opportunity, which, however, was but seldom; for over and above the vigilance with which her reputed parents watched over her, she herself studied to avoid them. Often did Mrs. W. surprise Matilda in her room in tears, and when asked the cause, she said she could assign none farther than that she frequently had an unaccountable depression of spirits which she in vain endeavoured to conquer; and that she felt a presage of some dire calamity hanging over her. Mrs. W. endeavoured to rally her spirits by every means she could think of.

Since Mr. W.'s family had been at Kingston, they had heard nothing from their much esteemed friend, Capt. Clifford, nor was this to be wondered at since every part was so guarded on both sides of the river. Matilda had now attained her 16th year, and was beautiful and engaging in an unusual degree. Her accomplishments had been regularly progressing, and were now highly finished. She played with uncommon skill on the various musical instruments in which young ladies are usually instructed, and her vocal performance was, if possible, still superior. Fitzgibbon had contrived to be in her company three or four times, and was so delighted with her that he demanded her in marriage of Mr. Wilson, who threw no particular obstacle in the way of his suit, but merely said that such a step required reflection, and that he would give him an answer soon.

On Mr. W. mentioning this proposal to his wife, she said that from the attentions which she observed Fitzgibbon pay to Matilda, it was only what she expected, but that she was confident her consent would never be obtained, even when they disposed to exercise their influence, which neither of them would of course do in a matter of such vital importance; that from what she had observed of Matilda for some time past, she was fully convinced that her affections were engaged, and almost certain that Captain Clifford was their object; she firmly believed that there was not an individual on earth whom Matilda could love, but him; and that it was also evident from what they witnessed, that that gentleman was in love with her. Mr. W. readily agreed with his wife in her opinion, and said he had made similar observations ... at the same time remarking, that they could not permit her to be married to any one without first making her intended husband acquainted with her history, which might possibly induce him to change his opinion, but this disclosure it would be prudent to defer to the last moment. Mrs. W. said she would mention Captain Fitzgibbon's proposals to Matilda, though she already was certain of her sentiments, and then they could communicate her answer to him, which would save them the disagreeable necessity of equivocation, which to the ingenuous mind is always painful.

Accordingly Mrs. W. cautiously communicated Fitzgibbon's offer to Matilda, when they were alone ... Matilda appeared much astonished, and after a pause, said she felt much obliged to Captain Fitzgibbon for the honour he intended to confer upon her, but it was totally out of her power to accept his offer, or indeed that of any other gentleman whatever; but here she stopped for a moment, and said she had no wish to alter her condition; that she considered herself as being too young for a change in life of so serious a nature, and she wished these sentiments to be communicated to Captain Fitzgibbon as being her unalterable determination. Mrs. W. represented to her husband Matilda's answer, which he accordingly communicated to Capt. Fitzgibbon the next day, who, upon being made acquainted therewith, appeared to labour under mortified pride, rather than disappointed love. He assumed a haughty sullen air, stood for an instant in silence, and, wheeling round in a most contemptuous manner, left the store.

It being now the fall of the year, Mr. W. was necessitated to go to Montreal for his winter's supply of goods, and his American friend (a Mr. Willard) of whom mention had been made as residing about a mile above Kingston, accompanied him. The day previous to Mr. W. departure, he settled with the officers of a regiment which was about to remove to York, such accounts as he had with them. The day following Mr. W.'s leaving home, Mrs. W. received a note from her friend Mrs. Willard, containing the unpleasant intelligence that Miss Willard was seriously ill, and earnestly begged for Matilda's company for some time. Painful as it was at all times for Mrs. W. to part with her ... nevertheless the present was a case wherein the common feelings of humanity were called upon loudly, and those of friendship still more so. The horse was accordingly put to the caleche without delay, and she took her departure, under the greatest anxiety on account of her friend, attended by the servant man. On her arrival, she found her friend, Miss W. indeed far from being well, but much better than she anticipated, and in hopes of a speedy restoration to perfect health. Matilda spent the day with Miss W., and used every means she could think of to amuse her, being well aware, that from the inexplicable sympathy which subsists between the mind and its earthly tenement, the state of the one has a very material influence upon the other.

In the evening Matilda took leave on her return home, in the same conveyance by which she had come in the morning. She was then in a state of mind more than usually cheerful, so delighted was she at the favourable turn which her friend's illness had so suddenly taken, and left a promise of repeating her visit the next day. Matilda proceeded on her journey homewards, enjoying an agreeable train of ideas, only clouded a little by not having heard any thing of Captain Clifford; but her confidence in his fidelity was unlimited, so that the only source of her uneasiness was the uncertainty of his personal safety. When the caleche was at a turn in the road, about mid-way home, all of a sudden a man muffled up in a great coat, started from behind a tree, and seized the horse's bridle. The servant seemed to think of nothing but his safety, for he instantly leaped from the caleche and ran off, leaving Matilda unprotected. The stranger desired her to dismount and accompany him, which, if she did, she need not be under any apprehension, for no harm should befall her; to which mandate, Matilda could only reply by a loud shriek, and fainted. He took her out of the caleche, and was proceeding with her in his arms towards the river, where a boat was in readiness to receive them, and to convey the unfortunate young lady to some secluded retreat which the ruffian had in view, when he was arrested in his progress by an unknown person, who having heard a scream, concluded it proceeded from some person in distress. The betrayer of Matilda ordered this humane, but to him, unwelcome intruder, not to approach at the peril of his life, which menace was met by the reply, "Cowardly villain, (for such I take thee to be,) prepare to meet thy fate from the hands of a man who is ready at all times to relieve oppressed innocence, and to punish the guilty."

They both were provided with swords, and a dreadful encounter took place, being good sword's-men; but the ruffian fought with such fury, as to lay himself open to his adversary's attacks; and on one of these occasions he received a severe wound in the body, and immediately fell. The stranger then ran to the assistance of the lady, who by this time had partially recovered. He eagerly inquired who she was, and how she came to be in the power of the villain who was carrying her off, and what was the cause of it? These questions were answered in a few words. The darkness of the night prevented Matilda's features from being observed; but her brave deliverer, upon learning her name and hearing her voice, made no farther inquiries, but immediately put her in the caleche, and seating himself by her side, drove (by her direction,) to Mrs. Wilson's house. He found Mrs. W. under the greatest anxiety on Matilda's account, and seeing him bring the persecuted maid in the room in a state of almost insensibility, (and being a stranger wrapped up in a great coat with scarcely any part of his face visible) she fainted. Such stimulants as the house afforded were resorted to, which proved effectual, and she was speedily restored to animation. The first use she made of her reason was to enquire to whom she was indebted for the restoration of her child, to which the stranger replied, that she should ere long be informed on that head; but in the meantime he desired to know by what means she had heard of the fatal accident which had befallen Matilda. She said the servant man had arrived a little before them, and had given the alarming account of himself having been dragged from the caleche, and knocked down by an unknown person, and that he was in a state of total insensibility for some time; on his recovering he found the caleche gone, he knew not whither, and no person being near at the time, he had no idea of Matilda's fate.

The stranger inquired if the servant was in the house, and being informed that he was, he ordered him to appear; the moment he entered the room, the stranger drew his sword, and in a firm and resolute tone, declared that he would instantly plunge it in his heart, if he did not without the least prevarication, confess the whole of the treacherous part he had acted, and who they were who bribed or in any way instigated him to do so. The culprit was so much alarmed, that he fell on his knees, and said that Captain Fitzgibbon was the person, and he alone – that he had for some time past held out to him strong temptations to betray Matilda, by letting him know when she went from home, &c.; that he had resisted all his offers of money, but he had prevailed upon him to do, what he had done (and for which he was now heartily sorry) by threatening to impress him for a soldier; but solemnly protested that he had received no reward for his treacherous action. The servant was desired to withdraw, but upon the peril of his life not to quit the house, nor to hold conversation with any person upon what had happened, and the disgraceful part he had played; an injunction scarcely necessary, for the fellow, though weak and timid, was by no means an hardened villain, and really had, as he said, resisted all the temptations of money; but the dread of being forced in the army, so wrought upon his fears, that he lost all sense of duty, and regard, for the fate of others. Mrs. W. and Matilda, being now somewhat composed, the stranger threw off his great coat (or rather cloak) in which he had hitherto remained most completely enveloped, and to their inexpressible surprise and joy, they recognized their highly valued friend Captain Clifford.

Excerpted from *Matilda, or The Indian Captive*

LUCRETIA GILDERSLEEVE

Cockades and Poor People

LUCRETIA ANNE MARIE GILDERSLEEVE (1826–1909) was the eldest daughter of Henry Gildersleeve, shipowner and president of the Kingston Marine Railway. The lengthy interview she gave to Professor Richard A. Pierce of the History Department at Queen's offers domestic details and considerable insights into life within the "Old Stones of Kingston."

QUESTION: Could you describe a typical household – the number of servants, and how it was managed?

ANSWER: I could describe my own. When I was a small child quite a number of people dressed for dinner every night...

I started to tell you about the carriages. The Dean's daughter who had been a great horsewoman in Ireland, just drove a single horse, but she drove a phaeton – a low carriage with a little seat out at the back where the groom sat, and then there was a main seat, and then down in front just under the dashboard there might be a small seat where they put the children – and her groom was in full livery, and she had the right to have a groom wear a cockade, which everybody didn't have. You had to be a certain parentage and you had to descend from a certain kind of family for the coachman or groom to wear cockades. Hers did. They drove as a rule a pair of horses, but people who could not keep a single horse drove what they called a buggy; but then later on there appeared what I think was called a runabout.

Now, for instance, in your own house, when I was a child – [in] the house where my two brothers were born – we had a gardener, and in the house we had a cook, a housemaid, a nurse, a woman who lived in the house and did nothing but sew. She made all the children's clothes, and mother's less good things. She was with us for years. There were, I think, five altogether. Now in those days the cook got probably about $8 a month, the housemaid and the nurse perhaps about $6, the gardener about $10 – everything was ridiculously cheap, as prices go today, but money went much further…

QUESTION: And of course they got their board and room…

ANSWER: Oh yes, and in those days we'd keep servants so long that they'd – two of ours were married from our house…

QUESTION: How did the poor, those who couldn't pay for their medical help get along?

ANSWER: They must have been looked after somehow. But in the Cathedral, St. George's – I don't know if it was the same in the Roman Catholic Cathedral – (I have seen our Cathedral rebuilt twice. It was pulled down partly the first time because they were going to make it much larger, put the dome on it and extend it. The next time it was burnt down and then had to be rebuilt again.) I can remember that there was a very wide aisle in the middle of the Cathedral and there were chairs put up, two and two in the middle aisle, and the poor people were allowed to sit on those chairs, and I can assure you that in hot weather (and they *were* the unwashed), if you happened to be sitting at the end of the pew…it was pretty odoriferous sometimes. But they came and were welcomed there; those chairs were specially built for them. All the pews were rented in those days. And when I was very young they had square pews – family pews. Father used to tell an amusing tale about how one of the pews used to belong to the rector. And he had a son named Lawrence – he afterwards became head of the Northwest Mounted Police. Lawrence was a great admirer of pretty girls, and when he sat in the square pew he sat in the part that faced the congregation, and he used to try and make eyes and that sort of thing at the pretty girls. His father caught him at it and said, "Lawrence, if you don't stop that I'm going to make an example of you one day that you'll remember." Well, Lawrence didn't pay much attention, so one day the whole congregation was absolutely electrified by hearing the Rector, who was up in the pulpit at the time, say, "Call the sexton." They called him up, and when the sexton got quite close he said, "I want you to conduct Master Lawrence Herkimer out of church." And the sextons went over and opened the door of the pew, and Lawrence, looking very sheepish and crimson with embarrassment, was escorted out of the church. He was allowed to come back later, but after that he sat where his father told him to.

Excerpted from *An Interview by Dr. R.A. Pierce,*
in Queen's University Archives

CHARLES MAIR

When Gallants Praise, and Maidens Blush

CHARLES MAIR (1838–1927) was born in Lanark, Upper Canada, and studied medicine briefly at Queen's University. While a reporter for the Montreal Gazette during the first Riel Rebellion, he was taken prisoner and nearly shot. In the 1885 Rebellion he served as an officer of the Governor-General's Body Guard and was given a medal of honour and proclaimed as "the warrior bard." He spent the rest of his life on the Prairies and in British Columbia where he wrote poetry, prose, and the verse drama *Tecumseh*. He received an honorary degree from Queen's University in 1926.

Winter

When gadding snow makes hill-sides white,
  And icicles form more and more;
When niggard Frost stands all the night,
  And taps at snoring Gaffer's door;
When watch-dogs bay the vagrant wind,
  And shiv'ring kine herd close in shed;
When kitchen chill, and maids unkind,
  Send rustic suitors home to bed –
    Then do I say the winter cold,
    It seems to me, is much too bold.

When winking sparks run up the stalk,
  And faggots blaze within the grate,
And, by the ingle-cheek, I talk
  With shadows from the realm of fate;
When authors old, yet ever young,
  Look down upon me from the walls,
And songs by spirit-lips are sung
  To pleasant tunes and madrigals, –
    Then do I say the winter cold
    Brings back to me the joys of old.

When morn is bleak, and sunshine cool,
  And trav'llers' beards with rime are grey;
When frost-nipt urchins weep in school,
  And sleighs creak o'er the drifted way;
When smoke goes quick from chimney-top,
  And mist flies through the open hatch;
When snow-flecks to the window hop,
  And children's tongues cling to the latch, –
    Then do I sigh for summer wind,
    And wish the winter less unkind.

When merry bells a-jingling go,
  And prancing horses beat the ground;
When youthful hearts are all aglow,
  And youthful gladness rings around;
When gallants praise, and maidens blush
  To hear their charms so loudly told,
Whilst echoing vale and echoing bush
  Halloo their laughter, fold on fold, –
    Then do I think the winter meet,
    For gallants free and maidens sweet.

When great pines crack and mighty sound,
  And ice doth rift with doleful moan;
When luckless wanderers are found
  Quite stiff in wooded valleys lone;
When ragged mothers have no sheet
  To shield their babes from winter's flaw;
When milk is frozen in the teat,
  And beggars shiver in their straw, –
    Then do I hate the winter's cheer,
    And weep for springtime of the year.

When ancient hosts their guests do meet,
  And fetch old jorums from the bin;
When viols loud and dancers' feet
  In lofty halls make mickle din;
When jokes pass round, and nappy ale
  Sends pleasure mounting to the brain;
When hours are filched from night so pale,
  And youngsters sigh and maids are fain, –

Then do I hail the wintry breeze
Which brings such ripened joys as these.

But, when the winter chills my friend,
And steals the heart-fire from his breast;
Or woos the ruffian wind to send
One pang to rob him of his rest –
All gainless grows the Christmas cheer,
And gloomy seems the new year's light,
For joy but lives when friends are near,
And dies when they do quit the sight, –
Then, winter, do I cry, 'Thy greed
Is great, ay, thou art cold indeed!'

Excerpted from *Dreamland and Other Poems*

EVAN MacCOLL

Cut and Cabbaged

EVAN MacCOLL (1808–1898) had written poetry in English and Gaelic and published *The Mountain Minstrel* before coming to Canada in 1850. A friend of the poet Charles Sangster, he was a customs officer in Kingston and for many years the bard of the St. Andrew's Society. His *Poems and Songs, chiefly written in Canada* (1883) went through four editions in five years.

My First St. Andrew's Night In Canada

REPORTED IN RHYME TO A DISTANT FRIEND

Never yet in "houff" or hall, sir,
Was there such a Carnival, sir,
As we "Kingston Scots" had all, sir,
At our last St. Andrew's.

Verily we feasted rarely,
Merrily we preed the barley;
Good Glenlivet had no parley
From us on St. Andrew's.

The Piob-mhor, so justly vaunted,
Each and all of us enchanted:
"Mac" seemed by Macrimmon haunted,
Piping on St. Andrew's,

MacIntosh, with jibe and joke there,
Saints to laughter would provoke there;
Whitehead ably played the "gowk" there,
For us on St. Andrew's.

Shaw was great in whoop and yell, sir,
Gunn in grinning did excel, sir;
Kinghorn's horse-laughs bore the bell there,
    Keeping up St. Andrew's.

Judge MacKenzie, as he cast there
A proud glance at Scotland's past, sir,
All her foes, in fancy, thrashed there
    Bravely, on St. Andrew's.

The MacEwen clan was there, sir,
Emblem'd by spirit rare, sir,
Charming every heart and ear there,
    Singing on St. Andrew's.

John Kinnear, MacKay, and Keeley
Cut and cabbaged pretty freely;
In them each enough for three lay,
    Keeping up St. Andrew's.

To our host, small gain could grow out
Of such forks as Scott and Mowatt; –
By the powers, but they did show it
    Fiercely on St. Andrew's.

With the haggis fairly stuffed there,
Losh, how Rammage groaned and puffed there
The mere flavour o't set Duff there
    Dancing on St. Andrew's.

Little wonder though old Dixon,
Lured by Drummond's hot-scotch mixing,
Took of it enough for six in,
    Blythly, on St. Andrew's.

'Twas no feast of scones and scuddan
Made MacDonald to unbutton;
Dan on sheeps-head plays the glutton
    Aye at a St. Andrew's.

Far too narrow for his orbit
Was the door to Sheriff Corbett
With the good things he absorbéd
With us on St. Andrew's.

When the bree had thawed Carruthers,
Who but *he* above all others
Claiming all mankind as brothers,
Blythly on St. Andrew's!

Not one Saxon guest attended
But spake Erse ere all was ended;
Pat, of course, is "Scotch-descended"
Always on St. Andrew's!

The finale – fitting close there –
Was a dance of Macs and O.'s, Sir;
Ending with three grand hurros there
For our next St. Andrew's!

From *The English Poetry of Evan MacColl*

S. F. WISE

The Many Kingstons

SYDNEY FRANCIS WISE (1924–) was Dean of Graduate Studies and Research at Carleton University from 1981 to 1990. He graduated from the University of Toronto as gold medallist in history and received a Master of Arts degree from Queen's in 1953. He taught at the Royal Military College and at Queen's before leaving to become Director of History at the Department of National Defence. He was awarded the Cruikshank Gold Medal of the Ontario Historical Society for outstanding service to the cause of history in Ontario; he was awarded The Order of Canada in 1989. His "A Personal View of Kingston" first appeared in *Historic Kingston*, the annual publication of the Kingston Historical Society.

MANY years ago, shortly after I had left the University of Toronto to take my first teaching job at Royal Military College in Kingston, my mother in Toronto was asked by a person compiling a questionnaire of some kind where her eldest son was. "He's in Kingston," she said. The poll-taker, in a most sympathetic way, tried to comfort her by saying: "It happens in the best of families; I am sure everything will turn out right in the end." My mother is a shy person, and was unable to correct the impression she had given. What is interesting, however, is the poll-taker's automatic reaction to the word "Kingston." It reflected an historical identification of Kingston on the part of people living in other parts of Ontario that goes back to the establishment of Kingston Penitentiary in the 1830s. For many people Kingston is synonymous with the high stone walls of the penitentiary and with what appears to be an increasingly mobile prison population.

When my wife and I first came to Kingston, we lived for some time in an apartment in the north side of town (my salary as a "demonstrator in history," which is what R.M.C. somewhat mystifyingly called me, was not up to anything more grand.) We discovered that to Kingstonians, Princess Street was more than the main street – it was a division between two sections of the community. Later, as my salary edged upward and our family expanded, we were able to rent a house near the university, and it became a pleasant duty to act as chauffeur for one of our neighbours, a dear old lady in her eighties, whom I would occasionally take for a drive along the Bath Road or some other scenic route. On one occasion, I took her on a tour north of Princess Street. She told me, and I have no reason to doubt what she said, that she had never been in that part of the city before. She had lived in Kingston all her life, had travelled widely in Canada, the United States and Europe, and had a large acquaintanceship in Kingston itself. But the north side of town was as unfamiliar to her as Albania.

Behind this remarkable instance of the Kingston local culture there were, of course, historical reasons which went back to the origins of the town. At first, Kingston grew up along the harbour front at the mouth of the Cataraqui River, and as population increased, settlement extended westward and northward. The preferred lots were those along the lakefront, a sector which provided homes for Kingston's established families. To the north of the York road (now Princess Street), where land values were lower, came the humbler members of Kingston's expanding population, reinforced from time to time by the settlement of labourers, chiefly Irish, from the building of the Rideau and St. Lawrence canals. From a very early time, then, the York road divided the town not only geographically, but socially and psychologically as well. During the years I was in Kingston, the city's northern edge continued to expand, not only from the European immigration of the post war years, but also as a result of the movement from country to town that has been so much a part of urban development in the province as a whole.

The Kingston pattern in this respect differed considerably from most Ontario urban centres. The land in Frontenac County, with some exceptions, is not very good – a thin clay overburden on top of the limestone bed of ancient Lake Iroquois. Moreover, the Canadian Shield dips down through Frontenac and neighbouring counties, ultimately to give us the magnificent Thousand Islands. This harsh hinterland, settled first by Loyalists and later by other generations of immigrants in the 19th century, not only sentenced tens of thousands of pioneers and their descendants to a marginal existence along a broad swath of sub-Shield land from Kingston north in a great arc through Haliburton and the Muskoka District to Georgian Bay, but it deprived Kingston of the great promise of its early years. It was its rival York, planted on Lake Ontario at the front of the wealthiest farming region in Canada, that became the great metropolis.

When I lived in Kingston, the St. Lawrence Seaway was completed, and many Kingston license plates bore the added marker: "Kingston, Gateway to the Seaway." There was some historical poignancy in that typical booster's phrase. Kingston's early merchant class – men like Richard Cartwright, Thomas Markland, John Kirby, John Macaulay – had dreamed of empire for their town. With their allies in the great mercantile houses of Montreal and London, they had aggressively sought to improve upon nature's works by canal construction on the St. Lawrence, Welland and Rideau, and had been the leaders in the development of lake shipping. The first steam vessel on Lake Ontario, the Frontenac, owned and built by Kingstonians, was launched just along the Ontario shore from here, near Bath, shortly after the end of the War of 1812. Across Kingston's magnificent harbour, on Garden Island, in the 1820s a favourite site for garrison picnics, where officers and their ladies listened to music from the regimental band and watched pleasure craft in the bay, the Calvin family established a major timber and shipping centre, with a company town on the island under the austere sway of the head of the family. When I first came to Kingston, the *Rapids Prince*, the last survivor of that baroque fleet of passenger steamers that plied the St. Lawrence and Ottawa Rivers, was being broken up for scrap. Garden Island, where we spent three summers, had long since ceased to be a thriving timber and shipping centre, and the worker's cottages, though still under the benevolent rule of the Calvins, were filled with university faculty getting away from it all. A gateway, as the hopeful successors to Kingston's first commercial élite learned rapidly, is something that one passes through. Behind the causeway across the Cataraqui were laid up the discarded ships of the Canada Steamship Line and the Key Line, while past Kingston (and usually on the American side of Wolfe Island) powerfully steamed the enormous successors to the old lake fleet, bound for Toronto, Hamilton, Cleveland, Detroit and Chicago with not a thought for the historic aspirations of the Kingston commercial community.

Because Kingston never experienced the transformation that industrialization and enormous population growth brought to Toronto, it managed to preserve certain social attitudes that date from colonial times. (Such attitudes exist in Toronto, too, especially in those havens for élites whose time has passed, Rosedale and King township.) After several years of city living, my wife and I were able to make a down payment on a small house in a country subdivision, well to the west of Kingston. It seemed to me then an ideal place to live and to bring up children, with its open spaces, lack of traffic noise and congestion, and contact with the country (this feeling was not to survive experiences with sump pumps, power failures, and isolation from city amenities.) It seemed to me also to be a significant agency for social change. Many of the young couples who moved out of the city were from the north side of Princess Street. In effect, they were escaping the traditional social identification which a Kingston address inevitably brought about, and I said as much to a Kingston lawyer from one of the old families. My innocent idealism won nothing but scorn: "Yes," he said, "and they'll be the first to default on their mortgages."

Class lines were drawn quite sharply in early Kingston between the little upper class composed of officers of the garrison and members of the business and professional élites, and the rest of the community. And to a remarkable extent, class lines persisted through the long Victorian afternoon of the later 19th century, and well into the 20th. When, while teaching at Royal Military College, I first embarked upon a study of our early colonial élite, I was told by a descendant of one of the Compact families that she was gratified that someone, at least, was interested in reconstituting the principle of aristocracy. A colleague of mine, just joining the staff at R.M.C., was given a lift over to the College gates by a lady in a large, black chauffeur-driven car. On learning that he had come from the graduate school of a large American university, she observed, as he was stepping out of the car, that "the main trouble with Americans is that they are trying to drag us all down to the level of the middle class." She did not wait for his reply – and indeed, he has not thought of one yet.

The persistence of older, more traditional social attitudes in Kingston is not really a matter for surprise. Almost from its origins, this city has been the beneficiary of a kind of golden shower of institutions. It is a diocese of the Anglican Church and an archdiocese of the Catholic Church. It has had a military presence from the beginning: the early garrison, the substantial naval and military establishment built up during the War of

1812, the massive fortress of Fort Henry and the complex system of harbour defence represented by the Martello Towers, one of the first permanent force units of the Militia, Royal Military College, the Canadian Army Staff College, the National Defence College and the major defence establishments at Vimy and Barriefield. Kingston Penitentiary dates from the 1830s, Queen's University from the 1840s. Major hospitals, sanatoria and asylums have had a long history in Kingston. These institutions have had an incalculable effect upon Kingston life. Their presence has cushioned the blows Kingston's ambitions to be a major commercial centre have suffered, and have atoned for her failure to remain the capital of Canada, as she was for a brief period after the Act of Union. They have given a continuity and stability to Kingston life that few other cities of her size have enjoyed, besides providing her with cultural and other advantages that would be envied by cities several times her size. And since all these institutions are, in one measure or another, hierarchic in nature, they have tended to reinforce the ordered character of Kingston society which, from the very beginning, has been so marked. When I first joined the staff at R.M.C., one of the first objects to strike the eye after passing through the Memorial Arch to the R.M.C. ground was a small, neatly lettered sign which read as follows: "NO ACCIDENTS PLEASE, BY ORDER, THE COMMANDANT." That was a source of great comfort: somehow, there in the sheltered precincts of Point Frederick, the mishaps and sudden shocks of ordinary life had been repealed, and one could live one's life free from the worries of contingency and happenstance.

Another effect this array of institutions had upon Kingston life was to divide its society into segments or cells. Some might belong to several, but on the whole it was possible to live a good part of one's life in one segment or another of the community without having very much to do with what was going on in another part of the community. Of course, such compartmenting occurs in larger cities, too, but it is not so visible as in Kingston, so, in a sense, there have been several Kingstons rather than one, quite apart from the major division that every newcomer to Kingston encounters almost immediately: the division between "old Kingstonians" (three generations in Cataraqui Cemetery) and everybody else. The oldest Kingstonians of all (aside from the long-vanished Indians who opposed settlement here in the first place) are of course the Loyalists. When my wife and I bought an old three story brick house on Frontenac Street, near the university, I was delighted to find, on examining the deeds turned over to me, that the property was part of the original Herchmer grant. The Herchmer family, Dutch in origin, had been among the early settlers of New Amsterdam, which later became New York. Like other families, they split at the time of the Revolution. Captain Johann Joost Herchmer was a Loyalist, and came to Kingston after the war; his brother, General Nicholas Herchmer, became an American revolutionary hero, dying at the Battle of Oriskany in 1777. As it happened, my work as a graduate student at Queen's had concerned the use of Indian forces by the British during the American Revolution, and I had been much interested in Oriskany, where a party of Indians and Loyalist Rangers had, according to my reading of the battle, defeated the New York militia opposed to them. When I actually visited the battlefield, I was much surprised to find the engagement treated as a famous American victory in the plaques and markers erected there. In the friendliest possible way, I attempted to explain the true nature of the battle to the curator of the museum on the site, who listened politely and then observed: "Oh yes, we often get the Canadian version here."

The Loyalist element in the Kingston community surfaces only rarely, but when it does it provides the attentive historian with interesting perceptions. When, in the course of its peregrinations across Canada, the Bilingualism and Biculturalism Commission held hearings in Kingston, one of the first persons to give evidence in the well-attended open meeting was a French-speaking Canadian from Quebec. He declared that the chief difference between French and English-speaking Canadians, and the cause of many of our problems in Canada, was the fact that whereas for the French Canadian, Canada was home, English speaking Canadians had two homes: Canada and Britain. The first man on his feet to protest was Henry Cartwright. He forcefully pointed out that he and his ancestors had lived in Kingston from its beginnings, and that for the founder of the family, the Honourable Richard Cartwright, Loyalist, merchant, member of the Legislative Council of Upper Canada, "home" had not been England, but New York colony, to which Cartwrights had come some generations before the Revolution. While the audience was still applauding this sturdy assertion of North Americanism, an old gentleman next to me, also a Loyalist descendant, leaned over and whispered to me: "The Cartwrights always were unsound about the Mother Country."

Kingstonians have, in fact, always been united in their loyalty, as typified by the career and pronouncements of John A. Macdonald. (That, Mr. Chairman, is the mandatory reference to John A. that any discourse on Kingston history must contain.) Above all, native Kingstonians have been united in their local patriotism, though sometimes these brimming feelings have been rather indiscriminately disposed. I understand that to the chagrin of the Kingston Historical Society, a recent release of the Chamber of Commerce fabulously and posthumously confers upon John A. a Kingston birthright – *honoris causa*, no doubt.

Because Kingston has been, in reality, many Kingstons co-existing in time and place, it has been rich in "characters." I do not intend to say anything about Kingston characters, partly because some of them are with us tonight, and partly because Robertson Davies has already exploited that vein of Kingston life to the full in his wonderful comic novels, which Kingstonians read with shocked delight and nervous glee.

But what pulls this many segmented community together, other than war and similar calamities? One of the things that has done this is sport, for Kingston has as rich an athletic heritage as is to be found in Canada. For a couple of years when I was at R.M.C. I had the good fortune to coach the basketball team and was led to take an interest in Kingston's sporting history. Just fourteen years after the first curling club (the Royal Montreal) was founded, Kingstonians, in 1820, started their own. At first, curling was something for Kingston's Scots alone; it was said that St. Andrew's Church was the Kingston Curling Club at prayer. Later, other, non-Scots began to play the game, despite being called "barbarians" by the sons of the heather, and together Scots and non-Scots made Kingston rinks formidable throughout Ontario and Canada. Of course, when one thinks of Kingston athletics, one thinks of Queen's and especially of football and all those legendary teams. It may come as a surprise to some that it was R.M.C., not Queen's, that first played the game of football which Montreal's McGill University had invented. Queen's at that time was a stronghold of soccer, and it was the R.M.C. cadets who taught Queensmen that the proper thing to do with a football was to pick it up and run with it. The first championship won by Queen's was in 1883, when the university defeated Knox College of the University of Toronto for the "Central Association Championship" (a better name for it might have been the Calvinist Cup). According to the *British Whig*, the score was "one goal for Queen's and one (under protest) for Knox", which seems a very Scotch kind of verdict. For some reason, too, a major contribution of Kingston to Canadian unity in Confederation year itself has been overlooked by our historians. On 26 September 1867 in the Sons of Temperance Hall in Kingston there met 52 delegates from 29 lacrosse clubs in Ontario and Quebec to form the Canadian National Lacrosse Association and to lay down rules for Canada's national game. They issued a manifesto praising the sport:

> Lacrosse stimulates nutrition, invigorates and equalizes the circulation, quickens and frees the function of respiration, strengthens the appetite and digestion, and purifies the blood. Its sociability calls forth a nervous stimulus which acts enticingly on the muscles. Lacrosse knocks timidity and nonsense out of a young man, training him to temperance, confidence and pluck. It shames grumpiness out of him, schools his vanity and makes him a man.

The language of this manifesto seems to me to be peculiarly Kingstonian in its emphasis upon the relationship of good health, morality and manliness.

From *A Personal View of Kingston*

ALAN BROWN

Cupidity Inlaid

ALAN BROWN is one of the foremost translators of French-Canadian literature. In 1974 he was awarded the first Canada Council translation prize. This poem appeared in *Quarry Magazine*.

Lines Written in a Kingston Doss-house

My papered wall for some square feet's displaced
(It's not as villainous as lots I've had)
By a landlady figure. She, dog-faced,
Tells why her life in Sudbury was sad.

Her eye that has cupidity inlaid
Brightens and gleams. She retells, with her laugh,
His peccadillos with a Polish maid
And how the lawyers talked, and she got half.

And so, instead of verse to grow the rage
Of Winnipeg and Montreal (*O dieux!*),
I launch loon-syllables tittering on the page.
You'll recognize, I hope, a *faute de mieux.*
I could send fleets of loving words. A pity
The docks and ways lie in another city.

From *Quarry Magazine*

GERARD BESSETTE

Primeval United-Empire-Loyalist

GERARD BESSETTE (1920–) was born and educated in Quebec, and has taught at the Universities of Saskatchewan and Duquesne and at the Royal Military College of Canada. He was a member of the Queen's French Department from 1960 until his retirement in 1979. In 1966 and 1972 he won the Governor-General's Award for French Fiction for the novels *Le Cycle* and *L'incubation.*

I was standing there casting my mind or rather my besotted eye over these book covers which were supposed to stimulate sexual thoughts and which had at least the virtue which at least fulfilled the function (an indispensable one) of setting forth of spreading out in the broad light of day fantasies too often repressed, infinitely more useful therefore (these books) than the ones I watched over back in Narcotown, books that I classified catalogued dusted off and that practically nobody ever looked at (back in the labyrinth of shelf-lined catacombs) save one halting half-blind octogenarian, a retired professor of German (inconsolable since the death of his wife in a concentration camp), buried down there these volumes (among them a few rare finds) on account of the war (just like Gordon and his Antinea in their Underground) thanks to a Jewish collector from Vienna, supposedly at first deposited there only temporarily (these precious volumes) in this little university library at a time when the collector still nourished the hope of returning one day to Austria (but he was to die of cancer in 1942), finally therefore bestowed upon this little university which (like all North American institutions of higher middle or lower learning) was in search of an Area of Specialization, so that this little university, swelling with pride in its new standing its new prestige thus acquired by accident of circumstance, had subsequently received a generous grant from some American foundation to complete its collection, in fact the grant was a bit over-generous for the problem of housing the new inflow of storing these volumes down in that dank dusty cellar three storeys below the street had become insoluble maddening claustrogenic ... I went on to explain that in consequence of all this – that is following the flight of the rich Jewish collector from Vienna and his death in Canada, which had indirectly opened the floodgates of the funds of the American Foundation for the Advancement of the Arts and Sciences (better known simply as AFAAS) – my role of librarian had cast me into these nethermost dungeons of the Sir Joshua Roseborough Narcotown University Memorial Library where I discharged a task of the most total the most unassailable futility, while the university, mired down and floundering helplessly in the rising flood of books fed continually by inexorable American generosity, had twice been compelled to demolish remodel transform its stacks then in sheer desperation to undertake the construction of an added wing which unfortunately threatened to compromise the aesthetic balance the architectural harmony of the library building (the landscape architect went so far as to add: and of the whole campus; but he was a notorious sourpuss and anyway the campus in question had been 'developing' catastrophically, for the past couple of decades, mushrooming higgledy-piggledy right and left, torn and twisted by relentless growing-pains as though stricken with a glandular disorder that threatened to end in a gigantism of monstrous proportions) ... Gordon's voice had gone hoarse and raspy, hollow shadows played over his drawn countenance, the motor hummed softly through the empty silence of the sleepy village, off to the left of the main intersection the sea-green streak of the St. Lawrence appeared briefly at the bottom of the deserted street, Gordon was wondering aloud what he would do what he would tell Maggie, perhaps he just wouldn't tell her anything at all (how could he tell her, what could he say?), for myself, I'd resume my functions midst the dusty shelves in the catacombs of the stocks (haunted by the ghostly presence of that ancient teutonic pedagogue Weingerter devouring volume after volume as he limped myopically from shelf to shelf), I'd go back to cataloguing copying slips notes manuscripts like a medieval monk in the stony labyrinth of his monastery, sneaking off every afternoon around three-thirty or four o'clock (nostrils mouth and throat still coated with a fine powder of grainy black dust) to have tea with Maggie, Maggie of the perfect manner and the no less perfect figure reigning over her sunny living-room with its Louis XV décor, in these conversations Gordon's name never came up, he was never present on these occasions, supposedly busy in his office between classes though on the rare occasions I dropped in to see him there he never appeared to have much to do of a pressing nature merely leafing through books and reshuffling the papers that littered his desk (no doubt a mannerism acquired in London in the course of his military functions under the blitz), in this living-room done in imported silk and furnished after Louis XV, sipping our tea (Maggie and I) from cups of English bone china inherited from her grandmother (who had died a few days after landing in Canada on a visit) already prepared (these cups) set out on the little oblong table each day in anticipation of my arrival around three-thirty or four, my own cup already containing the prescribed two lumps of sugar the tea (good and strong) already steeping in the tiny swan-necked teapot, prattling on (Maggie and I) flirting delicately making chit-chat about everything under the sun for thirty or forty minutes until the children Cutie and Alexander came to greet me politely almost ceremoniously on their return from school whereupon I always arose to take my departure steeling myself to reinterment in my catacombs, for old Weingerter (his cane tapping metallically on the cement floor) would limp in regular as Kant or clockwork sharp at four-thirty to shuffle about among the shelves peering and puttering among the volumes sniffing at the books getting them all out of order snorting like a team of work-horses (I wonder why I always wanted to be there when he came, I didn't owe him anything in particular but then this was his only pastime his only consolation) gluing his nose to the print, his two great bulbous eyes floating like dead fish behind the thick lenses of his heavy glasses, gabbling at me in a hash of German English and French, quizzing me on obscure microscopic details of the literature of the sixteenth seventeenth and eighteenth centuries on evasive elusive philological source-materials which he had somehow managed to run to earth (always pretending astonishment that I – *ein Bibliothekar, nicht wahr?* – should be unfamiliar with them), I always heard him out in silence assuming as attentive an air as I could muster (was this not after all one of his few consolations having lost his wife back there in that totalitarian nightmare and now alone in a foreign land of which he knew nothing save the dusty shelves of a library, the tiny cottage he lived in and the shortest route between the two?) so, I would take my leave of Maggie and the children (Cutie and Alexander) who I always felt despite their impeccable manners were glad to see me go this being the hour of their own afternoon snack, and so I would direct my steps toward the library crossing the park with its curved maple-bordered pathways its green wooden benches where the old men from the nearby Home for the Aged gathered to sun themselves in the fine weather.

What would Maggie say to all this? Gordon didn't know, perhaps it could be kept from her (but how could you hope for that in a small city still a village really like Narcotown?) perhaps at least she could pretend not to know, a bloody mess all round godammit (presuming of course that Nini came on to Narcotown at all but then she was bound to come) he couldn't anyway he wouldn't just drop her cold, he had been in love with her still was maybe no not maybe for sure the fact was that he had never hot over loving her...

THIS curator a certain Archibald Dorchester Roseborough colonel (retd.) of a cavalry regiment and universally known as Ripcord (this nickname a tribute to his heroic but futile struggle in the period between the wars against the birth and monstrous growth of the RCAF in the armed forces of His Britannic Majesty the King of Canada) had as his sole qualification in the field of library science (as was recognized by one and all) the fact that he was linked by direct descent with his grandfather Sir Joshua millionaire and devoted book-collector, this Archibald Dorchester Ripcord (possibly because of his long years of service in a cavalry offering nothing better than tanks and other motorized vehicles of a similar nature) had distilled out of devotion to tradition had conceived and cultivated a single-minded devouring passion for horses which he kept trying in vain to communicate to the members of the Bookworm Club who had the distressing habit of inviting him as guest speaker once a year...turned up as he did regularly every three months to scurry through the shelf-lined corridors of the nethermost stacks as a prelude to his customary Quarterly Report to the trustees stopping in his tracks every so often...to bellow: Will they never stop in God's name when will they ever stop? the 'they' referring of course to the Americans whose implacable generosity provoked in Ripcord a towering but helpless rage forcing him to call meeting upon meeting with the trustees with a view to new disturbances fresh rearrangements more enlargements when it would have been so easy too easy in fact too simple (and that was just the point by God too simple for those half-wits to consider it) to refuse politely but firmly thus damming up this constant flow this inexorable flood pouring over us from across the frontiers of those United States of America whence the loyalist ancestors of Archibald Dorchester had once fled (no doubt on horseback) in the innocent belief that they were thereby escaping the Yankee grasp for all time to come, but Ripcord stuck grimly to the saddle through it all letting nothing throw him putting a paternal paw upon my shoulder as he surveyed the heaped-up bundles of my index-cards: Magnificent work my dear fellow must carry on chin up we'll beat 'em yet; then disappearing again around the immovable frame of old Weingerter to return for another three months to his horse-stables (and presumably to his supposedly orgiastic parties) ...I knocked at her door at the door of her father the judge, she opened and said how-do-you-do-won't-you-please-come-in as though we'd just seen each other the day before: It may seem a bit early for tea but I'll just put the kettle on anyway; in voice and intonation just that faint suggestion (imperceptible to the uninitiated) just that quarter-or-half-tone of dissonance (like those latter-day twelve-tone musical compositions, a little oriental in flavour), her springy step at once light and decisive just enough swing of the hips to impart a shimmering wave to the bell-shaped skirt that swirled about the well-shaped legs, she left me sitting in the great drawing-room with its grand piano its ancestral portraits clinging mazo-de-la-rochean to the woodwork in the descending order from the primeval united-empire-loyalist-orange-lodge-rep-by-pops through the half-orange and the quarter-orange to the gradual emergence over the decades of the bonententists the a-mari-usque-pan-Canadians evolving in the fullness of time at just the right rate, reasonably bilingual sensibly bicultural prudently anti-American, moving cautiously along in the rearguard of the vanguard tragically torn between the Ensign and the Leaf choosing after agonies of indecision (having resigned themselves at last to the necessity of making a choice) that miserable unheraldic vaguely indecent excrescence of the vegetable kingdom, swept along like the rest of us by the inexorable winding current of history, carried on the crests of those rolling waves seeking like the rest of us to swim with the current while trying from time to time to surface for a gulp of air, seizing from time to time a laughably deceptive rudder and trying like Ripcord Weingerter Nini Gordon to sustain the illusion of living their lives, like Maggie coming into the room bearing her tray of china tea-things.

Translated by Glen Shortliffe, from *Incubation*

FRED EURINGER

Centennial Portrait

FRED EURINGER (1933–) is an actor, director and writer who has also been Professor of Drama at Queen's since 1963. He has appeared at the Stratford Festival, the Crest, the National Arts Centre, and many other theatres. He has also written plays and the short story collection, *A Dream of Horses*.

THREE am. From the darkened oblong of her window on the second floor overlooking Macdonald Park, the girl watched the latter part of her graduation eve unfold itself. She sat, as before, on the ledge of the window, her back against the sash, one bare foot on the ledge and the other trailing outside to the floor of the tiny balcony below. The saucer in her lap was filled with mutilated cigarette butts. A tumbler half-filled with the last of a bottle of Portuguese rosé was balanced loosely between the ribs of the radiator and the wall just inside the window. On one end of the radiator, neatly piled and tied with string, were the half-dozen or so books that she planned to take with her. On top of them lay a single copy of *Franny and Zooey*. On the balcony outside, within easy reach of where she was sitting, was a plain round metal waste-basket, in which were the charred remains of most of her notes and nearly all of her personal letters, which she had, without apparent emotion, incinerated during the preceding two hours. The unpleasant odour of charred wet paper was faintly persistent. Perfectly posed in the frame of the window, the glowing button of her cigarette only now and then visible, she appeared to be waiting for something.

Most of the night's activities were over as far as West Street was concerned. The tail ends of most of the parties had wagged themselves into exhaustion. From down the way, toward King Street, the sound of the Beatles indicated that the party on the top floor of number 62 West was still twitching. Most likely Dennis Roe and a couple of his never-say-dies stretched out on the floor in front of the stereo, finishing the precious last beers in the house and listening to the final record play itself over and over ad infinitum. One or two distant voices, punctuated now and then by a woman's laugh, suggested some activity up on the right, perhaps along Bagot Street, or down Lower Union on the other side of the block, but the direction was difficult to pinpoint. And down below somewhere, within the next couple of houses, the indistinguishable murmur of two voices could be heard partaking of an everlasting good-night on one of the porches. Now and then the sound of squealing tires or the slamming of a car door way off in the directionless distance. If one listened very carefully, one could make out the sound of Gerry Wilder's typewriter, high up, over all the other sounds, out across the park from his gable up the street, where, in his studio overlooking the park, he laboured long and late over a never-ending thesis. And regularly, distant, a shrouded clock-chime. Other than that, the sounds were those of the park itself. The occasional bleat of a very early robin, a faded dog, and as a background, the ever-present blend of nearby insects, distant traffic, and the movement of the trees. In her own house, a pipe moaned somewhere in the walls. And if you concentrated very hard, you could just make out the sound of her Westclox Baby Ben marking off the passing of the night. Her own breathing. Once in a while, wildly out of proportion, the scream of a mosquito as it whined in and out of the range of her ear – or the whirring panic of a june-bug, perhaps followed by a flat, ugly spat as it crashed into the wall, or the top part of her window, or her face.

Visually the park was a sea washed by the moon. A quiet sea, in which misty halos of green and yellow light were given life by the almost imperceptible motion of the leaves in the still night. Through the scrim of the night light in the trees, she could discern the soft dividing and uniting forms of two young lovers necking their progress across the park toward West Street. Along to the right, on the sidewalk at the corner of West and Wellington, under the pyramid of the lamp, two cats stalked one another soundlessly. Across the park one could see the moving lights of a couple of cars up Barrie Street, and on her right, the light from Gerry Wilder's window applied a subtle accent to the tops of the nearer trees. Now and then, between herself and her cigarette, the outsized silhouette of a moth or a june-bug would present itself, neurotic, violent, yet strangely hesitant. At 3.30, down to her left, a door opened, the light changed, and a noisy exchange of drunken good-nights from Dennis Roe's late guests brought sound and sight together for a moment. Then the lights, the voices and the Beatles went out, and a new equilibrium established itself along the West Street side of the park.

The girl in the blue dress in the window of number 68 got up and disappeared into the black oblong that was her room. She moved about in the dark, back and forth, sounding the dark space of her room which had become her universe. She moved like a bat, or a moth in the dark – there was something about her movements that was large, despite the confinement of the room. Short, strong movements which brought her to full stops each time at the edge of the room, or up against the bed or the mirror or her wardrobe. She returned frequently to the window, where she responded to the mélange of sounds and lights with what seemed to be mounting anxiety. She put the full length of her hands against the full of her face for a moment, to shut out the unbearable barrage of sensations emanating from the park, and then, suddenly, with determination, she went to her dressing table, where she turned on the little pink lamp that stood amongst the paraphernalia of her toilette. On the dressing table was a large tumbler of water which she had poured nearly three hours before. She emptied the contents of the large aspirin bottle out onto the debris on the table and began picking them up, the aspirins, and swallowing them, two at a time, each pair with a small measured amount of water. She was able, by this means, to get sixteen down with the first glass. She watched herself calmly in the mirror, sitting at her dressing table swallowing aspirins two at a time until the glass was empty. Then she went to the little sink in the corner of the room and poured another glass of water. She took the next three glasses at the sink, less controlled, hurrying now, spilling some water and choking a little as she swallowed them. She was counting out loud, very determined now, trying to keep track of the number. When she reached 50 – she had to fight to keep from gagging on the last dozen – she found her way to her bed, where she threw herself into a foetal heap. Not once did she pass a tear during the seven minutes required to take the 50 aspirins into her body.

Excerpted from "Centennial Portrait" in *A Dream of Horses*

DIANE SCHOEMPERLEN

Myrna at the A&P

DIANE SCHOEMPERLEN (1954–) was born and raised in Thunder Bay and graduated from Lakehead University. After ten years in Alberta she came to Kingston to conduct a creative writing workshop. "I thought it was a beautiful town, so I packed up my cat and my kid and all my stuff, and went." And stayed. She has written four books of short stories, including *The Man of My Dreams*, which was nominated for both the 1990 Governor-General's Award for Fiction and the Trillium Award, and *Hockey Night in Canada & Other Stories*. The following is an excerpt from the story, "How Myrna Survives."

... AGAINST all odds, Myrna is a writer, and every morning, to prime the pump, she likes to read a few chapters of some book good enough to be inspiring but not so good as to induce paralysis with its shameless brilliance. Over her third and fourth cups of coffee (a fresh-ground blend of Brazilian and French Roast which she invented herself last week and is justly proud of, though no one else has ever tasted it), she makes notes of the ideas that have come to her lately from one place or another. Things like:

1. While dressing herself up for the date, she couldn't help but think about chickens.

2. The man at the bar in the black cowboy hat ordered up another round for the house. He liked to play the big shot. Nobody else's money was good around him.

3. I was pushing the stroller up to the A&P to get the baby some prunes and there was this ambulance coming towards us. It turned left at the lights, heading over to Rideau Street, and there was me, pushing the baby in the heat and hoping it was for you.

4. At moments like this, Dorothy's husband, Sven, would

always say, "Kooks, Dotty. The whole world is full of kooks. What's the world coming to? That's what I'd like to know." And at moments like this, Dorothy would always wonder how she'd come to be living here in Houston, married to a man named Sven, of all things, and he's wearing a sombrero and never been anywhere near Sweden in his life.

Myrna fully intends to expand on these ideas later in the day. For now, she likes to get them down before she loses them. She likes the feel of her favourite pen in her hand first thing in the morning.

An odd phrase comes to mind and sticks, like a song or a name, knocking: it says, "All the length of..." Feeling playful and creatively eccentric, she writes:

1. All the length of the dead garden
there were raspberry canes.

2. All the length of the clothesline
there were pink baby clothes and beach towels.

3. All the length of the roof
there were loose shingles slapping in the wind.

4. All the length of the street
there were empty garbage cans, up-ended and rolling.

5. All the length of the stadium
there were blonde cheerleaders waving red pom-poms.

6. All the length of the forest
there were trees burnt black in the fire.

7. All the length of her arm
there were bruises.

8. All the length of her life
she was happy.

Myrna does not expect anything much to come of this exercise but it was fun, like flexing, and she calls it "Longing."

4. Myrna smokes too much.

5. Myrna drinks too much coffee.

6. Myrna has often been told she thinks too much.

7. Myrna waits for the mailman, who finally trudges up the driveway at 10:36 a.m., looking red in the face and grim. He leaves three bills, an envelope full of discount coupons for diapers and dog food, a flyer from Beaver Lumber where they have two-by-fours and padded toilet seats on special. Myrna is fed up.

8. She drives downtown with the window open and the rock-and-roll radio up full blast so the handsome young construction workers at the corner of Princess and Division will notice her and know she isn't exactly what she appears to be in her dark-blue compact with her seat belt on. She sings along loudly and puts a look on her face she thinks of as saucy.

9. She parks in the Marion Springer Memorial Lot on Queen Street which is out of the way but there is always a space. She walks three blocks to her bank. It seems to be one of those days when every second person she passes has something wrong with them. There is a man with one arm, the empty sleeve of his white jacket pinned across his chest like a beauty queen's banner. There is a little girl with a bulging pocket of lumpy scar tissue on one side of her mouth and her left eye is three times as big as her right, protruding and watering, pointing right at Myrna. There is that smelly man she always sees, in greasy jeans and a lumberjack shirt, talking to himself and barking. There is a mongoloid woman riding in a shopping cart, wearing short white gloves and waving like the Queen, pushed along by a woman old enough to be her grandmother but who is probably her mother. Myrna knows that's how these things can happen because her own mother, on ugly occasions requiring excuses, apologies, or some vague kind of justification, often reminded her, "I was nearly forty when I had you. You're lucky to be normal."

Standing in line in the bank, she tries to shake off the insidious fear these poor people have put in her. She's hoping she won't run into anyone she knows, someone who will corner her, and then she will actually have to smile at them and make some street small talk, as if she were happy to see them. She concentrates on not catching anyone's eye. By the time she gets up to the teller's wicket, she is able to make minor pleasantries about the weather and the mechanic in Hamilton who won $2.2 million in the 649 draw Saturday night.

10. In the A&P she gets out her list and loads up her cart, immensely enjoying the way the purchase of yellow toilet paper, whole-wheat bread, and a family-size can of kidney beans on sale can give her such a sense of self-worth. Standing in the check-out line, she feels confirmed in her pursuit (disguise) of normalcy (domesticity) and would like to point this out to the woman behind her, who is talking baby talk to her little girl in the cart which is filled with jars of baby food and a jumbo pack of ninety-six ultra-absorbent diapers.

Once Myrna was buying a fig tree along with her usual groceries and the woman behind her explained all about how it would need lots of water and lots of sun and then half its leaves would fall off anyway but this was nothing to worry about because a fig tree will just do that sometimes, shedding. And then it was such a beautiful plant, and only $14.99, that the woman went back and got one for herself, even though the last thing in the world she needed was another fig tree. Every time Myrna waters her fig tree now, she thinks about that woman.

Myrna waits her turn and chuckles at the tabloid headlines:

CHOCOHOLIC MOTHER GIVES BIRTH TO SUGAR-COATED BABY
BRIDE'S STOMACH EXPLODES AT WEDDING RECEPTION
79-YEAR-OLD PRIEST MAKES 15-YEAR-OLD TRIPLETS PREGNANT.

The cashier seems pleased when Myrna fishes around in her wallet and quickly comes up with the exact change.

11. Myrna likes to take herself out to lunch. But she doesn't go to the Pizza Hut any more because they always bring the food so fast that she thinks they feel sorry for her, having to eat lunch all alone. Either that or they want to get rid of her. She gets so nervous eating there, what with all the good cheer and rushing around, that she's afraid she'll choke and terminally disgrace herself, face-down in her food.

She doesn't go to Bonnie's Bistro any more either because the last time she did, there was an elastic band in her french fries.

She doesn't go, at least not very often, to The Waterworks Café, which is a popular place where all the local artists, writers, musicians, and aspirants like to congregate. She does go there once in a while because every time she walks by, she feels like she's missing something.

The Waterworks is tastefully decorated in trendy pastels, mint green and dusty rose, with original artwork on the walls, oil paintings and silk-screen prints with price tags in the corners. They play eclectic music. The menu features soups, salads, pâté, a selection of items which can be attractively served on a croissant, and twenty-seven varieties of mineral water, domestic and imported, sparkling and still. It is a small place, meant to be intimate, but there is not even a decent space between tables, so you are always bumping the back of your chair into the back of the chair of the person at the table behind you. And they are always bumping your chair just as you are trying to get a spoon full of hot soup (home-made minestrone, or cream of broccoli) up to your mouth.

The other patrons wander from table to table, carrying their cappuccino or Perrier, congratulating or commiserating. Myrna must be feeling impervious and relatively intelligent in order to go into The Waterworks because, once inside, she feels like an impostor or an intruder. She secretly yearns to be part of this group but knows she will never pull it off.

Myrna likes to have lunch at Martin's Gourmet Burger Palace where the efficient waitress named Donna brings her a coffee and says, "The usual?" while Myrna is still taking her coat off, arranging it on the back of her chair. She sits so she can see out the window. She has bought a lottery ticket before coming in and sits for a while with it in her hand, trying to decide if, when she scratches and wins, she will jump up and down screaming her head off, "I won! I won!" or if she will just sit there smiling gently, sure of herself, her secrets, and the future.

She reads *The New Yorker*, especially the "Goings On About Town", though she's never been there and doubts she ever will because she is afraid of big cities.

She observes the people at the next table, a party of five, three men and two women, drinking pear cider and wearing quiet office outfits. One young man in a grey trench coat passes around a blue binder with the title "Focus on Dermatology" on the cover. Myrna cannot imagine what these people are going to do with the rest of their lives, once this lunch is over. No matter how often she comes here, she never sees the same people twice.

Sometimes, by the time Donna brings her food (a mushroom and bacon burger with Caesar salad instead of fries), Myrna has got to feeling guilty for being there, wasting time when she should be home washing the floor, doing laundry, cleaning that mildew from the bathroom window-sill because sometimes she thinks she can SMELL it. She should be at home THINKING. Mostly, she should be at home WRITING. At the very least, she should be finishing up the rest of the things on her list because these are the parameters she has set for herself, these are the promises she must live up to
in order to feel justified
in order to wrest
              wring
              rake
              rescue
              resurrect order out of chaos
                              value out of worthlessness
                              or the tidal fear of it.

While in Martin's she writes in a small hard-covered notebook which she carries in her purse at all times. She writes about how the sight of Canada geese travelling across the sky in their V spring and fall always gives her a lump in her throat which she has never been able to figure out. But suddenly, in the act of writing it down, she sees that this natural phenomenon is an affirmation that all is right with the world, that things indeed are unfolding as they should. And the lump in her throat comes from the precious duplicity of simultaneously believing this and knowing that it's not true.

Myrna likes the image of herself writing in restaurants and, for a few minutes, everything makes sense.

Myrna leaves a good tip and waves at the waitress on her way out. She has seen this Donna several times on the street but they do not acknowledge each other, as if they keep a shameful secret between them, as if Myrna keeps having lunch at Martin's with somebody else's husband instead of alone...

Excerpted from *The Man of My Dreams*

MATT COHEN

Folded into the Dark Groves

MATT COHEN (1942–), one of Canada's most accomplished novelists, was born in Kingston General Hospital. After a varied academic career, one day "many years after his birth, he suddenly realized that he had strayed far from home – at which point he immediately returned to the county of his birthplace." He says he is sure Kingston has had a tremendous influence on his work, in which the city has gained, he ventures to hope, "a metropolitan dignity worthy of its history." He is the author of four "Salem" novels set in the region north of Kingston – *The Disinherited, Colours of War, The Sweet Second Summer of Kitty Malone*, and *Flowers of Darkness* – as well as *Emotional Arithmetic* and *Freud: The Paris Notebooks.*

... SOMEHOW he managed to draw it out of his pocket. It was crumpled and stained with beer. "What I wanted to know exactly was if there was going to be a wedding to follow after this or if, you know, wc just wasted ten dollars on this piece of paper. Not that it matters. I mean I've gone forty-nine years without getting married and I don't know why I should be getting married now."

Kitty tried to shove her feet deeper into her paper slippers. On the table were Sandra's cigarettes. When she had one lit and the smoke sucked deep into her lungs, she felt her blood slow down, trying to ready herself for this.

"It's late," Sandra said.

"That's okay."

"People are very quiet at night."

"Quiet," Pat said. "There's only one place more quiet than here and that's where they go after. Present company excepted if you know what I mean."

"People come to the hospital to get cured," Sandra said. "Not to die." Her voice was like dry gold. "Mrs. Malone is receiving the very best of care."

"You betcha," said Pat. "You know just this very night I says to myself. Pat, you know you should be thankful they've taken Kitty in under their big downy wing in the downy-town hospital."

"I'll have to ask you to leave."

"I'll have to ask you to leave," mimicked Pat, wiggling his hips as he spoke.

"If you don't leave nicely, I'll have to call the police."

"I'll have to call the police," piped Pat in a falsetto. *"We're in the downy-down-town of the town and the gown; and if I don't eat my fleas you're gonna call the police."* All this while standing at the door, his legs crossed over themselves, like Sandra's, one foot held tentatively forward, like her clubfoot, his voice as high and pure as he could make it.

"That's very good," Sandra said. She clapped her hands. "You should come back on the weekend. They love to make rhymes in the children's wing on Sundays."

"My rhymes," said Pat, "are not suitable for the pink pure minds of city babies. I am the goddamn fucking bard of Salem, and I don't strut my goddamn god-gobbling wares in the maternity ward of this smelly atheistic grave of a hospital." He was holding the wedding licence before him, curled into a scroll, and was edging towards Kitty as he spoke, making her nervous, waving it at her as if it was the Ten Commandments.

"I mean," Pat said, except that he was not saying, he was shouting, "what in the hell do you intend to do about this thing?" He was so drunk his face was purple. He was so drunk he couldn't hear anything but the sound of his own voice. He was so drunk Kitty wanted to be cured, to be out of this hospital and at her own house where she could stand up and walk towards him with his eternally gnawing gut and kick him out of her house, out of her sight, out of her consciousness.

"Go away," Kitty whispered.

"Don't tell me," Pat shouted. He was standing over her, waving the licence like a club.

"I'll have to ask you to leave," Sandra said again. She was on her feet now, beside him, diminutive and golden and one hand on his arm.

"Don't tell me."

And then the other hand flashed forward. Kitty could see Pat twist towards her, his arm caught by Sandra, pinned by the needle. He was so surprised he only stood there. And then, his face gradually draining from purple to deadly white, crumpled to the floor.

"There there," Sandra crooned. She was kneeling beside him. "Don't you worry lover. Don't you worry now."

SANDRA'S golden mantra, the squeak of Pat's shoes as they slid along the tile floor, Kitty's quick intake then slow-breathing release: all of these Ellen had heard. And through the wet window of tears pressed between eyelids and cheeks she had taken in the whole scene: poor beaten-purple Pat skunking into the room with his stinky temper and babbly tongue, Sandra sneaking up on him like a golden snake, striking him to the ground.

As for Kitty, Ellen didn't have to look directly at her to know how she was, strung between anger and resigned amusement. Kitty was exactly as usual, charmed and disgusted; and although Doctor Connors, that stupid round-faced squirt of a doctor, hadn't been able to find any baby in her, at least he hadn't killed her. She wouldn't be dying in the hospital, not Kitty, she'd be going home soon enough.

"You'll be all right?" Sadie had kept asking. "You sure you'll be all right?"

"Christ yes," Ellen insisted. "You'd think I was a little kid who shouldn't be let out." And stood up for them, walked around the kitchen and sat down. Hardly puffing. Just to prove she still had it in her. Christ yes. And though she let Mark help her skate-walk out to the car, she was strong enough to turn and wave to Sadie before climbing in. Good-bye, she was saying; Good-bye you skinny-shanked fish-eyed bitch and I hope you're happy with the goddamned house you tore right out of me. Had the crust to make me sit in my own kitchen without moving for twenty years. Now you can sit your own bony arse in that wicker chair and see how you like it.

She heard their voices.

Pat was slumped against the wall and Sandra had resumed her conversation with Kitty.

Her eyes rested on a thin river of tears; it was a comfortable, almost happy way for them to be: her eyes relaxed and swimming, her skin feeling moist and young.

She had left the house, just as she had needed to, and she was now thinking again of her father's wonderful and cryptic last good-bye.

What he had said was, "Them Indians sure know how to die."

In the old days she had remembered him saying this, but thought nothing of it, thought only that he meant Indians were no good for living.

But now, sitting in the clean white shadows of a Kingston General Hospital nursing station, she let there be a different meaning to his words.

Because there was a way to die, a high highway, a whole beautiful surge of dying that was built into a person, an inner fantastic flower that took a whole lifetime to seed and grow and then burst into violent exploding bloom just at that very moment you slide off that old barn roof and into the one long final free fall; and now at the end of this long night and day it seemed she had spent the last twenty years getting ready to know this; the knowledge had been growing beneath the surface of her mind, waiting to be released, growing with beautiful wildweed berserk speed, racing through her cells in a crazy undammed rush, just waiting to be discovered, to burst out and take her sliding off the roof and up to heaven in one last great long-stemmed rosy-petalled leap.

The moon was sliding down the old barn roof; the wonderful secret of her dying had rushed through her so completely that she was now happily afloat in the sensation of her own expiring, every breath, every last sweet breath feeling as sweet as the silver shining moon.

And not only was she dying, but she had realized something else – that she, Ellen Malone, eighty-two years old and an old wrinkled-skin bag of shit, was headed straight for heaven.

Heaven Now.

Beautiful, eternal, blood-clearing heaven was up there somewhere and she knew by the silver rush of her blood through her veins, by the clear feeling of every last countdown detail that this dying rush, this last slide off the edge was leading not down but up, not into the snide snaky vacuum of doubt but into the blue undeniable sky that the prophets had visited and that the after-shave-swallowing ministers bragged about without knowing. But she knew it, knew it as certain as she knew her own name, knew that her father's words about the Indians, all that long-worded stuttering stuff she had read in the Bible, the whole last wasted decades of her life were coalescing into one last beautiful upwards swan dive that would lead her into that perfect oasis, straight into heaven as sure as Moses led the Jews out of the desert.

She wanted to sing.

"I'm me," she wanted to sing. "Me, just pure perfect Ellen Malone me and I'm dying high, flying like a goddamn bird, raising my soul up into heaven like a cloud in the sky, goddamn I'm going to heaven and you don't know how it is, you poor arse, no you don't."

It was a gift.

Some people, like Stanley Kincaid and Henry Malone, they just died by accident; their lives were smashed and crashed into oblivion like chickens run over by a bulldozer, their bodies destroyed before their souls knew how to survive without.

A gift: and it had been so long, almost a whole lifetime, since she had run into a gift like this: an easy joyous overflowing in the centre of her being, a sure knowledge that came from the inside and couldn't be deflected by others – that it was making her cry.

She didn't want them to see her tears, know she was conscious, be forced to deal with them or worse explain that the only thing that had made her happy in the whole time since her husband's death was the prospect of her own. Not that she could see why she had missed the stupid bugger, Henry Malone, so dumb he couldn't tell the hole in his sock from the holes in his ears; and if there were mornings enough she had woken up missing him, there were equally the number of mornings she had said to herself, good riddancc. But it was true, anyway, so good-bye Henry, or maybe hello, because if *she* was going to heaven maybe he would be there too, why not, the whole stupid world was probably going.

"Ellen."

No, don't talk, go away.

"Ellen."

She squinched her eyes tighter, trying to suppress the tears.

"What's wrong, Ellen. You feeling sick?"

"I'm okay," she finally whispered.

"Ellen, what's wrong?"

She looked at Kitty. Who was leaning forward, concerned, her housecoat open so Ellen could see how her own very youngest daughter was getting old too, the skin on her throat growing rough and bumpy, the folds in her neck V-ing down to the cleavage between her breasts.

"I'm okay," Ellen said. "I am being raised up to heaven."

"What?"

"You heard me, Kitty. The Good Lord is taking your poor old mother away."

"Jesus."

"My soul is rising up in the sky like the angel Gabriel in his fiery chair."

"Ellen, you want a cigarette?"

"I should have taken you to church more. I should have set a better example.

"It's okay. Here."

The cigarette felt fat and round in her fingers: distant.

She leaned forward to Kitty's match. Then sucked in the smoke, trying to fill her lungs, trying to force a whole heaven-wafting cloud into her lungs. They should have gone to church the whole time, the whole family there every Sunday, preparing for this.

"I just come down here," Ellen said. "I wanted to see you." She rolled the tip of her cigarette on the ashtray Kitty held for her, surprised to see half its length had already burned away. "You can't hang on too long, you know. But you can't give up too early, no." She was looking at Kitty and thinking that she, like Mark Frank on the drive down, was paying her no special attention, seemed to have no knowledge that this occasion was unique and final. The goddamn fools were thinking she was going out ranting; after all these years of gaming they couldn't tell the real beef from the baloney.

"I'm serious, child. Do you know I'm telling the truth now?" She looked at Kitty, waiting for her answer. "Do you know? My soul has lifted and I feel myself spread out across the whole sky. I am a whole cloud covering the whole earth and I feel the whole sun shining down on me alone. Kitty, that is God's truth. It is shining down on me."

"Hey," croaked Pat, "Hallelujah."

Ellen looked over to where Pat was sitting on the floor, his foolish grin spread over his drunken face. And behind him now appeared a grey limping shadow! Charlie her firstborn; Charlie who understood.

"Oh Charlie," Ellen greeted him. "Hallelujah." She was almost shouting as she said it, she realized it had been years since she shouted. "Hallelujah. HALLELUJAH!" The sound of her own voice filled her skull, walloped around in her brain like a giant fish leaping to the surface. "HALLELUJAH CHARLIE. HALLELUJAH."

"Hallelujah," Pat groaned. "Halle-fuckin-lujah." He had changed from his stiffened-out drunk to his jellyfish stage. He struggled to get up and then collapsed again.

"I'm going to heaven," Ellen whispered. "I'm going to heaven and it feels so good."

"Oh Lord," said Pat, "em-brace me." He had his arms spread out wide, ready to be crucified. "Hallelujah."

"Shut up," Sandra screeched. "Get out of this place." She was descending on him, waving the needle like a knife; and as Ellen sat in her chair she saw the four of them converge: Pat, his hands now covering his face, Charlie, his cane raised uselessly in the air, Sandra swooping down on Pat like a great golden bird, and Kitty, one hand to her side and the other tugging at Sandra.

"No," Kitty was pleading. "No, please don't."

"I can't help it," Ellen whimpered. "I can't help it." For one last time she sensed them all: Kitty, Charlie, Pat – they were all reaching out to each other, their love a beautiful golden net; and then the room jolted and the air was so bright and liquid she could hardly see anyone, they were all changing now, turning into each other and then there were only bright and shimmering shapes moving like burning shadows in the air.

And then she was in the forest again, folded into the dark groves and mysterious trees, in the deep wind-rushing forest, God's breath blowing clear her veins, in the forest, her own soul gleaming like a full moon from her belly as she tumbled dark and shapeless through the rush of her dying.

Excerpted from *The Sweet Second Summer of Kitty Malone*

JUDITH THOMPSON

Lookin Like That Madonna

JUDITH THOMPSON (1954–) was born in Montreal, grew up in Connecticut and Kingston and is a graduate of Queen's and the National Theatre School in Montreal. She learned the language for her harsh, violent, compassionate plays during a summer job with the Ministry of Community and Social Services. Of the playwright's role in society, she has said: "You've got to be the leopard on the outside, not one of the grazing cattle." She has won many awards, including two Governor-General's awards for drama for *White Biting Dog* and *The Other Side of the Dark*. Her first play, *The Crackwalker*, is set in Kingston.

ACT ONE, SCENE FOUR

THERESA *and* ALAN *are in a restaurant.*

THERESA: Where d'ya think Joe took off to?

ALAN: I don't know probably drinkin, maybe the Shamrock.

THERESA: You think they're splitting up?

ALAN: I hope not.

THERESA: Me too. I love Sandy, she my best girlfriend.

ALAN: I – Joe – he and me are good buddies too. They go good together anyways.

THERESA: Could I have a doughnut?

ALAN: What kind, chocolate? I know you like chocolate.

THERESA: I love it.

ALAN: Sandy's nuts, you're not fat.

THERESA: Don't say nothin about it.

ALAN: You're not.

THERESA: I don't like talkin about it.

ALAN: Here. Two chocolate doughnuts.

THERESA: Thank you Alan.

ALAN: Jesus you're a good lookin girl. You're the prettiest lookin girl I seen.

THERESA: Don't talk like that.

ALAN: I love screwin with ya. Do you like it with me?

THERESA: I don't know – don't ask me that stuff dummy-face.

ALAN: I like eatin ya out ya know.

THERESA: Shut your mouth people are lookin don't talk like that stupid-face.

ALAN: Nobody's lookin. Jeez you're pretty. Just like a little angel. Huh. Like a – I know. I know. I'm gonna call you my little angel from now on. People gonna see ya and they're gonna go "There's Trese, she's Al's angel."

THERESA: Who gonna say them things?

ALAN: Anybody.

THERESA: They are?

ALAN: Yup.

THERESA: You're a dummy-face.

ALAN: So beautiful.

THERESA: Stop it Al you make me embarrass.

ALAN: You're – I was always hopin for someone like you – always happy always laughin and that.

THERESA: I cryin sometimes ya know.

ALAN: Yeah but ya cry the same way ya laugh. There's somethin – I don't know – as soon as I seen ya I knew I wanted ya. I wanted to marry ya when I seen ya.

THERESA: When, when did you say that?

ALAN: I never said nothin, I just thought it, all the time.

THERESA: We only been goin together for a little while, you know.

ALAN: Let's get married.

THERESA: Al stop lookin at me like that you embarrassin me.

ALAN: Sorry. Did you hear me?

THERESA: Yeah. Okay.

ALAN: When?

THERESA: Tuesday. I ask my sosha worker to come.

ALAN: No. Just Joe and me and you and Sandy. Just the four of us. I want Joe to be my best man.

THERESA: Sandy could be the flower girl. Uh. Oh.

ALAN: What?

THERESA: Hope you don't want no babies.

ALAN: Why. I do! I do want babies! I get on with babies good!

THERESA: Not sposda have none.

ALAN: How come? Who told you that?

THERESA: The sosha worker, she say I gotta get my tubes tied.

ALAN: What's that?

THERESA: Operation up the hospital. They tie it up down there so ya won't go havin babies.

ALAN: They can't do that to you no way!

THERESA: I know they can't but they're doin' it.

ALAN: They don't have no *right*.

THERESA: Yah they do Al I slow.

ALAN: Slow? I don't think you're slow who told you that?

THERESA: I ain't a good mum Al I can't help it.

ALAN: Who said you ain't a good mum.

THERESA: All of them jus cause when I took off on Dawn.

ALAN: Who's Dawn?

THERESA: The baby, the other baby.

ALAN: You never had a baby before did ya? Did ya?

THERESA: Las –

ALAN: You didn't have no other man's baby did ya? With another guy?

(Pause)

THERESA: No, it's Bernice's.

ALAN: Who's Bernice.

THERESA: My cousin my mum's sister.

ALAN: Well how come you were lookin after her baby?

THERESA: Cause she was sick up in hospital. Jeez Al.

ALAN: Well – what happened what'dja do wrong?

THERESA: Nothin it wasn't my fault just one Friday night I was sniffin, eh, so I took off down to the Plaza and I leave the baby up the room, eh, I thought I was comin right back, and I met this guy and he buyin me drinks and that then I never knew what happened and I woke up and I asked somebody where I was and I was in Ottawa!

ALAN: He took you all the way up to Ottawa? That bastard.

THERESA: I never seen him again I thumbed back to Kingston. (crying) I come back to the house and the baby's gone she ain't there so I bawlin I goin everywhere yellin after her and never found nothin then I see Bonnie Cain and she told me they took her up the Children's Aid she dead. So I go on up the Aid and they say she ain't dead she live but they not givin her back cause I unfit.

ALAN: Jeez.

THERESA: I ain't no more Al I don't sniff or nothin.

ALAN: Them bastards.

THERESA: Honest.

ALAN: I know. I know ya don't and we're gonna have a baby and nobody ain't gonna stop us. We're gonna have our own little baby between you and me and nobody can't say nothin bout it. You're not goin to no hospital, understand?

THERESA: But Al she say she gonna cut off my pension check if I don't get my tubes tied.

ALAN: Fuck the pension check you're not goin to no hospital.

THERESA: Okay Al.

ALAN: Come here. You're not goin to no hospital.

THERESA: You won't let em do nothin to me, will ya Al?

ALAN: Nope. You're my angel and they ain't gonna touch you... Hey! I know what ya look like now!

THERESA: What, an angel?

ALAN: That – that madonna lady you know them pictures they got up in classrooms when you're a kid? Them pictures of the madonna?

THERESA: The Virgin Mary?

ALAN: Yeah. Her.

THERESA: I love her I askin her for stuff.

ALAN: Yuh look just like her. Just like the madonna. Cept the madonna picture got a baby in it.

THERESA: It do?

ALAN: She's holdin it right in her arms. You too, maybe, eh? Eh? Hey! Let's go up to the Good Thief.

THERESA: Al I don't know you goin to church! You goin every Sunday?

ALAN: No I never went since I was five I just want to go now. We'll go and we'll – we'll like have a party lightin candles and that a party for gettin married!

THERESA: I love lightin candles.

ALAN: Maybe the Father's gonna be there. They're always happy when someone's gettin married we could tell him!

THERESA: Al I gettin sleepy.

ALAN: Well after we party I'm gonna put ya right down to sleep over at Joe's. I won't try nothin or nothin.

THERESA: What if Sandy be piss off.

ALAN: No Trese, they said we could stay there together. The two of us. And we're gonna.

THERESA: Okay...really I lookin like that madonna?

ALAN: Just like her. Just like her.

He is rocking her in his arms.

Lights fade.

Excerpted from *The Crackwalker*

ELIZABETH GREENE

Turning Vision into Line and Colour

ELIZABETH GREENE (1943–), a native of New York, came to Kingston in 1969 to teach English at Queen's University, and, like so many others, has been here ever since. Her short stories have appeared in *Quarry Magazine* and the *Kingston Whig-Standard Magazine. The Sorrow Gatherer* "grew out of the many Saturday mornings where I lingered with my son at the Kingston market listening to Tom Mawhinney play the autoharp – one of the songs was Richard Farina's *Pack Up Your Sorrows.*"

. . . HE went to Boston for a time, then hitched back west through the Berkshires and north to Canada, along the Saint Lawrence to Montreal. For a while he walked the streets, watching, listening. But Montreal was too sharp, too stylish, too intellectual. One August morning he was back on the road. His ride happened to drop him off in a small city at the end of Lake Ontario, and Martin had been soothed by the lake, the gray stones, the white triangles of sailboats.

Martin spent that first day walking along the lake, past the great old stone houses where there must have been brilliant parties a hundred years before, past the beach where children swam and shouted and gulls swooped ravenously for the crumbs of their sandwiches, through a grassy lawn marked with volleyball nets, past the power plant, past the prison, out to the conservation area at the end of the road. He sat among the rocks and stared at the lake, at the rippling expanse of blue, going black or gray as the light changed.

Something in him stopped churning. A great blue heron flew by; as dusk deepened, he saw an owl perched in a tree. He slept in the woods, and in the morning he walked back into town and rented a flat with north light on the north side of town. He bought canvases, a sketching pad. Then he began a half-light existence, knowing no one, speaking to no one. If time were a lake, he was floating. He looked at the canvas and turned away; the sketch pads remained blank. He began going to parks as if to an office. Without speaking, he acquired an acquaintance – the very old, sitting on benches, on front stoops, taking in sun like lizards; invalids in wheelchairs, glad to be out, though one or two were muffled against the cold even in August and seemed to be noticing very little. There were teenagers, of course, and well-dressed office girls, even some businessmen, on their lunch hours and coffee breaks. They were not on the edge of life as he was, and they did not interest him. But gradually he began to watch for the mothers with babies or toddlers. It was the mothers whose names he learned – Delphine with Jeremy, Valerie whose older daughter Rhianna was about seven and younger Gwenda was about Jeremy's age; Suzanne with five year old David and two year old Adam; Maude with grown-up Peter – nearly nine – and younger Wendy and baby Annabel who was just learning to walk.

The children were extraordinarily beautiful – had he been so as a small boy? – as they ran, slid, jumped, danced, swung, fought. From a distance the older ones were leggy like cranes or sea birds; the little ones were rolly and cuddly like teddy bears. Closer, they were a force field of energy and sound – laughing, crying, shrieking, screaming, with their mothers' voices, low but controlled, binding the whole thing together. They lived in the middle of a web of kleenexes, sweaters, crackers, juice, apples, toys, which somehow the mothers managed always to produce when needed. Had his own mother been like that? Then he began to notice the mothers. When they sat in the parks or when they paused with their children to listen to the long-haired autoharpist at the market on Saturday mornings, he eavesdropped shamelessly. He gradually perceived that each of these women had once been the center of a romance, that with motherhood (the most obvious consequence of romance) their lives had changed drastically – they now lived from crisis to crisis: Annabel's teething, the roof leaking, sibling quarrelling, children waking at night, ear infections, birthdays, doctors' appointments, dentist appointments…

AT first, he had to get his lines back and the feel in his hands. What had he been doing all these years? Then he began to feel the rhythm of the days more as a cradle than a torment. He got up with the light, dressed, breakfasted at a coffee shop, went somewhere, usually to a park, but sometimes to the open air market, sometimes to a street corner, and sketched. Then he would have lunch, often in a park, then walk, then return home and rework his sketches, occasionally translating them to canvas. Sometimes he wished for conversation, but more often he was grateful for the absence of disaster. When the mothers and children were elsewhere, he drew the drifters, the teenagers, the seagulls, broccolis and cauliflowers, men and women at outdoor cafés. When fall came, the parks were deserted in the mornings. He changed his schedule to accommodate the school day, painting in the morning and sketching in the afternoons...

AS the weeks went by and Delphine's friends began to trust him, he learned that each tapestry was woven over an abyss. Valerie's husband drank; Maud's had affairs; Tom was a workaholic; Suzanne's husband was a doctor doing his residency. Although they were married and not so long before had been beautiful girls who had been courted, wooed, cajoled and won, these friends were now essentially women without men. They ran their houses and raised their children. Their husbands worked. Romance had faded into routine. Or, romance had turned toward the children, into punctuating their days with periods of happiness.

"Not all marriages are like this," said Delphine when Martin asked her about it.

"I wonder if my parents' was," said Martin. He thought of his mother cooking, his father coming home from work and reading the newspaper. No one living could tell him.

All he knew was that he had felt liberated when he had left home for college and that no love yet had induced him to consider returning to that confinement.

He sketched children playing on kitchen floors, women peeling vegetables, washing dishes, talking on telephones. As his understanding improved, so did his sketches. He was not surprised when Valerie left Richard shortly before Christmas...

JANUARY came with cold, bright snow-covered days and brilliant red sunsets that sank quickly into night. Martin bought cross-country skis and glided along the paths he had walked only weeks before. He discovered the joys of flying over the frozen lake, past ice-fishermen, past skaters, past Breughelesque trekkers. The conviviality of the frozen lake, dotted with people and as various as a Dutch painting, constantly pleased him. He skied in the afternoons. On nursery school mornings Delphine came to his apartment and they breakfasted and made love....

He suddenly saw how his market picture would have to be, Delphine and Valerie, Maud and Suzanne, talking, buying food, the children playing or running or gazing spellbound at the auto-harpist, the husbands on the edges – he began to try out a design, then another, think of details – a teddy bear, a pacifier, a handkerchief – What season of the year was it? What were they wearing? Who else was at the market that morning? The aged artist? A photographer? An older woman with her shopping basket? Every detail would have to count. Even with the final design, the final details, unresolved, he knew this would be an ambitious picture, that he was in the middle of a moment of inspiration, such as Giotto, Rembrandt, Rubens, Brueghel must have felt – but what a gap between inspiration and realization! Still, he was excited as he thought and planned and then went to the market to sketch the buildings, even in the wrong season. Oddly enough, when he saw Delphine next, he did not tell her of this vision and his bare beginnings at turning vision into line and colour....

Excerpted from *The Sorrow Gatherer*

TOM MAWHINNEY

Nellie on the Shore

THOMAS ANDREW MAWHINNEY (1948–) came to study at Queen's University in the 1960s and now juggles dual careers as a psychologist and folk singer. He has released eight record albums since 1980 and has been a busker and TV host/producer. "*Nellie on the Shore* was written when the tall ships visited.... I visited a Polish ship and exchanged songs below deck with a Polish sailor with whom I could only communicate through music."

Nellie On The Shore

Chorus: Wave your hankie, Nellie on the shore
You won't see nothing of me no more.

Sailing on the ocean, sailing on the sea
There's few women looks at the likes of me
I've sailed down south and I've sailed all around
Thinkin' 'bout Nellie in Kingston town.

Wave your hankie, Nellie on the shore
You won't see nothing of me no more.

We sailed into port, I was looking for a bride
Nellie had three men by her side
I stepped right up and I asked for a kiss
She answered my question with her fists.

Wave your hankie, Nellie on the shore
You won't see nothing of me no more.

She stood on the dock, and I threw her a wink
She gave me a look that made me think
I shouted from the bow, "Will you wait for me, Honey?"
She shouted right back, "Jack, don't get funny!"

Wave your hankie, Nellie on the shore
You won't see nothing of me no more.

Well, fifteen years of a sailor's life
Give a man the notion to find him a wife
The women I've seen wherever I roam
Can't compare to my Nellie back home.

Wave your hankie, Nellie on the shore
You won't see nothing of me no more.

Sailing on the ocean, sailing on the sea
There's few women looks at the likes of me
I've sailed down south, and I've sailed all around
Thinkin' 'bout Nellie in Kingston town.

Wave your hankie, Nellie on the shore
You won't see nothing of me no more.

JANETTE TURNER HOSPITAL

A Safe Little Bourgeois Cage

JANETTE TURNER HOSPITAL (1942–) was born and educated in Australia. After several years in Boston she moved to Kingston with her theologian husband. Her first novel, *The Ivory Swing*, won the 1982 Seal First Novel Award. She is also the author of *The Tiger in the Tiger Pit*, *Borderline*, *Dislocations*, and *Charade*.

"IT'S always been done this way, dear," the woman on the telephone said to Juliet. There was only the gentlest hint of frost in her voice. "I don't think it would be very nice for a new young faculty wife to upset tradition, do you?"

Nice! Juliet thought with dismay. I have never wanted to be nice.

"It's the great occasion of the year," the woman continued. "When the alumnae return and the board of trustees gathers, we have tea and sandwiches in Winston Hall. And the young faculty wives have always poured tea. It's a great honour."

"Yes, I'm sure it is. I can fully appreciate ...." Juliet struggled to be politely regretful. "It's just that there must be many others to whom it would mean more ....And I'm terribly busy, teaching part-time you see, and working on a book."

"A book! Oh my dear, how sweet. Such clever young wives we get these days. A children's story for the little one on the way?"

"No, actually it's a history of political campaign strategies I began when I was –"

"But you *must* take a rest, dear. All work and no play ....Now we're assembling in the lounge of Winston Hall at three and I've got you on the first shift. And one more thing, it's traditional to wear white gloves for the occasion. The silverware, you know."

"I regret that I must decline."

"My dear, it simply isn't done, to decline."

And at three o'clock, gloveless, Juliet held a baroquely silver teapot as though it were a weapon, pouring tea into Royal Albert cups and thinking scalding thoughts. She was wearing a black turtleneck sweater, a black velvet mini-skirt – the year was late in the sixties, a decade which had left Winston untouched – and black mesh stockings.

"After all," she had told David furiously, "it's a wake, isn't it? The end of my life as a normal intelligent woman!"

Among the pastel silks and gloved hands and coiffed hairdos, she looked like a witch's foundling. She tossed the long blonde mane of her hair like an unbroken colt who will never consent to be bridled.

"Oh my dear!" The telephone voice, stricken, materialized at Juliet's side and Juliet turned to offer combat with flashing eyes. She knew what the woman would look like, had already pictured her when they spoke on the phone – silver-blue hair lacquered into place, figure corseted in rectitude, vapid bourgeois eyes – but in fact she was frail and bird-like, vibrant; and aghast as a robin who has found her nest wantonly smashed. Juliet thought of grandmothers and of gentle souls who mourn for the past.

Immediately contrite, she thought: I am just as judgmental and insensitive, just as dogmatic. What right do I have...?

"I am Mrs. MacDougall," the woman said, extending her hand in mournful reproof, "and I do reproach myself for not explaining adequately the formality of the ... you poor child, you must be dying of embarrassment."

"No, oh no, not at all," Juliet said hastily. She set the teapot down and took Mrs. MacDougall's soft-gloved hand in her own. "It's entirely my fault. I'm sorry, truly I am. I didn't even stop to think you might be hurt. I just thought it better to establish that I'm not the tea-pouring type. I'm only a faculty wife by a kind of accident. I mean I don't think of myself that way at all."

Mrs. MacDougall put a slightly trembling hand to the cameo brooch at her throat. "There are some of us," she said softly, "who made brief brave stands a few centuries ago when we were young. And had to spend our lives learning to take defeat gracefully. My dear – Juliet, isn't it? – I believe I will like you, but I fear for you. I hope Winston will not be too unkind."

It seemed a quaint warning and Juliet never gave it a second thought. But there were many guests at the alumnae reunion who were less inclined to make allowances, and though Juliet was indifferent to their disapproval she was to learn, over the years, that a small town has subtle and sometimes vicious ways of not forgiving deviations from the norm.

Excerpted from *The Ivory Swing*

DAVID HELWIG

To Hug Loneliness

DAVID HELWIG (1938–) was born in Toronto, and lived in Kingston from 1962 to 1992, and now lives in Montreal. He has taught at Queen's, was head of CBC-TV Drama for two years, but has been writing full time since 1980. He is the author of many books of fiction and poetry, including the four novels in the Kingston Quartet: *The Glass Knight, Jennifer, A Sound Like Laughter*, and *It is Always Summer.*

It would not be incorrect to suggest that the Wordsworthan sublime like the demonic sublime in Dickens is in which it was to be, by and large, expected to be achieved by the transposition of material from the genre the ethos of another genefic mode.

ROBERT stared at the page. The linotype operator must have been drunk. It was the worst set of proofs he'd ever read. Besides that, the book was written in double talk. He'd said so when the manuscript first came in, but the academic experts called the book important, and Robert had tried to get the style improved in a series of letters that grew more and more turgid until Robert gave up.

It wasn't his responsibility. He reminded himself of the reasons he had come here, to this unimportant editorial job, to escape large decisions, worrying responsibilities. In Toronto where his decisions cost money, his nerves had begun to go to pieces. Sometimes his vision would blur, he couldn't sleep, his head ached. So he had chosen to retreat to a mechanical job that cost him nothing but occasional irritation; a deliberate step down, away from challenges.

He saw Ray Statler's figure move past the door, in a flash of bright colours. He was the new graphic designer, just out of art school, the first designer hired by the university press after years of contracting out their books. Statler's trousers all seemed to be pink or purple and he tended to wear them with yellow or green shirts and ties of dark red or black. Just to look at his outfits was exhausting. He was an ambitious young man, with some talent and excessive self-confidence. He had told Robert in almost their first conversation that his former girlfriend had gone to Europe and he was on the lookout for a replacement. To be his mistress, clearly, was to be regarded as a splendid opportunity, and within a few weeks he had found a beautiful Czech girl with long dark hair and soulful eyes. A kind of Slovak princess. Ray accepted her astonishing beauty as no more than his due. They did make a handsome couple, for Ray had good features and reddish golden hair and beard, but Robert found it hard to believe that either one of them really existed.

They belonged on the pages of a magazine. They didn't exist firmly enough to make him jealous that they were young and beautiful and that he was tall and skinny and big-featured with thinning hair and weakening muscles.

Outside the window of the little house where the press had its offices, the grass and trees were still vibrant green in the September sunlight. Here and there a few leaves were turning yellow but it was still really summer. In a neighbour's yard, the bright flares of the zinnias hung in the light. Robert turned his head and Ray Statler appeared in the doorway.

"How are things?" he said.

"This is the worst set of proofs I've ever seen. The linotype operator must have been drunk."

"Those people are a pain in the ass. We gotta move to someplace else. Christ, they can't do much, and what they do, they do badly. There's a new outfit called Computex that I want to try. Get the type set there and print at that outfit in Barrie. It's stupid to work in letterpress these days unless you want to do limited editions."

"Have you convinced Wilson?"

"I've discussed it with him four times and I still don't know what he thinks."

"You never will."

"I'm going to do it whether he likes it or not."

"Oh he'll let you do it. Or at least he won't stop you. But if something goes wrong he'll be able to claim it was all your idea and that he never gave it approval."

"So he'll let me do whatever I like."

"Pretty much."

"Good. That's all I care about."

"I have a kind of picture of Wilson walking through the world backward bent over to cover his tracks."

"Perfect way to get buggered by the future."

Ray sat down in one of the office chairs.

"Can I sit down?" he said. After the fact.

"I'd rather do anything than work."

Statler leaned back, gave a self-satisfied stretch and yawn, arms and legs spread as if offering himself to any goddess who might be passing, hot with desire for just such a lovely golden body.

"Ever read any Czech poetry?" he asked.

Robert just shook his head. It was inevitable that the conversation should be about something he was ignorant of.

"Margita's been translating some for me to read. It's good. It's funny how you can feel right away that it's European. There's a poem about Edison, by Nezval. Only a European could have written it. I told Margita she should do a whole book of translations and we could put them through the press. I could do woodcuts to illustrate them.

"Are they good translations?"

"Yeah. She's really bright. I've only had to make a few suggestions here and there."

Passing goddess, tear out his tongue. To hear him patronize his lovely dark princess will kill me. I hunch misshapen in my chair and watch the autumn sunlight catch the edge of his golden hair. I see them both at the edge of some fairy tale.

"Do you want a cup of coffee, Robert? I'll make some if you like."

"Sure," Robert said, knowing that it was a mistake to drink coffee, but somehow unable to say no. Statler was making him irritable but he didn't want him to go away. Didn't know why.

Statler got up and went to the little kitchen of the house where they kept an electric kettle, instant coffee and occasionally cookies or a piece of cheese. At 10:30 every morning Wilson's secretary made coffee for them all, but at other times during the day they made their own. Robert stared out the window where the afternoon sunlight came across the trees and into the office, pouring itself on the chair where Ray Statler had been sitting. And on one half of Cindy's picture that hung on the wall, illuminating the left side of the round smiling face, a corner of a red dress with a white collar that set off the delicate colouring of the child's skin. Beside, in the shade, was Gavin, his son, his face smiling with a kind of eager boyish handsomeness that might turn into anything. He was small for his age, oddly, and worried about it. Robert tried to reassure him that he would be sure to inherit some of his father's height, but the boy knew that his maternal grandfather had been small.

Robert had left the Toronto job and come to Kingston hoping the improvement in his nerves would make him a better father to his children, but before that could happen, he had moved out. He wondered how the children felt about Jennifer's lovers. He didn't want to know these things.

Robert turned to his desk and had corrected a few more lines of the proofs when Ray Statler came in with two mugs of coffee, put one down on the desk and sat back down in the sunlight with the other. The sun now shone on his face, and he put his head back and spoke with his eyes closed.

"Are you planning to settle down here?" he said.

"I haven't thought that far ahead. My kids are still here. I'm comfortable enough for now."

"I love it. There isn't enough here. I need the experience, but within a year or so, I'm going to screw off and get something better."

Robert nodded.

"Books aren't my field anyway. Designing books is for old men. You have more fun in a faster game."

"I don't," Robert said. "You might." He lifted the mug to his lips. The coffee was strong and tasted good in his mouth, but he knew what it would do to his stomach. Swallowed.

"Aren't you lonely," Statler said. Robert was shocked by the brashness of the question, yet in a way he was pleased. It seemed to be the question he had wanted someone to ask him for a long time.

"Sometimes," he said. "But I'm getting used to it. I want a bit of rest before I explore any more emotional jungles." Robert was at the point of saying more, but the words were less than half true, and he silenced himself.

"Margita and I were talking about you last night. Actually she was asking me about you. You puzzle her."

"I'm pretty ordinary," Robert said.

"Nobody's ordinary," Statler said complacently.

Robert drank his coffee.

"I told her," Statler said, "that I thought you were one of those people whose talent and intelligence had never really found a shape to express themselves."

Again Robert was startled by the man's presumption, but

teased by it, for it might contain the truth.

"How long has Margita been in Canada?"

"Six years. She went to high school here. Her English is almost perfect, isn't it?"

Robert lifted his cup, his eyes moving to the back yard, where a cat was climbing along the edge of the old garage. He thought of the girl again, the Bicycle Girl. She had often come back to his mind in the last two weeks but he hadn't tried to see her, had thought of it but refused himself. In the drawer of the desk in front of him was a picture of Molly. Somewhere in the closet of his apartment was a picture of Jennifer. He didn't want any other pictures yet. For now he wanted to hug his loneliness...

ROBERT walked out the door of the small brick house and turned toward the lake... The traffic on King Street was heavy, and Robert did not look at the water as he waited to cross. He wanted to save it. Finally a break in the traffic allowed him to cross the road and the narrow corridor of grass to the sidewalk at the edge of the lake where he stood leaning against the iron fence. The lake was brilliant blue in the early evening sunlight. He looked across at the island. The trees and houses were small and clear, every detail sharply focused.

As if I could walk across the water and reach the island and say Yes, this is the place I wished to be.

Out on the lake he saw a single sailboat, the arch of its white sail drawing it down the course of the wind. Jennifer had never chosen to hear him, to let his mind truly touch her. Always she turned aside and chose silence and left him raging. So he had been turned back into himself, into a confused landscape of muddled insights, now and then dragging one to light, bringing it like a hunter his kill and faced again with silence. The few misshapen essays lay somewhere in a drawer.

He climbed through the iron bars and onto a pile of rocks at the water's edge. He began to toss stones into the water aiming each to land at the exact centre of the spreading circle of ripples left by the previous stone. When the handful of stones was gone, he stared across the water at the white sail that was moving away toward the island, and as he stood up, turning to leave, he saw the girl from the party disappear around a corner on her bike. He looked back to the lake, and the sailboat was gone, somewhere behind the island. It seemed like an omen.

Robert climbed back on the sidewalk and began to walk quickly along the shore, past the heating plant and through the park to West Street. He didn't want to go home yet, and he walked quickly to clear his head, then more slowly when he came to the park, moving in a strange calm under the high branches, past the tall columns of the trees that stood between the courthouse and the lake. A few dry leaves lay on the ground, but most were still holding to their branches.

As he reached the edge of the park, he looked at the bronze figure of a soldier in the uniform of the Canadian Army in the first world war. The arm was raised and the body angled as if the man were running forward, but as Robert moved past it, the figure seemed to be going backward into the trees to lie down in the leaves, not in death, but in a backward motion in which he became a child, his imaginary brother. Robert saw him as two figures, the brother running forward into battle, his arm raised, and the other lost brother who always fell backward through time. He stopped and stared at the figure, black and dramatic against the sky that was as blue as the sky of a postcard.

Robert turned and walked toward his apartment. What he wanted right now was a drink and some food. Later he might read or go to a movie. He would fill the time.

By the time he reached his apartment Robert was very hungry, and he cut himself a piece of camembert to eat while he drank his gin and tonic and cooked supper. He took some beef liver and began to peel and slice onions; by the time he had them in a frying-pan, his drink was finished and he mixed another and began to sip it as he sliced tomatoes and put them in with the onions, then put the liver on to fry in another pan. He remembered that he had some red wine in the bottom of a bottle and he poured it over the liver and covered the pan.

The phone rang. He turned down the heat under the two pans and went to answer it. The voice was Jennifer's, and at first there was pleasure in its familiarity, in his own response to it. Like a key that fitted some lost door. A touch.

"Hello Jenny."

"Do you have a minute?"

And at once the anger. There seemed to be no beginning, no reason, as if it was a response to the very rhythm of her speech. Asking if he was busy, as if his life was full and rewarding and he had no time for her or the children. When was he ever busy?

"Of course."
"Could you manage to take the children Saturday morning as well as the afternoon?"
"Why?"
Mentally Robert took that back, said no to his own impulse, agreed with her and hung up.
"I have some things to do."
He hated the vagueness whenever a man was involved. She patronised him, treated him with care, handled him. As if he were a child. He wanted to kill her.
"Have you told the kids? I don't want them sulking all day because they're stuck with me."
"They always tell me what a good time they've had with you."
"I'm glad they tell someone that."
"If they told you, you wouldn't listen."
"You know all about me, don't you?"
"I didn't phone to argue, Robert."
"But you're willing to join in."
Robert could feel the fury increasing, a pressure in his throat and in the back of his head.
"Can you take them Saturday morning?" Patiently, as to a child.
"Of course." He raged silently.
"Thank you." She hung up.
Robert put down the receiver and stood, with his eyes shut, beating his fist against the wall, screaming inside his head, until the anger wore itself out enough that he could open his eyes and look down at the black shape of the phone on the small table beneath him. Beside it stood the glass with his drink which he now took in his hand and drained, walking to the kitchen and filling it again, the drink stronger this time so the taste of the gin dominated. He stared at the food cooking in the two pans, then forced himself to turn his attention to it, each gesture consciously made, as if he were acting out this performance of getting supper, eating, drinking, mixing another drink.
By the time he finished, he was beginning to feel drunk, careless. When he stood up from the table he bumped against it and nearly dumped the plate. He walked into the small living-room of the flat and sat down in the armchair without bothering to turn on any lights. There was a little light from the kitchen, and Robert's eyes moved around the room assessing it, weighing it in

his mind and finding it without substance. A wooden bookshelf painted white, with a couple of novels, an anthology of poems, several paperbacks of Freud, some history and biography in paperback. A second-hand rocking chair painted brown with a red cushion on the seat. Molly had bought that for him. A coffee-table with the telephone and a small book of telephone numbers. On the wall an expensive calendar with reproductions of Picasso's drawings. Jennifer had given him that for Christmas.

He wondered if love was nothing more than the euphoria of beginnings, the pain of endings. Or was it a language he had never learned? As his eyes moved around the room, he thought again of Jennifer, and remembered the last time they'd been happy.

The year before they'd moved to Kingston, they'd taken a holiday together, driving a station-wagon throughout Quebec and around the Gaspé peninsula. It was May, and in Toronto the leaves were out, but as they drove northeast past Montreal and along the south shore of the St. Lawrence, they were driving back into winter. Past Rivière du Loup, they began to see snow still lying on the ground. Neither of them had been through this part of the country before, and they seemed detached and happy, separate from themselves, adventurous. Late in the second day, they were driving along the north coast of Gaspé, the St. Lawrence no longer muddy with tidal silt as it had been further west, but wide and blue, more like an ocean than a river. They stopped to cook supper on the Coleman stove they'd brought with them, and ate standing up in the chilly wind, looking out over the water. A freighter in the distance looked still, like a toy ship.

They drove on until it seemed close to getting dark, then pulled off the road and parked on a small sideroad that ran a hundred feet and stopped at a snowdrift. Robert opened a bottle of gin, and they cooled their drinks with snow. They were on a hilltop and could see for miles across the water. They stood together to watch darkness come out of the east.

They spread their large sleeping-bag in the back of the station-wagon. By now the air was cold, and they clung together for warmth, then made love, feeling exposed and vulnerable.

In memory they seemed hardly to have spoken that night or in the morning when they woke shortly after sunrise and began to drive through the sleeping towns, then inland over curving and precipitous roads, seeing on each side of them woods still filled with snow, the green of spruce and pine and red twigs of the birches bright in the sunlight. When they reached the seacoast, they stopped at the top of a hill to make breakfast. Looking east there was nothing between them and Europe but the weight of the Atlantic, and the sharp wind seemed to carry that weight. The grass and the trees were bent by it. There were no woods here. Everything was windswept, bleak and shining. Robert remembered a moment when he held a mug of hot tea in his hand and turned to look at Jennifer who squatted behind the car to urinate, her heavy body somehow concentrating all its reality tightly together to strike him more intensely.

As they went along the coast they drove into low cloud, the whole air a kind of pale fog, the sea reflecting the grey silver of the sky. Then out over the sea, a hole opened in the moving clouds and a patch of brilliant silver began to scud over the water, a shining focus to all the white and grey and silver. I am happy, Robert had said to himself. I am a happy man.

They drove on, and somehow it broke as it always did; something fell apart between them, the rhythms became jagged, awkward, until Robert began to wonder if all the hours before had happened only for him, if she had never been part of it.

The road along the south coast of Gaspé was rutted and pocked. The country was poor and ugly. They argued.

I don't want this pain, Jenny. I don't want all my memories to come to this. I will stand up from my chair as if I were a hero. I will walk to the table and pour gin in my glass. I will get drunk, then sleep.

Excerpted from *The Glass Knight*

CAROL SHIELDS

The Poet's Corner

CAROL SHIELDS (1935–) was born in Oak Park, Illinois, and came to Canada in 1957. She now lives in Winnipeg and teaches at the University of Manitoba, but often visits Kingston. She writes: "I've always loved Kingston and because we have good friends there, we've often spent time in the area." She is the author of several acclaimed books of fiction and poetry, including *Small Ceremonies, Various Miracles, Coming to Canada,* and *Swann: A Mystery,* which is partly set in Kingston.

Frederic Cruzzi: His Short Untranscribed History of the Peregrine Press: 1956–1976

THE *Kingston Banner,* even before Frederic Cruzzi arrived from England to be its editor, had perforce been something of an anomaly as a regional newspaper, its constituency being an uneasy yoking of town and gown, farmers, civil servants, and petit-bourgeoisie. Its advertisers were the owners of such small, conservative family business as the Princess Tearoom and Diamond Bros. Colonial Furniture Emporium, but its most vociferous readers were revolutionaries and progressives of the academic stripe. The *Banner*'s editorial policy, as a result, tended to be skittish, gliding between pragmatic waltz and feinting soft-shoe, and for that reason was always, and still is, perused with a knowing wink of the eye. This is accepted by everybody. It is also accepted that the real battles are fought on the Letters-to-the-Editor page, which occasionally spills over to a second page and once – in 1970, with the War Measures Act – to a third. Here, despite quaint temporary alliances and retreats into unanimity, the struggle assumes those classic polarities between those who would stand still and those who would move forward.

The boisterous, ongoing warfare of the Letters page has mostly been regarded by Cruzzi as analogous to a healthy game of societal tennis, both amusing and lifegiving. Sometimes, too, it yields an inch of enlightenment. But warfare abruptly stops at the Entertainment page. Even among those readers who would never dream of subscribing to the Kingston Regional Theatre or the fledgling Eastern Ontario Symphony, and who would rather dive naked into a patch of summer thistle than be caught reading one of the books reviewed in the *Banner*, there is a silent consensus that *art* is somehow privileged and deserving of protection. A dirty book discovered in a school library may raise a brief fuss, but the general concept of art is sacred in the Kingston region, and lip service, if nothing else, is paid to it.

When Cruzzi took over the *Banner* he was bemused, and so was Hildë, by a long-running feature on the Entertainment page known as "The Poet's Corner." A number of local poets, mostly elderly, always genteel, vied for this small weekly space, dropping off batches of sonnets at the *Banner* office on Second Street, as well as quatrains, sestinas, limericks, haiku, bumpity-bump, and shrimpy dactyls, all attached to such unblushing titles as "Seagull Serenade," "Springtime Reverie," "Ode to Fort Henry," "Birches at Eventide," "The Stalwart Flag," "Old Sadie," "The First Bluebird," "Sailors Ahoy," "Cupid in Action," "The Trillium," "The Old Thrashing Crew," "The Eve of Virtue," and so on. Payment, regardless of length or verse form, was five dollars, but this rather small sum in no way discouraged the number of submissions. Cruzzi, in his first month in Kingston, looked carefully at both quantity and quality and immediately announced plans to terminate "The Poet's Corner."

What a fool he was in those days, he with his heavy tweed suits and strangely unbarbered hair, his queer way of talking, his manners and pronouncements. The public outcry over the cancellation of "The Poet's Corner" was unprecedented and appeared to come from all quarters of the community. He was labelled a philistine and a brute journalist of the modern school. The word foreigner was invoked: Frenchy, Limey, Wog – there was understandable confusion here. Readers might be willing to tolerate the new typeface imposed on them, and no one seemed to miss the old "Pie of the Week" feature when it disappeared from the Women's page, but they refused to surrender Li'l Abner and "The Poet's Corner." Culture was culture. Even the advertisers became restless, and Cruzzi, in the interest of comity and suffering a heretic's embarrassment, capitulated, though he let it be known that there would be a two-year interregnum on seagull poems.

In time, because the Kingston literary community was small,

he and Hildë befriended and grew fond of the local poets. Cruzzi even took a certain glee in the awfulness of their product. Herb Farlingham's poem "Springtime Reverie," for instance ("Mrs. Robin in feathered galoshes/Splashes in puddles chirping 'O my goshes!' "), gave him moments of precious hilarity that were especially welcome after a day spent composing careful, pointed, balanced, and doomed-to-be-ignored editorials on the arms race or the threat of McCarthyism.

In 1955, toward the end of a long golden summer, Cruzzi opened an envelope addressed to "The Poet's Corner," and out fell a single poem, typed for once, titled "Anatomy of a Passing Thought" written by one Kurt Wiesmann of William Avenue, just two streets from Byron Road where Cruzzi and Hildë lived. The sixteen-line poem possessed grace and strength. Light seemed to shine through it. Cruzzi read it quickly, with amazement. One line, toward the end, briefly alarmed him by veering toward sentimentality, but the next line answered back, mocking, witty, and containing that spacey necessary bridge that in the best poetry joins binocular clarity to universal vision. Extraordinary.

It was 5:30 in the afternoon. He took a deep breath and rubbed a hand through this thick, still-unbarbered hair. Hildë was expecting him at home for a picnic supper with friends. Already she would have set the table under the trees, a red table cloth, wine glasses turned upside down, paper napkins folded and weighed down by cutlery. Nevertheless he sat down at his desk and wrote Mr. Wiesmann a letter telling him why his poem was unsuitable for the *Banner*. It was unrhymed. It had no regular metre. It did not celebrate nature, or allude to God, or even to Kingston and its environs. It did not tug at the heart-strings or touch the tear ducts and was in no way calculated to bring forth a gruff chuckle of recognition; in short it was too good for "The Poet's Corner." He ended the letter, "Yours resignedly, F. Cruzzi," surprising himself; he had not realized his own resignation until that moment. (Rationality won't rescue this scene the way, say, a footnote can save a muddled paragraph, but it might be argued that Cruzzi, by this time, had acquired an understanding and even a respect for his readers' sensibilities.)

Kurt Wiesmann, a chemist with a local cooking-oil manufacturer, was delighted with his letter of rejection, and continued to send the *Banner* unprintable poems. In a year's time Cruzzi and Hildë had read close to fifty of them, and they both urged Wiesmann, by now a friend and frequent visitor to their house, to approach a book publisher. They were astonished, moved, and entertained by what he wrote, and felt he should have an audience larger than the two of them.

But it turned out that publishers in Canada found Wiesmann's poems "too European"; American publishers thought them "too Canadian," and a British publisher sensed "an American influence that might be troubling" to his readers. Hildë, exasperated, suggested one night – the three of them were in the kitchen drinking filtered coffee and eating cheesecake – that they publish the poems themselves.

In a month's time they were in production. It was Kurt Wiesmann who suggested the name Peregrine Press. He was a restless man, tied down by a family and job, but a traveller by instinct. His book was titled *Inroads* (Hildë's idea) and was favourably reviewed as "a courageous voice speaking with the full force of the alienated." A Toronto newspaper wrote, "The newly launched Peregrine Press must be congratulated on its discovery of a fresh new Canadian voice."

Their second poet was the elegant Glen Forrestal of Ottawa, later to win a Governor General's Award, who wrote to the Peregrine Press introducing himself as a member of the Kurt Wiesmann fan club and a veteran of several serious peregrinations of his own. Their third poet was the fey, frangible Rhoda MacKenzie, and after that came Cassie Sinclair, Hugh Walkley Donaldson, Mary Swann, Mavis Stockard, W.W. Wooley, Burnt Umber, Serge Tawowski, and a number of others who went on to make names for themselves.

Printing was done during off-hours at the *Banner* and paid for out of Cruzzi's pocket. Hildë, who had set up an office in an upstairs bedroom, read the manuscripts that soon came flowing in. She had a sharp eye and, with some notable exceptions, excellent judgement. "Whatever we decide to publish must have a new sound." She said this in a voice that contained more and more of the sonorous Canadian inflection. To a local businessman, whom she attempted to convert into a patron, she said, "We have the responsibility as a small press to work at the frontier."

Along the frontier a few mistakes were inevitably made. Even Hildë admitted she had been taken in by Rhoda MacKenzie's work, that behind its fretwork there was little substance. And both she and Cruzzi regretted the title they chose for Mary Swann's book – *Swann's Songs.* An inexplicable lapse of sensibility. A miscalculation, an embarrassment.

For twenty years the press operated out of the Cruzzi house on Byron Road. Methodically, working in the early mornings after her daily lakeside walk, Hildë read submissions, edited manuscripts, handled correspondence, and attended, if necessary, to financial matters – though bookkeeping took little time since the Peregrine Press never earned a profit and print-runs were small, generally between two hundred and three hundred copies. Always, in the final stages before the publication of a new book, a group of friends, the official board as they called themselves, gathered in the Cruzzi dining-room for a long evening of plum brandy and hard work: collating pages, stapling, gluing covers, the best of these covers designed by Barney Ouilette, and remarkably handsome, with a nod toward modernism and a suggestion of what Hildë like to call "fire along the frontier."

Her only agony was the problem of what to do with unsuccessful manuscripts. Tenderhearted, she laboured over her letters of rejection, striving for a blend of honesty and kindness, but forbidding herself to give false encouragement, explaining carefully what the press was looking for. These explanations gave her pleasure, as though she was reciting a beloved prayer. "New sounds," she explained, "and innovative technique, but work that turns on a solid core of language."

Despite her tact, there was sometimes acrimony, once an obscene phone call, several times scolding letters impugning her taste. Herb Farlingham, who would have financed the publication of his *Seasoned Sonnets* if Hildë had let him, wept openly. "I'm so terribly sorry," Hildë said, supplying him with tea and a paper towel for his tears. "It's nothing personal, you may be sure." The Peregrine Press, she explained, thankful for a ready excuse, had very early taken a stand on self-publication and was anxious to avoid even the appearance of being a vanity press...

Excerpted from *Swann: A Mystery*

IRVING LAYTON

Unspeakably Colonial

IRVING LAYTON (1912–) came to Canada from Romania with his parents in 1913. He served with the Royal Canadian Artillery in World War II, then attended McGill University where he studied and subsequently taught with F. R. Scott, Louis Dudek, and other " McGill poets." He is the author of many books of poetry, including *Red Carpet for the Sun*, which received the Governor-General's Award, and *Waiting for the Messiah*. He attended the founding meeting of the Writers' Union of Canada at Queen's University in 1955, organized by poet and scholar George Whalley.

Anglo-Canadian

A native of Kingston, Ont.
– two grandparents Canadian
and still living

His complexion florid
as a maple leaf in late autumn,
for three years he attended
Oxford

Now his accent
makes even Englishmen
wince, and feel
unspeakably colonial.

From *Collected Poems*

AL PURDY

Quarrelling Poets

ALFRED WELLINGTON PURDY (1918–) was born on a farm in the Kingston region near Wooler, Ontario, just outside Trenton, and educated at Albert College in Belleville. His memories of growing up in the area are chronicled in his first novel, *A Splinter in the Heart*, published when he was seventy-two. After serving in the Second World War, he lived and worked across Canada and for the past thirty years has lived on Roblin Lake near Ameliasburgh. He has received the Governor-General's Award for Poetry twice, for *The Cariboo Horses* and for *Collected Poems of Al Purdy*.

House Guest

For two months we quarrelled over socialism   poetry   how to
  boil water
doing the dishes   carpentry   Russian steel production figures
  and whether
you could believe them and whether Toronto Maple Leafs
  would take it all
that year and maybe hockey was rather like a good jazz combo
never knowing what came next
Listening
how the new house made with salvaged old lumber
bent a little in the wind and dreamt of the trees it came from
the time it was travelling thru
and the world of snow moving all night in its blowing sleep
while we discussed ultimate responsibility for a pile of dirty
  dishes
Jews in Negev   the Bible as mythic literature   Peking Man
and in early morning looking outside to see the pink shapes of
  wind
printed on snow and a red sun tumbling upward almost
  touching the house

and fretwork tracks of rabbits outside where the window light
had lain
an audience watching us
quarrelling
but keeping all our loves and hates inside the skin of friendship

Of course there was wild grape wine and a stove full of Douglas
fir
(railway salvage) and lake ice cracking its bones in hard Ontario
weather
and working with saw and hammer at the house all winter
afternoon
disagreeing about how to pound nails
arguing vehemently over how to make good coffee
Marcus Aurelius   Spartacus   Plato and Francois Villon
And it used to frustrate him terribly
and even when I was wrong he couldn't prove it
and when I agreed with him he was always suspicious
and he must be wrong because I said he was right
Every night the house shook from his snoring
as if there was a motor driving us on into daylight
and the vibration was terrible
Every morning I'd get up and say 'Look at the nails –
you pulled them all out half an inch in the night –'
And he'd believe me at first and look and get mad and glare
and stare angrily out the window while I watched irritation
drain from his eyes onto fields and farms and miles of snow

We quarrelled over how dour I was in early morning
and how cheerful he was for counterpoint
and I argued that a million years of evolution
from snarling apeman had to be traversed before dinner
and the desirability of murder in a case like his
and whether the Etruscans were really Semites
the Celtic invasion of Britain   Europeans languages   Roman
law
we argued about white being white (prove it) & cockroaches
bedbugs   separatism   Nietzsche   Iroquois horsebreakers on
the prairie
death of an individual and the ultimate destiny of man
and one night we quarrelled over how to cook eggs

In the morning driving to town we hardly spoke
and water poured downhill outside all day for it was spring
when we were gone with frogs mentioning lyrically
other important things besides breakfast
I left him hitch hiking on #2 highway to Montreal
and I guess I was wrong about those eggs

From *Collected Poems of Al Purdy*

SEYMOUR MAYNE

Come, Dance

SEYMOUR MAYNE (1944–) was raised and educated in Montreal and has been teaching at the University of Ottawa since the early 1970s. A prolific poet, he has also been active as an editor of anthologies and founder of little magazines and literary presses. His poetry publications include *Mouth*, *Name*, and *The Impossible Promised Land: Poems New and Selected.*

Flesh Light

Back there in Kingston
friends and poets
stone blind in flurries of October's
leaves and flakes

Hovering into phosphorous night
with large firefly mouths
they eat into night's soft meatiness
and still avoid each other's desperate love

Come, dance, you, you and you
Can't you hold your palms to each other's
like warm applause of friendship

Your autumn eyes are being eaten out
by the dying drones

Go run into cold and heavy streams
Shriek as Ontario silveriness
folds you under heavy scales
Your buzzing heads aglow are lanterns
upon water, hallowed and weened hives
distilling within
                    molten honey
of fragrant dying flesh and light

From *Name*

ERNST LOEB

Canada

ERNST LOEB (1914–1987) was born in the Rhineland, the son of Jewish parents. Arrested in 1933, he was forced to flee to Italy, then to Palestine, and finally in 1938 to America, where he worked as an unskilled labourer until his marriage in 1944. After a belated academic start, he turned to a university career that included writing books, articles, and reviews on widely ranging topics – Goethe, Heine, Rilke, Brecht, and Kafka – that were published internationally. In 1970 he came to the German Department at Queen's University, and between 1974 and 1986 he published four volumes of poetry. In 1985, for his services to German culture in Canada and the U.S.A., he was awarded the Commander's Crest of the Order of Merit of the Federal Republic of Germany.

Canada: A Realistic Note of Thanks

You love this young and untried land,
for here no memories torment,
and every footstep in the sand
anew and for itself is bent.

In its vast peacefulness you may grow old,
the visions of a sombre past receding.
Your neighbour greets you, smiling bold,
and only sees another being.

And that is much: not homeland, true,
but more than you possessed, much more;
because you paid once, dearly too,
for what you thought lay at your door.

Translated by Anthony W. Riley,
from *Quarry Magazine*

GEORGE WHALLEY

A Millimetre of Green

ARTHUR GEORGE CUTHBERT WHALLEY (1915–1983) was born in Kingston and educated at Bishop's University, after which he went to Oxford as a Rhodes Scholar. He was a naval officer during the Second World War and taught at Bishop's before returning to Queen's, where he was head of the English Department for many years and a noted Coleridge scholar. His poetry appears in *The Collected Poems of George Whalley*, edited by George Johnston; autobiographical and biographical essays appear in *Remembrances: George Whalley*.

Poem In Hospital (6–7 January, 1980)

night
the voice of the wind making snow
(in the dark)
the voice of
– a great white melancholy snow-braving owl-ferocious bird
crying in the dark for the cold in its beak
and the cruel dark light in its huge eyes

Nansi – moth-like in the dark
dust on wing:
where an old voluble carbon candle gutters;

Not to be frightened
to feel no premonition of death
to have no sci-fi stories in full technicolour
about coming back from lighted corridors
& high celestial choirs
to the miracle of taxes, corrupt politicians, a society
degenerated into a decayed

& self-consuming economy
is no virtue
but perhaps the composure was, the quietness,
like an old leafless tree in a blizzard
not determined to survive, heroically & interestingly determined
but simply standing still, fires banked, cherishing
what little little fire was left (   ) greek word
like a black spruce in the barren ground
never flamboyant like brown butterflies or the tiny Alpine flower
rooted in permafrost
but growing for 400 years, maybe a millimetre of green a year.

From *The Collected Poems of George Whalley*

TOM MARSHALL

Looking Back

JOHN ALEXANDER MACDONALD (1815–1891), affectionately (by most) known as "Sir John A.," was born in Glasgow, Scotland, but emigrated to Upper Canada as a small child with his parents in 1820. He grew up and was educated in the Kingston area. During a life of alternate triumph and tragedy, he became Canada's first, and arguably greatest, prime minister. Partisan, cynical, intelligent, tolerant, and humane – despite his flaws – "he was, and he is, tremendous company," as the historian P.B. Waite writes. Much as Sir John A. presides over the political and social life of Kingston, so Tom Marshall is the genial spirit of the literary and cultural life of "this wood."

Macdonald Park

(The yellow tree
that stands
in my window
delicate, imperial
moves to some end
I cannot see
some paradox
some lie

that I begin
to formulate
here

Sir John may know.
It's his park.
All this scattered
gold is his,

Perhaps
under the great
roots that coil
he lies
a giant
or a gnome.

A red-nosed gnome.
Lord of Misrule.
Alberich
scattered under gold.

Given to earth, earthy.
Thus alive.

Capricorn.
The prancing goat.
Bibulous, sly.
Kingston's Pan.

The picnicking god
among his people.

(later
the plucked
tree
naked

The eyes are glazed, fixed
on some unseen skyline.
The mouth bestows blessings.

He does not bore them
with facts. Dances
among the cakes. Dances.

The whiskey-throated folk
murmuring; their proud horses
tied outside the grove.

On the crisp air
images of coming
apple-thud.

(sunlight
perpendicular
on
limestone

promises
the snow

(perhaps
a lie
may be
true north

Years later,
climbing the snow-hill, he looked back
a moment – trees striped with white
shadows, negative. The waste lake
between and beyond. And he said
then, something might be made
of this wood. Nodded to himself
and went on.

Bibliography

Bailey, Don. *Homeless Heart.* Kingston: Quarry Press, 1989, pp. 29-31, 35-39.

Bessette, Gerard. *Incubation.* Trans. Glen Shortliffe. Toronto: Macmillan, 1967, pp. 15-17, 30-34, 62-64, 131-132.

Brooke, Rupert. *Letters From America.* New York: Charles Scribner's Sons, 1916, pp. 45-79.

Brown, Alan. "Lines Written in a Kingston Doss-House." *Quarry* 4 (Spring 1955), p. 16.

Brown, Allan. *This Stranger Wood.* Kingston: Quarry Press, 1982, p. 19.

Champlain, Samuel de. *The Works of Samuel de Champlain, 1615 – 1618.* Trans. and ed. H.H. Langton and W.F. Ganong. Toronto: The Champlain Society, 1929, III, pp. 86-91.

Clifford, Wayne. *An Ache in the Ear.* Toronto: Coach House Press, 1979, pp. 59-65.

Cohen, Matt. *The Sweet Second Summer of Kitty Malone.* Toronto: McClelland & Stewart, 1979, pp. 164-170; rpt. Kingston: Quarry Press, 1993.

Davies, Robertson. *Tempest-Tost.* Toronto: Clarke, Irwin, 1951, pp. 11-16.

Dickens, Charles. *American Notes. The Works of Charles Dickens.* New York: Bigelow, Brown & Co., 1868, IV, pp. 267-270.

Drache, Sharon. "The Mikveh Man." In *Great Canadian Murder and Mystery Stories.* Ed. Don Bailey and Daile Unruh. Kingston: Quarry Press, 1991, pp. 172-83.

Euringer, Fred. *A Dream of Horses.* Ottawa: Oberon, 1975, pp. 92-95.

Finnigan, Joan. *The Watershed Collection.* Kingston: Quarry Press, 1988, pp. 32-34.

Folsom, Eric. "Graveyard Where the Trillium Grows." *Quarry* 26, 1 (Winter 1977), pp. 7-8.

Fox, Gail. "Love Poem." *Quarry* 20, 4 (Fall 1971), pp. 5-7; rpt. *End of Innocence: Selected Poems 1988.* Ottawa: Oberon Press, 1988.

Gildersleeve, Lucretia. "Interview." Queen's University Archives.

Greene, Elizabeth. "The Sorrow Gatherer." Unpublished.

Hale, Katherine. *Canadian Houses of Romance.* Toronto: Macmillan, 1926, pp. 117-120.

Hamm, Jean-Jacques. *Entre Zorn et Saint-Laurent: Poemes.* Paris: Editions Saint-Germain-Des Pres, 1985, p. 48.

Head, George. *Forest Scenes and Incidents in the Wilds of North America Being a Diary of a Winter's Route from Halifax to the Canadas And During Four Months' Residence in the Woods on the Borders of Lakes Huron and Simcoe.* 2nd ed. London: John Murray, 1838, pp. 171-173, 342-343.

Heighton, Steven. "Walker." *The New Quarterly* 4,2 (Summer 1986).

Helwig, David. *The Glass Knight.* Ottawa: Oberon, 1976, pp. 19-28-34.

Hennepin, Louis. *A New Discovery of a Vast Country in America.* Rpt. from the second London issue of 1698. Introduction, notes and index by Reuben Gold Thwaites. Toronto: Coles Publishing Ltd., 1974, pp. 44-45.

Henry, Walter [A Staff Surgeon]. *Trifles From My Port-folio; Or Recollections of Scenes and Small Adventures During Twenty-nine Years' Military Service in the Peninsular War and Invasion of France, The East Indies Campaign on Nepaul, St. Helena During the Detention and Until the Death of Napoleon, and Upper and Lower Canada.* 2 vols. Quebec: William Neilson, 1839, II, pp. 89-91, 98-102.

Hospital, Janette Turner. *The Ivory Swing.* Toronto: McClelland & Stewart, 1982, pp. 110-112.

Itani, Frances. *Rentee Bay: Poems from the Bay of Quinte (1785-89).* Kingston: Quarry Press, 1983, pp. 8, 21-22, 28, 47-48, 50.

Kirkconnell, Watson. "Fort Henry Revisited." *Queen's Quarterly* 30 (1913), p. 122.

La Rouchefoucauld-Liancourt, François-Alexandre Frédéric, Duc de. *Travels in Canada, 1795.* Ed. William Renwick Riddell. Trans. Henry Neuman. Toronto: 1917, pp. 65 ff.

Layton, Irving. *Collected Poems.* Toronto: McClelland & Stewart, 1965, p. 158.

Le Chasseur, Jean. *Journey of My Lord Count Frontenac to Lake Ontario.* Intro. and trans. James S. Pritchard. Kingston: Downtown Business Association, 1973, pp. 24-33.

LePan, Douglas. *Something Still To Find: New Poems by Douglas LePan.* Toronto: McClelland & Stewart, 1982, p. 27.

Loeb, Ernst. *Hoffen darf die Erde. Gedichte.* Andernach: Atelier Verlag, 1985.

Lower, Arthur R.M. *Canadians in the Making: A Social History of*

Canada. Toronto: Longman, Green & Co., 1958, pp. 229-230.
MacColl, Evan. *The English Poems of Evan MacColl*. Toronto: Hunter, Rose & Co., 1883, pp. 220-222.
Machar, Agnes Maule. *The Story of Old Kingston*. Toronto: The Musson Book Co. Ltd., 1908, pp. 284-286.
Mair, Charles. *Dreamland and Other Poems*. Montreal: Dawson Brothers, 1868, pp. 71-74.
Marshall, Tom. *Dance of The Particles*. Kingston: Quarry Press, 1984, p. 25.
Marshall, Tom. "Macdonald Park." *Quarry* 16, 2 (January 1967), pp. 19-21.
Mawhinney, Tom. "Nellie on the Shore." Unpublished.
Mayne, Seymour. "Flesh Light." *Quarry* 23, 3 (Summer 1974), p. 30; rpt. *Name*. Oakville: Mosaic Press/Valley Editions, 1976.
Miller, Linus. *Notes of an Exile to Van Diemens Land*. Fredonia N.Y.: W. McKinstry, 1846, pp. 99-108.
Montgomery, John. "Account of an Escape from Fort Henry." In *The Life and Times of William Lyon Mackenzie*. Ed. Charles Lindsey. Vol. III. Toronto: P.R. Randall, 1862, pp. 369-73.
Moodie, Susanna. *Life in the Clearings*. London: Richard Bentley, 1853, pp. 207ff.
Moore, Thomas. *The Poetical Works of Thomas Moore*. New York: Johnson, Fry & Co., no date, pp. 155, 161.
Ondaatje, Michael. *In the Skin of a Lion*. Toronto: Macmillan, 1987, pp. 179-86.
Purdy, Al. *Collected Poems of Al Purdy*. Toronto: McClelland & Stewart, 1986, pp. 107-09.
Roy, James A., *Kingston: The King's Town*. Toronto: McClelland & Stewart, 1952, pp. 334-336.
Russell, James. *Matilda: or the Indian's Captive: A Canadian Tale, Founded on Fact*. Three Rivers: George Stubbs, 1833, pp. 52-53, 66 ff.
Ryan, Oscar, E. Cecil Smith, H. Francis and Mildred Goldberg. *Eight Men Speak: A Political Play in Six Acts*. Toronto: The Progressive Arts Clubs of Canada, 1934, pp. 5 ff.
Sangster, Charles. "The Saint Lawrence and Saguenay." In *Nineteenth Century Narrative Poems*. Ed. David Sinclair. Toronto: McClelland & Stewart, 1972, pp. 44-48.
Schoemperlen, Diane. *The Man of My Dreams*. Toronto: Macmillan, 1990, pp. 80-86.
S [Shanly, Charles Dawson]. Shanly Family Scrapbook (c. 1830-1850). Queen's University Archives.

Shields, Carol. *Swann: A Mystery*. Toronto: Stoddart, 1987, pp. 200-205.
Simcoe, Elizabeth. *Mrs. Simcoe's Diary*. Ed. Mary Quayle Innis. Toronto: Macmillan, 1965, pp. 71-74, 153-156.
Sterns, Kate. *Thinking About Magritte*. New York: Pantheon, 1992, pp. 12-14, 40-41; Toronto: HarperCollins, 1992.
Thompson, Judith. *The Crackwalker*. Toronto: The Playwrights' Union, 1981, pp. 24-31.
Viger, Jacques. *Reminiscences of the War of 1812-14*. Translated by J.L. Hubert Nielsen, M.D. Kingston: News Printing Co. (privately printed), 1895, pp. 7.
Wallace, Bronwen. *The Stubborn Particulars of Grace*. Toronto: McClelland & Stewart, 1988.
Whalley, George. *The Collected Poems of George Whalley*. Ed. George Johnston. Kingston: Quarry Press, 1986, p. 128.
Whitman, Walt. *Walt Whitman's Diary in Canada*. Ed. William Sloane Kennedy. Boston: Small, Maynard, and Co., 1904, pp. 21-26.
Wise, S[ydney] F. "A Personal View of Kingston, an Address to the Annual Meeting of the Ontario Historical Society, Kingston, 21 June 1973." *Historic Kingston* 22 (1974), pp. 1-8.

Further Reading

Angus, Margaret. *The Old Stones of Kingston: Its Buildings Before 1867*. Toronto: University of Toronto Press, 1966.

Armstrong, Alvin. *Buckskin to Broadloom*. Kingston: Kingston *Whig-Standard*, 1973.

Bell, Michael. *Painters in a New Land: From Annapolis Royal to the Klondike*. Toronto: McClelland & Stewart, 1973.

Errington, Jane. *Greater Kingston: Historic Past, Progressive Future*. Burlington: Windsor Publishing in cooperation with the Kingston District Chamber of Commerce, 1988.

Farr, Dorothy. *The Artist Inspired: A History of Art in Kingston to 1970*. Kingston: Agnes Etherington Art Centre, 1988.

Finley, Gerald. *In Praise of Older Buildings*. Kingston: Frontenac Historic Foundation, 1976.

Finnigan, Joan. *Celebrate This City*. Toronto: McClelland & Stewart, 1976.

Glover, T.R. and Calvin, D.D. *A Corner of Empire*. Toronto: Macmillan, 1957.

Harper, J. Russell. *Early Painters and Engravers in Canada*. Toronto: University of Toronto Press, 1970.

Lamontagne, Leopold. *Royal Fort Frontenac*. Toronto, The Champlain Society, 1958.

Mika, Nick and Helma. *Kingston: Historic City*. Belleville, Mika Publishing, 1987.

Osborne, Brian S. and Donald Swainson. *Kingston: Building on the Past*. Westport, Butternut Press, 1988.

Preston, Richard A. *Kingston Before the War of 1812: A Collection of Documents*. Toronto: The Champlain Society, 1959.

Smith, Arthur Britton, ed. *Kingston! Oh Kingston!* Kingston: Brown & Martin, 1987.

Stewart, J. Douglas and Ian E. Wilson. *Heritage Kingston*. Kingston: Agnes Etherington Art Centre, 1973.

Swainson, Donald, ed. *St. George's Cathedral: Two Hundred Years of Community*. Kingston: Quarry Press, 1991.

Much valuable information both literary and visual can be found in *Historic Kingston*, the Transactions of the Kingston Historical Society; the Kingston Public Library; the Queen's University Archives; and the Lorne Pierce Collection at the Douglas Library at Queen's University. The Agnes Etherington Art Centre has a collection of paintings and sketches of the city.

Many of the works excerpted contain much of interest, and several authors – Matt Cohen, Robertson Davies, David Helwig, and Tom Marshall, to name a few – have written extensively about the area in prose and poetry.

Enthusiasts should consult *Kingston: A Selected Bibliography*, compiled by Deborah Dafoe; and "A Brief Guide to Archival Sources Relating to Kingston," by Ian E. Wilson, in *Historic Kingston* 21 (1973), pp. 76-101.

Permissions

"Skating on Navy Bay" from *The Watershed Collection* by JOAN FINNIGAN is reprinted by permission of Quarry Press, Inc. "Astrolabe" from *Something Still To Find* by DOUGLAS LEPAN is reprinted by permission of the Canadian Publishers, McClelland & Stewart. Excerpts from *Rentee Bay: Poems from the Bay of Quinte (1785 – 89)* by FRANCES ITANI are reprinted by permission of the author. "Love Poem" from *End of Innocence: Selected Poems 1988* by GAIL FOX is reprinted by permission of Oberon Press. "Lakeshore, Kingston" from *This Stranger Wood* by ALLAN BROWN is reprinted by permission of the author. "Graveyard Where the Trilliums Grow" by ERIC FOLSOM is reprinted by permission of the author. "Robert Frost in Kingston" from *Dance of the Particles* and "Macdonald Park" are reprinted by permission of Quarry Press, Inc. "Building the Stone Wall" from *An Ache in My Ear* by WAYNE CLIFFORD is reprinted by permission of the author. Excerpt from *Tempest-Tost* by ROBERTSON DAVIES is reprinted by permission of Janet Turnbull Irving. Excerpt from "The Mikveh Man" by SHARON DRACHE is reprinted by permission of the author. Excerpt from *Thinking About Magritte* by KATE STERNS is reprinted by permission of HarperCollins Publishers Ltd. Excerpt from *Homeless Heart* by DON BAILEY is reprinted by permission of Quarry Press, Inc. Excerpt from *In the Skin of a Lion* by MICHAEL ONDAATJE is reprinted by permission of the Canadian Publishers, McClelland & Stewart. "Neighbours" from *The Stubborn Particulars of Grace* by BRONWEN WALLACE is reprinted by permission of the Canadian Publishers, McClelland & Stewart. "Walker" by STEVEN HEIGHTON is reprinted by permission of the author. Excerpt from the papers of LUCRETIA GILDERSLEEVE is reprinted by permission of the Queen's University Archives. "A Personal View of Kingston" by S.F. WISE is reprinted by permission of the author. "Lines Written in a Kingston Doss-House" by ALAN BROWN is reprinted by permission of Quarry Press, Inc. Excerpt from *Incubation* by GERARD BESSETTE is reprinted by permission of the author. Excerpt from *A Dream of Horses* by FRED EURINGER reprinted by permission of Oberon Press. Excerpt from *The Man of My Dreams* by DIANE SCHOEMPERLEN is reprinted by permission of Macmillan of Canada. Excerpt from *The Sweet Second Summer of Kitty Malone* by MATT COHEN is reprinted by permission of the author. Excerpt from *The Crackwalker* by JUDITH THOMPSON is reprinted by permission of Coach House Press. Excerpt from "The Sorrow Gatherer" by ELIZABETH GREENE is published by permission of the author. "Nellie on the Shore" by TOM MAWHINNEY is published by permission of the author. Excerpt from *The Ivory Swing* by JANETTE TURNER HOSPITAL is reprinted by permission of the author. Excerpt from *The Glass Knight* by DAVID HELWIG is reprinted by permission of Oberon Press. Excerpt from *Swann: A Mystery* by CAROL SHIELDS is reprinted by permission of Stoddart Publishing Co. Limited. "Anglo-Canadian" from *Collected Poems* by IRVING LAYTON is reprinted by permission of the Canadian Publisher, McClelland & Stewart. "House Guest" from *Collected Poems of Al Purdy* by AL PURDY is reprinted by permission of the Canadian Publisher, McClelland & Stewart. "Come, Dance" from *Name* by SEYMOUR MAYNE is reprinted by permission of Mosaic Press. "Canada" by ERNST LOEB is published by permission of Anthony W. Riley. "Poem in Hospital" from *The Collected Poems of George Whalley* by GEORGE WHALLEY is reprinted by permission of Quarry Press, Inc.

Illustrations

COVER: *Harbourfront* by Gwyneth Travers, reproduced by permission of Peter Travers. Gwyneth Travers (1911-1982) was a native of Kingston who graduated from Queen's University in 1933 and trained with André Biéler, Ralph Allen, and George Swinton, from whom she learned the colour woodcut printing techniques she used to portray the architecture of Kingston.

FRONTISPIECE: *Kingston from Fort Henry* by James Gray, aquatinted by J. Gleadah, reproduced by permission of The Royal Ontario Museum. James Gray travelled throughout Upper Canada during 1828 sketching views of Niagara Falls, Belleville, Kingston, and other towns. A series of these sketches was published in London, aquatinted by J. Gleadah.

FIRST IMPRESSIONS: *Thousand Islands* by William Roebuck, reproduced by permission of the Agnes Etherington Art Centre. William Roebuck (c. 1796-1847) attended the Royal Military Academy and came to Upper Canada with his family in 1818 where he was attached to Lord Dalhousie's service.

SYMPHONY IN STONE: *Fort Henry* by Carl Schaefer, reproduced by permission of the Agnes Etherington Art Centre. Carl Schaefer (1903–), who studied at the Ontario College of Art under Arthur Lismer and J.E.H. MacDonald, taught at Queen's University Summer School of Fine Arts from 1946 to 1950.

NEIGHBOURS: *Hockey Players* by David Brown, reproduced by permission of the artist. David Brown (1936–) grew up in Kingston and graduated from Kingston Collegiate and Vocational Institute. He played one season with the Montreal Junior Canadiens before attending the Ontario College of Art. Since 1966 he has worked as a painter, art teacher, and set designer in the Kingston region.